BATTLE OF FORCES:

SERA TOUJOURS

Acclaim for the Cain Casey Saga

The Devil Inside

"Vali's fluid writing style quickly puts the reader at ease, which makes the story and its characters equally easy to get to know and care about. When you find yourself talking out loud to the characters in a book, you know the work is polished and professional, as well as entertaining."—*Family and Friends*

"Not only is *The Devil Inside* a ripping mystery, it's also an intimate character study."—*L-Word Literature*

"*The Devil Inside* is the first of what promises to be a very exciting series…While telling an exciting story that grips the reader, Vali has also fully fleshed out her heroes and villains. *The Devil Inside* is that rarity: a fascinating crime novel which includes a tender love story and leaves the reader with a cliffhanger ending."—*MegaScene*

The Devil Unleashed

"Fast-paced action scenes, intriguing character revelations, and a refreshing approach to the romance thriller genre all make for an enjoyable reading experience in the Big Easy…*The Devil Unleashed* is an engrossing reading experience."—*Midwest Book Review*

Deal With the Devil

"Ali Vali has given her fans another thick, rich thriller…*Deal With the Devil* has wonderful love stories, great sex, and an ample supply of humor. It is an exciting, page turning read that leaves her readers eagerly awaiting the next book in the series."—*Just About Write*

The Devil Be Damned

"Ali Vali excels at creating strong, romantic characters along with her fast paced, sophisticated plots. Her setting, New Orleans, provides just the right blend of immigrants from Mexico, South America and Cuba, along with a city steeped in traditions."—*Just About Write*

Praise for Ali Vali

Carly's Sound

"Vali paints vivid pictures with her words…*Carly's Sound* is a great romance, with some wonderfully hot sex."—*Midwest Book Review*

"It's no surprise that passion is indeed possible a second time around"—*Q Syndicate*

Calling the Dead

"So many writers set stories in New Orleans, but Ali Vali's mystery novels have the authenticity that only a real Big Easy resident could bring…makes for a classic lesbian murder yarn."—*Curve*

Blue Skies

"Vali is skilled at building sexual tension and the sex in this novel flies as high as Berkley's jets. Look for this fast-paced read."—*Just About Write*

Balance of Forces: Toujours Ici

"A stunning addition to the vampire legend, *Balance of Forces: Toujours Ici,* is one that stands apart from the rest."—*Bibliophilic Book Blog*

Visit us at www.boldstrokesbooks.com

By the Author

Carly's Sound

Second Season

Calling the Dead

Blue Skies

Love Match

The Dragon Tree Legacy

<u>Forces Series</u>

Balance of Forces: Toujours Ici

Battle of Forces: Sera Toujours

<u>The Cain Casey Saga</u>

The Devil Inside

The Devil Unleashed

Deal with the Devil

The Devil Be Damned

The Devil's Orchard

BATTLE OF FORCES:

SERA TOUJOURS

by

Ali Vali

2013

BATTLE OF FORCES: SERA TOUJOURS
© 2013 By Ali Vali. All Rights Reserved.

ISBN 13: 978-1-60282-957-2

This Trade Paperback Original Is Published By
Bold Strokes Books, Inc.
P.O. Box 249
Valley Falls, NY 12185

First Edition: November 2013

Credits
Editors: Shelley Thrasher and Stacia Seaman
Production Design: Stacia Seaman
Cover Design by Sheri (graphicartist2020@hotmail.com)

Acknowledgments

Thank you first to Radclyffe for your support and advice, and for allowing me to follow my imagination with these characters. Any time your boss encourages you to put a swordfight in your work, that's a sign of an awesome job.

Once the words are written and the story is finished, the editing begins, and I'm grateful to Shelley Thrasher for all the hard work and time she puts into each book. Thank you, Shelley, for your patience, your friendship, and for everything you've taught me.

Thank you to the BSB team who all work so hard to bring every book to print: thank you to Stacia Seaman for your final edits and comments, Sheri for another great cover, to the other authors who are always there to offer encouragement, and to my beta readers. All these years later and Connie Ward and Kathi Isserman are still saying yes when I ask them to read something new. Thank you both for your input and for keeping me on track.

Thanks to you the reader for all your support and great emails. Everything I write is always done with you in mind.

Life is always changing, and while every day is different, for me there is always one constant. Thank you, C, for loving me and for making me laugh even when it's the last thing I want to do. You sure have made my life a fun adventure, and I'm always looking forward to what comes next. You're my best friend, my joy, and I love you. *Verdad!*

For C
A lifetime is not enough

CHAPTER ONE

Do you promise you'll bring me back here one day?" Piper Marmande stood on the balcony of Kendal Richoux's Venetian home and stared out over the water. She'd enjoyed the view for the last six months, but every day she found something new and beautiful in the postcard-worthy scene.

"Time isn't a problem for either of us, so I'll bring you back whenever you like," Kendal said from the doorway. The casual clothes had been put away and Kendal was wearing the type of business suit Piper had always seen her in when they'd met. "Thank you for the memories you've given me of this place."

"I'd say we're going home, but my home will be wherever you are," Piper said as she walked toward Kendal and put her arms around her waist. "Until I met you, I never thought I'd say that to another soul because I didn't trust anyone that much with my heart."

"The car is ready, signora," the maid said from the hallway.

"Tell them to wait, please." Kendal returned her full attention to Piper. "Your heart is safe with me. You've brought someone who can't die back to life, and I'll spend eternity trying to give you the same happiness."

Eternity—the only meaning that word had ever held for her was fluff that sappy people wrote on cards, but she had drastically changed her interpretation in six months. In that short time, she and her grandparents had been about to lose their family business, so she'd made a deal with a man she detested to keep it out of Kendal's hands. When her grandfather Mac had mentioned they were in Kendal's sights, she'd become frantic to save everything her family had built through generations.

She'd been so hostile and immature in their initial meetings that she was still surprised Kendal hadn't lost patience with her. When she'd finally let her guard down she'd found not only a savior, but love. Kendal gave her what she thought was the most important thing to her—only it wasn't Marmande Enterprises, but the raider who'd tried to sink it.

"What are you thinking so hard about?" Kendal whispered.

"The day I realized I'd fallen in love with you was the night you faced Henri. At least it was the first time I'd admitted it to myself." Kendal's brother was as old as her slayer but, unlike Kendal, he'd chosen the darkness. He was a powerful vampire who'd killed their father to torture Kendal's soul, but their fight had finally ended at Kendal's house outside New Orleans. "When Henri drove that sword through your chest I knew I'd be alone until I died. I didn't want anyone else."

"Do you have regrets?" Kendal's voice was still soft and seductive.

"Regrets about spending eternity with you?" she asked as she tugged Kendal out into the sun. "My regret started the second I thought you'd died. You were gone and I hadn't told you how I felt about you." All that blood and that sword sticking out of Kendal's chest had dropped her into a hell of her own making, and she thought she'd be trapped in it until death came for her. The only relief she'd find was Kendal waiting on the other side.

"I should've given you more time to decide."

Piper heard Kendal's remorse. "Let me finish before you get all glum on me." She took Kendal's jacket off and pointed to the double chaise lounge they'd spent their mornings on. "My regret and despair were my salvation, so as painful as that night was, I'd relive it continuously because it proved to Morgaine and Lenore how much I loved you."

Piper hadn't known what to expect when she stepped into the large library located over a bar in New Orleans. There she'd met Lenore and been trusted with the secrets of the Genesis Clan and their greatest achievement—the elixir of the sun. Lenore was their chief archivist and had read her the story of the Clan's best slayer, Asra, a soldier born during the reign of the only female pharaoh over three thousand years before.

"It sounded so real, those stories in your book, but I didn't want to let myself believe them," she said as she stretched out next to Kendal. "To believe it was to hope, and to hope for anything always ended in disaster for me."

"What changed your mind?"

"Morgaine," Piper said with a smile.

The beautiful Morgaine, who'd delivered the Elders' invitation to Kendal, had mixed the elixir for Asra and trained her, but broke the rules when she fell in love with her recruit. That wasn't part of Lenore's story, but Piper knew the instant Morgaine spoke about Kendal. "Your watcher was so adamant I make up my mind right then to either come here or be locked out forever. It scared me to gamble with my heart like that, but I had no other options."

"Your longing led you here, but what happens when the darkness that's dominated my life for so long comes back? Death holds no power over us, Piper, but the elixir you drank won't protect you from things like Henri."

"The people who've known you the longest say you're the best slayer they have, so I'm not worried."

Kendal finally laughed. "It's that easy for you?"

"At first it wasn't because I thought you were all crazy, but seeing you sitting in a field of daffodils that'll never die brought *me* back to life. I still find it a little crazy, but I haven't needed to sleep in three months, and I'm a woman in love."

Kendal smiled, and Piper was sure that same smile had melted hundreds of hearts throughout the years. Kendal's generosity and her gentle nature had been the core theme of Lenore's tales, and no amount of fighting or aging had dimmed either.

"You're the woman I've waited for." Kendal kissed her as she lowered the zipper of her dress.

"Do you think the maid will come back to tell you about the car again? Or maybe to show you her cleavage one more time on the off chance you might want to see it up close?" Piper asked, but didn't stop Kendal from undressing her.

"Not if she wants to keep her job."

They stood to make it easier to get naked except for her underwear, since Kendal liked to strip those off herself, and it still amazed Piper how quickly her body reacted to Kendal's touch. One long look and her nipples got hard, and Kendal's fingers anywhere on her body made her wet. "I can't blame her for the crush she has on you. You've made me a maniac, and I never really liked sex. I can't imagine what you'd do to someone who undresses you with her eyes every chance she gets."

"You do know how to flatter, my love, but you don't have to worry about the maid or anyone else." Kendal unfastened Piper's bra with one hand and squeezed her breast as soon as she got it off.

"Practice really has made you perfect in this arena, and I don't ever want to disappoint you." They'd made love every day since her arrival, but she still cursed her inexperience. Worry over that always made her think about all the women who'd shared Kendal's life and her bed.

Kendal must've picked up on her insecurity because her touch went from teasing to nurturing. "You sweet idiot."

"Don't tell me that's my new nickname," she said as she tried to look away.

"It will be if you doubt my loyalty and love. You've got nothing to fear."

"The way you touch me doesn't make me afraid," she said with her face pressed to Kendal's shoulder. "I don't want us to have secrets, so I hope you don't mind a few of these crazy conversations along the way. I don't doubt your love. I just wish I knew more so I could make you as crazy as you make me."

"You're making me crazy now."

She snorted at Kendal's sense of humor, which encouraged her to go on. "In a good way, Asra. Not a pull-your-hair-and-howl-at-the-moon crazy."

"Skill's only important in swordplay," Kendal said as she moved so she could see Piper's face. "How I touch you isn't about technique, but about how much I love you. My past holds a mixture of good and bad memories and experiences, but not one of them makes my heart pound like it does when I feel you against me. All that's important to me is today and every tomorrow I'll have with you."

"You are sweet, but I might as well spill all my insecurities before we go back to real life." Piper tried her best to maintain eye contact. "It's your last chance to run screaming up the hill of indestructible flowers."

"I'm old, not insane, so let's hear your list. The only way I'm leaving is if you tell me you're in love with the maid."

"You'd be okay with that?" Piper narrowed her eyes to slits.

"Only if you'd be okay with me planting our maid under all the indestructible flowers."

"I'm being serious," she said, but laughed anyway as she pressed her head to Kendal's shoulder.

"You can tell me anything, so be honest."

"Throughout your life you've had one constant no matter what you were doing," she said, not really sure how to go on.

Kendal moved so they were facing each other, their joined hands between them. "Can I tell you a story before you say anything else?" Piper nodded and appeared relieved. "When you got here, did you come for eternal life?"

"You know better. I came for you, and only you."

"When Morgaine visited me the first time, she told me my father was dead. After the shock of losing the one person in my life I loved and trusted, she told me my brother Abez had killed him. Like you, I never knew my mother, so my father was my whole world. He taught me the sword, about honor and commitment, convinced the pharaoh of my worth, and then in a moment of horror he was gone."

"At least I had Gran and Pops," Piper said, then kissed Kendal's knuckles.

"When I saw what Abez had done, and what he'd become, I accepted the cup Morgaine mixed for me. I drank only for a chance at avenging my father's murder." Kendal closed her eyes and thought back to that oasis she'd shared with Morgaine all those years. They'd made love so many times, but it didn't compare to being totally and hopelessly in love with the woman in her arms.

"Finding Abez drove me from the day I reentered the world, but he proved an elusive adversary, so I made a decision that I felt would honor my father as much as killing Abez."

"You'd already chosen immortality. What else was there?"

"I chose to find things to enjoy. The world had become a wondrous place, and I reinvented myself like Abez did numerous times. But I did it so I could enjoy the changes in the world, not find dark corners to hide in. Through the years Lenore told me I had an adventurous heart, and she was right, but it kept me sane. In time I learned as much as I could, and with Lenore's help I found out about the Elders and the Genesis Clan. The lessons and the adventure kept me going until I found the monster that once was my brother."

"Thanks for sharing that with me, but what does it have to do with the crazy stuff in my head?" Piper shrugged. "It makes me sound juvenile, but the Viking goddess loves you and she's been in your life so long that I get insanely jealous when I think about it. I can't ever share you or this," Piper said as she lifted their hands.

"I told you because you need to realize how we got here. You drank for love, and I drank for vengeance, not because of my love for the Viking goddess, as you put it."

"So Morgaine doesn't matter?"

"I've only mixed the elixir twice, for you and Charlie. But only you mattered enough to me that I didn't want to go on without you. Charlie begged me for the same reason I decided to drink," she said of the man who'd come into her life as a slave at Oakgrove. "He wanted revenge, but you simply wanted me, so Morgaine isn't someone you need to worry about."

"You forgot the daffodils outside," Piper said, and moved to straddle her hips.

"I was smart enough to know the right woman would come along and appreciate them." She ran her fingertips along Piper's shoulders. "I love you, and because you're here I've sent word to the Elders that I'm done. I've given them what they wanted, and Ora and Abez are dead. All I want now is peace and to enjoy my life with you."

"Are you sure?" Piper grabbed her hands and squeezed. "Will they let you do that?"

"They can try to keep me, but no soldier is worth his sword when forced to fight." Piper smiled as if she wanted more than anything for what she was saying to be true. She'd enjoyed that relaxed smile all winter as they walked through the streets of Venice and the surrounding countryside. They'd talked and she'd told Piper stories of the things she'd witnessed, but she'd balanced them with her hopes for the future. She'd been honest about her life so Piper would be sure about her decision.

"You won't be sorry?"

"Did you fall in love with me for my slaying abilities?"

Piper released her and ran her hands down her own body until they were between her legs. "I fell in love with you because you're a sexy beast who makes me wet." She brought her hand back up and ran her fingers around Kendal's lips, painting them with her desire and making Kendal groan. "I never thought I'd be the kind of person who craved sex, wanted to be romanced, and ended up with the kind of partner I didn't think existed, but my patience paid off."

"You are the definition of desire." Kendal moved her hand between Piper's legs and curled her fingers from the slick opening of Piper's sex to her hard clit. Piper tipped her hips forward and jutted her chest out. Her nipples looked as hard as the small stone under her fingers, and Kendal sucked the one nearer to her mouth.

"Do you mind being late?" Piper asked as she tugged her head back by the hair.

"With a chartered plane I can make love to you as long as I want, and we won't miss it."

Piper pulled Kendal to her and kissed her hard before she lay down. When she was on her back, she reached down and spread her sex open for Kendal. "If you're mine—prove it."

Kendal slid two fingers in to the knuckle and Piper spread her legs wider. The sight of her made Kendal think that another three thousand years wouldn't make the pleasure of being with Piper fade. She'd gladly put her sword down for this woman. It was someone else's turn to keep the darkness at bay.

She'd found her light.

❖

"Exactly what do you want me to do?" Hill Hickman asked the guy who'd arranged an appointment after hours. The gun she kept taped to the bottom of her desk was pointed at his gut, so she wasn't afraid of him, but he did give off a weird vibe.

"I need background information on a few people my boss is hoping to do business with." He crossed his legs and held his fingers over the folder in his lap. "I suggested you because of your relationship with Piper Marmande."

"Is that a nice way of asking me to spy on Piper?"

"He's more interested in Kendal Richoux than Ms. Marmande, but I understand they're together." He made air quotes and smiled on the last word.

"We're getting ahead of ourselves," she said as she thought about the offer Kendal had called her about. Maybe it was time to retire from the private-detective field and go into corporate security. A job with Kendal would mean fewer meetings with assholes like this. "Your assistant only gave your name as Leonardo." He nodded at the information. "Is there more to it, or are you the Cher of the corporate world?"

"Unless you can't continue without more, I'd prefer to keep this as informal as possible." He reached down and she leaned forward to make sure he didn't produce any nasty surprises. The stack of money he took out was thick with hundred-dollar bills. "We'll start with a twenty-five-thousand retainer, if that's acceptable."

"I'll give you the file I put together for Piper on Richoux for a lot cheaper than that," she said, sure now there was more to this than Leonardo was saying. "Do a Google search, and the five articles or so you'll find is all there is. I might find more now, but I'm not willing to lose a good friend over it."

Hill stood and hoped she wouldn't have to shoot this guy to get rid of him. "I'm going to pass, so good luck."

She waited until he drove away from the front of the building before checking to make sure he hadn't left anything behind. When she was sure the room was clean she checked the surveillance camera to print out a picture of Leonardo.

"Oakgrove residence, may I help you?"

"Charlie, it's Hill Hickman," she said as she scanned the photo into her computer. "I need to talk to Kendal as soon as possible. Do you think you can arrange it?"

"I'm sure Piper hasn't had a chance to call you, but they'll be home this week," Charlie said. She liked his slight French accent. "Can I help you with something?"

"Does the name Leonardo sound familiar?"

"Nothing comes to mind, but I'll check with Kendal if she calls."

She studied the picture on her screen, trying to detect anything about him she'd missed. "Whoever he is, he just offered me a stack of money for information about Kendal, and he thought he'd get further than I did when I tried finding information about her for Piper because Piper and I are friends. He evidently figured he could exploit that angle to get to her."

"No matter what I ask, please don't take offense," Charlie said, and laughed.

"Let me give you some answers before you have to. I didn't take him up on his offer because I'm planning to take Kendal up on hers, and I can email you the picture I took of him. It came out pretty clear."

"Then come by the house whenever you like. Kendal left a set of keys for you, and I have your paperwork."

"She was that sure I'd say yes?"

"Kendal's always more hopeful than sure about a lot of things."

As soon as the email left her out-box she shut her computer down and clipped her backup gun on her waistband. She had a feeling she'd need more than the one on her shoulder. "Are you free for dinner, Charlie?"

"I'm putting steaks on the grill for us, so don't take long."

"See you in a few." The coming months would be interesting, she thought as she locked the door, but she was ready for a change. Piper had certainly found happiness by trying something completely different.

It was time she did the same.

❖

"She's done what she set out to do," Morgaine said.

"And our bidding along the way without complaint," Lenore said as a follow-up.

They'd come above ground for this meeting, and the only shade in the Egyptian desert came from the tent Rolla's men had erected close to the door of the Elders' compound. It was the Genesis Clan's oldest and largest holding, and the only one completely hidden underground. Everyone who'd consumed the elixir at the Elders' invitation had rooms here; how many and how opulent depended on age and rank.

The palatial library and large span of space filled with treasures any museum would kill for belonged to Rolla, the oldest of the Elders and the closest thing they had to royalty. His word wasn't law, but he had a tremendous amount of influence over the group, whose job it was to set rules and dole out punishment.

"From what you're telling me, she's broken her word *again*, and she shouldn't be surprised with the punishment. The slave she brought to us was warning enough, but this...it's too much."

"Two in three thousand years, Rolla, isn't something to complain about," Lenore said.

"The Elders meet at the next full moon, and I expect you both to have her here."

"Why are they meeting?" Morgaine asked, running her glass of ice water across her forehead. The last time she'd been this hot was when she'd trained Kendal leagues from this spot.

"To decide punishment or reprimand."

"You'd seriously force her to sleep?" Morgaine said as she jumped to her feet. "Have the years you've spent in that library finally made you snap?"

"This infraction won't be so easily overlooked." Rolla closed his eyes and turned his face to the sun.

"Do you think because Ora and Henri have been destroyed that Asra isn't needed? They weren't our only two problems."

He tossed a rolled-up scroll at her feet and waved his hand. "Asra is the one who feels she's no longer needed. She wishes to be released from her obligation to us."

"She's in love. Give us a chance to talk to her before we take drastic action."

"Love is the excuse you're giving as her defense?" He opened his eyes, looked at her, and laughed. "If it is, you've made this easier for me. Love is the last reason to bring another forth."

Morgaine laughed as well before staring over Rolla's shoulder to the handsome man fifty feet away, sunning himself on a towel and wearing a small bathing suit. Whoever he was had held Rolla's hand until he'd sat down. "If her defense is lust, will that make it wiser?"

"Leave my decisions out of this discussion because I made them with the consent of the others."

"What did you tell them about that?" She pointed to Rolla's pet and ignored Lenore's hand on her forearm. "What worth could he possibly have aside from your pleasure?"

"Travis's worth is as a future slayer. He's good with the sword, has been tested in battle, and like Asra, he accepted the challenge. We found him after he served the British in the War of 1812. He was the only one in his unit to survive, so he was invited into our ranks and has been in training ever since."

"You're comparing him to Asra?" Morgaine asked, and laughed. "Usually the only survivor in any battle is someone who runs from the fight. Are you sure it was because of bravery?"

"I *am* comparing him, and I believe he'll be twice as valuable because he truly wants to serve." Rolla spoke with almost a growl and glared at her as if daring her to continue.

"His place with you is no different than Piper Marmande's with Asra," she said before she walked through the sand toward Travis and kicked him in the side. His reflexes were good enough that he rolled to his feet with his sword in his hand. It appeared Roman in design but too long to be effective.

"I can't kill you, but you're going to hurt for that," Travis said, cocking his head back to flick his blond hair out of his face.

She laughed at his cockiness like she had with Asra when they'd first started. When they'd trained together she hadn't picked up a sword against Asra until well into their fortieth year. You couldn't learn to fight with the sword until you learned to keep it in your hand, she'd said repeatedly until Asra understood.

"How old is this brave slayer, Rolla?" she asked sarcastically.

"He's been training with Zanga for close to a hundred and eighty years."

"Zanga, your messenger?" When Travis brought his sword down toward her head, she kicked him in the knee as she grabbed his wrist. His sword was in her hand before he fell and in his chest before he could offer any more threats. "If this is part of our defense, the scales will tip before Asra is back to full strength, if you bury her and Piper." She pulled the sword from Travis's chest and threw it as far behind him as she could. "Tell Zanga his value is in delivering messages, not training slayers."

"That wasn't fair, he wasn't ready," Rolla said, but without conviction.

"The most unfair thing will be Asra's refusal when you wake her because you'll have no choice. The world will know darkness and you'll have only yourself to blame, because I won't lay it at her feet."

Lenore said, "Neither will I, and I'll be happy to say that at the gathering unless you exclude Morgaine and me because you've changed the rules. It's your right, I know, but it'll taint the outcome if she has no defenders."

"Bring her, or there will be consequences."

"For her or for the people we've sworn to protect?" Morgaine asked as Rolla went to Travis's aid.

Lenore shook her head and led her to the helicopter that Rolla had sent for them. "Don't provoke him anymore, or Asra will pay the price."

"I wonder if he's considered what happens if she refuses and changes her allegiance."

"Asra would never fight against the Clan," Lenore said.

"Even if he gives her no choice?" Morgaine stopped Lenore before they boarded. "She'll fight on the side that'll keep Piper in her life, and if Travis is Rolla's line in the sand, may the gods help us."

If pushed, their slayer certainly would fight anyone who tried to hurt Piper, and there was little chance they'd be able to stop her even with Morgaine's help—but she kept those thoughts to herself.

CHAPTER TWO

Does not sleeping eventually drive you crazy?" Piper asked as the last remnants of land disappeared below them.

"I'm sure you'll find some way to entertain yourself." Kendal lay stretched out next to her with her eyes closed.

"You're not planning to go back to New York, are you? I mean, what happens next?"

"Eventually we'll head north, but not for long. Unless you have other plans I'd like to stay in New Orleans. I don't want to rob you of any time you have with your grandparents." Kendal sat up straighter and smiled, but she appeared almost melancholy.

"Is it hard?" she asked, guessing what had upset Kendal.

"It can be, and those were the only times along the way I felt true regret, even if I've never had anyone I loved enough to mix the elixir for. I've had close friends, but I lost them because I left, not because they died from old age." Kendal slipped her fingers though the hair at the side of Piper's head, and she leaned into the touch. "I still miss my father, and you've been lucky to have your grandparents. Not everyone had been so fortunate and been loved so fiercely, so it'll be the same for you one day."

"I can't imagine my life without them."

"If the gods are kind, you won't have to worry about that for years to come. Having you back and seeing you happy will add years to their lives."

Piper crossed her legs so she could put her foot behind Kendal's knee. "What I'm sure about is Pops telling me 'I told you so' with relish when I see him." Now that they were airborne she encouraged Kendal to the plane's sofa with a kiss. "While I'm working, what will you be doing?"

"I'll open some offices in the city so I can get out of the limelight in New York. Kendal Richoux still has a few years left, and I'll enjoy riding them out at Oakgrove or wherever you want to live. Maybe Charlie and I can bring some of those fields back to life."

"You'd look good as a farmer, honey. Thanks for understanding how much my family means to me. Will you always be so amenable?"

"Enjoy it while you can, pipsqueak. In a few hundred years you'll be constantly complaining about how cranky I can be."

Piper laughed and shook her head before she kissed her in a way to inflame her passions. "If I can't sleep on long flights anymore, then let's try something else."

"What'd you have in mind?"

"Are we a mile up yet?" She took Kendal's hand and put it on her knee.

"You will be when we're done." Kendal moved her hand under the hem of Piper's dress and up her thigh.

"I've never felt this beautiful with anyone," Piper said as she pulled Kendal to cover her. That Kendal wanted her this much would be the balm to any hurt she'd experience. As wonderful as the sensation of Kendal's touch was, the honeymoon was almost over.

Piper didn't know any Elders other than Morgaine and Lenore, but they didn't seem like the types to let go so easily. It wouldn't matter to them if Kendal was tired of their game, and she expected a fight before it was over.

But they needed to understand that the slayer belonged to her now, and she'd fight to keep her.

❖

The weather outside Marmande Enterprise's offices in New Orleans was gloomy, with gray skies and a driving rain that'd been falling for two days straight. The yard was a mud pit off the main pathways, and with no letup in the weather, it'd stay that way for a week or more. Most of their employees were under makeshift shelters since they were too busy to stop outright. Only the welders had gotten the day off.

Their expansion, made possible with Kendal Richoux's help as well as bankroll, had brought contracts flooding in, swelling the number of workers both outside and in the office, and even with all that, they had a waiting list of clients. Men and women in company-issued blue hardhats were busy with the Coast Guard cutters Kendal's connections had gotten the contract for, while close by another group in white hardhats was busy with the construction of new dry docks on the expanse of riverfront property next to them. They owed Kendal every bit of the chance to bring Marmande back from the extinction of bankruptcy or takeover, and Mac hated to think ill of their savior, but success had also brought change.

He stood in the corner office that overlooked the business his grandfather had founded and waved to the few who'd noticed him as they walked by. It was gratifying to be able to give all these people job security, but it wasn't enough to make up for losing Piper. He didn't mind the long hours and the endless piles of paperwork, but he missed the fun his granddaughter added to his day.

"Leave her be." He repeated what his wife, Molly, had said that morning when he'd complained *again*. The words didn't shake off his bad mood, so he sat and forced himself to concentrate on something productive. "Gene, would you bring in the Navy contract, please, as well as the blueprints? I want to review them before their design team gets here," he said into the intercom.

"Right away, sir. Can I get you anything else?"

"My granddaughter, from wherever she is." He didn't say it out loud, but it didn't hurt to wish. His dad used to say that if you threw wishes out into the universe, sometimes they were answered.

It wasn't that he begrudged Piper the long vacation, but she hadn't given too many explanations, no matter how much he pressed when she called. "Just the paperwork, thanks. Molly said I had to lay off the coffee."

"You got it," Gene said as she tensed to get up but dropped back down again.

"Will we lose the contract if he misses the meeting or reschedules?"

"What?" Gene said, and appeared stunned.

"This meeting he's getting ready for? Is it necessary for Pops to be there?" Piper asked with a smile so wide she doubted Gene recognized her. She'd never been known for her sunny disposition around the office. "Miss me?" she said when Gene still hadn't moved.

"Hardly noticed you were gone," Gene said, but Piper knew she was teasing when she laughed. "I know someone, though, who hasn't smiled in weeks since you left."

"Can't find them?" Mac's voice came through the small speaker when Gene pressed the button.

"Actually, someone's here who wants to say hello but doesn't have an appointment."

"I'd love to chat on any other day, but I can't keep these guys waiting. I don't think it's a good idea to piss off the Navy as a first move."

Piper said, "How about if we send over their good friend Ms. Richoux to take your place? Will you see me then? I'm sure when she's done we'll have to double the size of the operation."

Before Gene could take her finger off the device, the door to Mac's office opened, and he stopped as if afraid his eyes were deceiving him. He hesitated only a moment before he lifted Piper into his arms and swung her around like he had when she was a little girl.

"You're a good-looking sight for these old eyes, sweetheart," he whispered in her ear before kissing her cheek. Kendal walked in and smiled, as her feet were still hanging a few inches off the ground because of Mac's bear hug. Piper was too content to move, so she held her hand up to keep Kendal and Gene still.

"I missed you too, Pops. Can you to take the rest of the day off so we can catch up?" She squeezed his neck again, loving the familiar scent of his cologne. "I have a lot to tell you, but I want to tell you and Gran together."

"Is everything all right?" Mac asked when he put her down but kept his arms around her.

"Everything's great." Her comment came out sultry.

"Mr. Marmande, it's nice to see you again, sir," Kendal said as she held out her hand to him.

"Kendal, I didn't expect you." Mac kept hold of Piper's hand as he shook hands with Kendal. "If you had anything to do with bringing this pretty little girl home, though, I owe you the meal I'm always trying to buy you."

"Not necessary, sir, and I believe the pretty little girl said something about wanting to see her grandmother, so why don't the two of you take off?"

"I wish I could right this minute, but I have a meeting with—"

"Dell and Harry from the Navy," Kendal said. "If you don't think I'm overstepping my place, I'd love to meet with them for you. If something needs your stamp of approval I promise to call you before I commit you to anything not outlined in the contract."

"Let me grab my coat," Mac said as he slapped his hands together.

When he stepped back into his office Piper looked first at Gene, then at Kendal. "Gene, could you tell him we had to make a phone call if he's quicker than usual?"

"You can use my phone," Gene said as she held up her receiver. Piper locked eyes with Kendal, and the half smile Kendal gave her made her wish for a moment alone. "Or you can use the one in your office if you need more privacy."

"Thank you." With what Piper hoped was a sexy sway of her hips, she led Kendal down the hall.

"Well, if that's what it takes to mellow her out a little, I'm all for it," Gene said, and both Piper and Kendal looked back and smiled.

When her office door closed, Piper slid her hands up the lapels of Kendal's coat and pulled until she bent to her level. "I wanted to thank you personally, before I take him home, for giving us this time together. I'm sure meeting with these two guys was the last thing you wanted to do after that long flight." The wool of Kendal's coat was soft under her fingers, and she closed her eyes when Kendal kissed her in a way that made her believe she finally belonged. She belonged somewhere and to someone, and in turn Kendal was hers. "I promise to make it up to you later. Will you meet me at Riverbend when you're done? I want to introduce you to my grandmother."

"I'd love to, and I love you," Kendal said, and followed her out.

Her grandfather was ready to leave, but he was staring so intently at Kendal, she turned around to see what the problem was. Mac rocked on his feet and stayed quiet as Kendal wiped her lipstick off. If he didn't have a clue about their relationship, the pink shade of Kendal's lips was his first hint.

"Ready to go?" Mac asked.

"I can't wait to see Gran. There's so much I want to tell you both."

"Kendal, are you sure you don't mind filling in for me?"

"The boring twins and I go way back, sir, so take Piper home and have fun."

❖

As the car pulled away Mac held Piper's hand and almost bounced in his seat. "Today I'm finally glad I gave in to the driver you and Molly insisted on."

"Yeah, I get you all to myself," she said, and kissed his cheek.

"You look so different." His innocent statement made her whip her head up and stare at him.

"What do you mean?"

"For the first time in your life you look happy, sweetheart. I mean really happy. Am I wrong about that?"

She was immensely relieved, thinking for a minute he'd guessed what was really different about her. "I wanted to wait and tell you and Gran together, but you're right. I'm really happy."

"So Miss Richoux isn't so bad after all, huh?" He laughed, and she shook her finger at him and smiled.

"Don't be smug, and no lectures about how you're always right."

"Does she realize how lucky she is?"

Tears suddenly filled her eyes but didn't fall. "I hope you're not disappointed with my choice, but I love her. She's changing her life so we can be together and I can stay close to you guys. You probably wanted different for me, but Kendal…she completes me."

"I wanted you to be happy, Piper. Your grandmother and I have known for a long time that the right person would come along. Someone who'd cherish you and love you like you deserve to be loved. If Kendal's that person I'm happy for you. I just need to know if she realizes how lucky she is to have won your heart."

She hugged him for his answer, glad to have him accept Kendal into their family. "I'm blessed, and I don't mean just because of Kendal. Thanks, Pops."

They talked about business for the remainder of the ride since she wanted to save the rest of her story for her grandmother. When they walked into the old plantation house, Riverbend, they had another tearful reunion when Molly saw them there together.

"It's been too quiet without you here," Molly said as she held her tight.

"I missed you both, but it's been one of those life-changing vacations, so I'm glad I went." She kept her arm around her grandmother's waist and walked with her to the large comfortable sofa in the formal parlor. Both of her grandparents were happy and healthy for now, but she thought about what Kendal had said. The time would come to let them go, but today wasn't the time to dwell on it.

"Really?" Molly said as she sat and kicked her shoes off. "Tell us about it."

"The whole mess with the company and how I handled it is something I'm not proud of, especially how I treated Kendal, but she came through for us anyway." All the worry over that seemed like a distant past, and Kendal's touch had erased Kenny Delany from her memory. Of all the great things Kendal had done for her, removing Kenny from her future was one of the best. Like Pops had said, Kendal had fought for her honor and left Kenny mortally wounded—in business anyway.

"Mac told me about that, and it's too good to believe Ms. Richoux doesn't want anything in return."

"That's not entirely true," she said, and Mac's back came off his wingback chair.

"Piper, if you think—"

"Wait, let me finish," she said, to calm them down. "I went to see Kendal right before we left and asked why she'd help us without wanting anything. No one is that generous, right?" She remembered how easy it'd been to stand with Kendal in the shower, and how much she'd desired her hands anywhere Kendal wanted to touch her. It was the way she'd spoken to her that had unlocked her heart.

"What happened?"

"She just wanted me to be happy and never be in the position where I'd have to turn to someone like Kenny again. If I'd needed it in writing that she'd never come after the business, she'd do that too."

"My mother was a fan of fairy tales. Maybe heroes on white horses are still riding around," Molly said, and laughed.

"I love you both, but no one aside from you would've done this for me. She gave us the company free and clear because it was important to me, so I chased her to Venice to thank her."

"That's the only reason?" Molly asked.

"No." She glanced at her grandfather for encouragement. "I've been waiting for a glimpse of one of the heroes in the stories you were fond of too, and I was getting tired of the disappointment of never coming close. I was starting to believe I'd have to settle because what you share with Pops, and what my parents had, doesn't happen often."

"You don't look like a woman who's settled, sweetheart," Molly said as she reached for her hand.

"I love her, and I can't believe how much I was missing because I've never felt like this before." She laughed even though she was crying. "Kendal's fun, and she's made falling in love so easy it took me a while to realize she'd been courting me from the day we met."

"Things built carefully with time, patience, and love last through the ages," Molly said, and Piper laughed again. If only Gran knew how profound her statement was.

"Let's celebrate," Mac said, slapping his hands together and heading to the bar.

❖

With the serious part of their talk over, Piper told her grandparents about the trip and adventure she'd shared with Kendal. Molly sat back and enjoyed the lightness of Piper's voice as much as her tale. They'd certainly come full circle from the first mention of Kendal's name months before; back then, a curse always followed it.

She was looking forward to meeting the miracle worker who'd transformed her granddaughter into this happy, relaxed woman in love. In one short afternoon she had lifted the burden of her son's suicide and the scars it had left on Piper. No matter what they'd done once Piper had come to live with them, she'd thought they'd never strip away Piper's protective shroud of sadness.

Piper was making Mac laugh with something Kendal had talked her into when they heard the knock at the front door, and Molly went to answer it. Their visitor, who stood a few feet from her, had broad shoulders, tan skin, and the most interesting blue eyes. They were almost colorless, as if at one time they'd been a brilliant blue, but with age and time they'd faded in hue but not beauty.

Kendal Richoux seemed both confident and sexy, and Molly had no problem seeing how easy it'd been for Piper to fall for this charmer. They hadn't exchanged a word, but she instantly knew Kendal was as enchanting as she was gorgeous.

"Welcome to our home, Kendal. I'm Molly Marmande," she said, and extended her hand.

"It's a pleasure, ma'am." As Kendal bowed slightly over her hand her face got hot, and she almost laughed at the thought of how long it'd been since anyone but Mac had made her blush. "Piper's told me so much about you I feel as if I've known you for years."

"That's amazing to hear, since she's hardly mentioned anything about you except a rather colorful description of your first meeting." She led Kendal to the parlor and sighed at the way Piper's face transformed at the sight of Kendal.

Kendal shot Piper a teasing glare, making her raise her hands in a defensive posture. "I plead ignorance, and you have to admit you were here to steal from us at first. Leave it to me to fall in love with the pirate known better as the Great White."

"Would that make you the damsel in distress?" Kendal's quick answer made Piper laugh as she stood.

"In your dreams, honey." Piper held her hand up and closed her eyes for a moment when Kendal didn't hesitate to take it. Molly smiled as she looked at Mac. Their son and daughter-in-law could finally rest in peace—Piper had found her champion.

Piper stared into Kendal's eyes and hoped her family really was okay with this, since she couldn't fathom another day without Kendal and the love she felt for her. "I missed you," she whispered, since Kendal's back was momentarily to her grandparents.

"I missed you too, but you'll be busy for months to come because of my meeting today." Kendal turned around but didn't let go of her hand. "Mr. Marmande, you'll be happy to know they agreed to a few more vessels and a broader service agreement once the new dry docks are in place."

"Are you sure you don't want a job? This is a family business and I'd like to keep it that way. From the looks of things the family's future is looking bright." He pointed to their linked hands.

"I wouldn't worry about the family business, sir. I'll do whatever I can to assure that you're successful for many years." Kendal then turned to Molly and smiled. "I'm not sure what Piper has told you, but I want to assure you both that she's in very good hands. I love your granddaughter with all my heart, and I'm going to do so for an eternity." The declaration made all of them smile, especially Piper since, because of the elixir of the sun, that was their reality.

"It's all we ask of you, dear. That and for you to start calling us Mac and Molly," Molly said as she opened her arms to Kendal.

"Take your coat off, Kendal. You two are staying for dinner." Mac held up the bottle they'd been drinking from, and Kendal nodded.

"Actually, we should've had you over before now since Piper tells us we're neighbors," Molly said.

"I tend to the trust set up to maintain the house and grounds, but my recent visit was the first time I've been in New Orleans in years."

"Our cat burglar next to you was forever trying to get over the wall and take a look around," Mac said, laughing. "Once she knew some of the folklore about your place, and that not much was written about it, we practically had to tie her down."

"If Piper doesn't find it too spooky, we'll be moving in so we can see each other often. She makes me so happy I'm sure any ghosts still lingering there will settle down."

Piper kissed Kendal's knuckles and rested her head on her shoulder.

"Did the deed come with the true story of what happened over there?" Molly asked, and Piper almost snorted at the anticipation on her grandmother's face.

Gran had mixed a lot of history in with the bedtime stories she'd read to her every night of her childhood, and Piper was glad she was still teaching European history when she'd entered college so she could witness the way Gran wove her spell, enticing her students to love history. Her passion for the subject had filled her classrooms over the years.

"I might know a little bit." Kendal was teasing her. "Would you like to hear it?"

For the rest of the night she and Mac sat quietly as Kendal spoke and answered all Molly's questions. Kendal knew something about practically every subject, and by the time dinner was over Piper was sure Gran was as smitten as she was.

Kendal had definitely awoken her passion, but she also possessed such a history and so much intelligence that Piper wanted to know everything about her. No matter where their conversations led them, Kendal was always patient as she explained anything Piper didn't know. She used her intellect to make the evening flow smoothly, never to humiliate or degrade. Kendal also had a quick wit that made her as good at verbal sparring as she was with the thousands of swords she owned.

"It's amazing someone so young has been able to become so successful and still get all that reading in." They'd gone back to the front room for coffee and Molly sat without her shoes again. "You'd have made a wonderful teacher. You talk about things as if you'd experienced them. What a gift."

The beautiful antique clock struck twelve, and Kendal squeezed Piper's fingers before she stood and helped her to her feet. "Let me quit while I'm ahead, then. Thank you both for an enjoyable evening," Kendal said.

"Piper, are you staying?" Molly asked as if trying to gauge just how far this relationship had gone.

"Thanks, Gran, but we're heading back into the city tonight. I've kept Kendal away from her business long enough, and I'm sure she has things to do. We promise to come back tomorrow and have dinner again. One night isn't enough to really catch up."

Molly winked and smiled at her. "Good girl. I wanted to make sure you're keeping Kendal as happy as she's obviously making you. Don't let this one get away."

Even though Piper had the ability to live forever, Gran's teasing could still make her blush, if Kendal's soft laugh was any indication.

Her grandparents kissed them good night, laughing at the remaining pink tint to her cheeks.

"I don't think life could get any better," Piper said when they were alone, and regretted instantly saying it out loud. Tempting fate was never a good idea.

❖

Travis refused Rolla's offer to wash his face and chest free of blood, so the Elder walked back into the compound, most probably to his library. Morgaine had caught him unawares and embarrassed him to prove how lacking he was compared to the legendary Asra. Only soon she'd see how badly her plan would backfire on her when he made her pay for the humiliation.

The gate behind him squeaked, but it couldn't be Rolla since he never asked for anything twice. That was one reason he'd accepted a place so close to the Elder. Rolla asked for physical pleasure but didn't seem to need it as much as the feel of old parchment in his hands.

"Did they suspect anything?"

"Bailey, were you the same nervous ninny before you drank the elixir?" The intensity of the sun had almost healed the puncture in Travis's chest, and he thought of the sensation as it had gone in. He'd never experienced such quick and agonizing pain. "Any more of this hovering and wringing your hands, and even the clueless idiots in there with Rolla are going to figure you out."

"Maybe it's because I realize the consequences more than you," said Bailey, one of the Elders' archivists.

"More like you fear the consequences more than me." He waved Bailey closer so they could walk together. "Are you ready for the next part of our plan?"

"I've been saving the scrolls I found years ago, and once I hand them over to Rolla, he should be engrossed for days. If you want I can come with you."

"We've been through this," Travis said in anger. "You've got to stay and cover for me if he figures out I'm gone. He's agitated over what the great and wonderful Asra's done, so that might trump an old paper. It's about the only time he likes to blow off a little steam doing something that requires very little thought."

"Unless you're very attached to Rolla, I'll gladly take your place until you return," Bailey said softly.

"Rolla's already given me what I was interested in," he said, lifting his hand and flexing it. Rolla had told him it didn't work that way, but when he was in the sun he swore he could feel the power grow inside. "He gave me the elixir and provided the time I need to get what I want."

"But you promised to help me." Bailey pressed his hands to his chest and appeared desperate. "We're halfway there."

"We all want something, Bailey, but don't worry. I gave you my word." He caressed Bailey's cheek to calm him. "And I don't do that often."

"I'm grateful." Bailey kissed his palm.

"How grateful?" He turned Bailey around and pushed him to the ground. The weak little bastard looked back and smiled at him. It wouldn't be long now before he had the world at his feet like this, happy to do his bidding.

It wouldn't be long at all.

❖

At the gate to Riverbend, Piper put her hand on Kendal's arm so she slowed the car to a stop. "Would it be all right for us to stay at Oakgrove tonight?"

"Sure, but why does it sound like you think I'll say no?" Kendal took her hand off the stick shift and put it on Piper's knee.

"I don't think you'll say no, but feel free to if you want." Piper stared out the passenger window as if she suddenly couldn't face some horrible truth.

"Okay," Kendal said as she moved her hand to Piper's shoulder. "Do you want me to say no because you'd rather live somewhere else, or do you want me to say yes? Neither one is a wrong answer, but I'm not sure which way you want me to go."

"Oakgrove is loaded with memories. If it's special to you, I don't want to intrude." Piper turned around, but it appeared like the words were harder to get out than carrying her and the car next door on her back.

"I own lots of real estate that's special to me, but not because of any history I've had with a woman. Oakgrove is one because the first time I saw this place I had a need to tame it and make it my home. That was long before I met Angelina and Tomas, so it doesn't stand as a testament to how I felt about her. If that were true, I'd have had it burned to the ground to not have any memory of it and what happened. To me there are so many happy memories of Oakgrove, and they have nothing to do with the du'Pons."

Piper looked at her for a long moment without saying anything, her face illuminated by the dashboard light. "I asked because of the painting in the sitting room. I love you, but I respect that you might need to keep some things separate from us."

"I want you in all aspects of my life, Piper. What I own, what I've collected, and what I've experienced are all open and available to you. All you have to do is ask and I promise to always be honest."

"You really are sweet, considering what you've done for a living."

"Don't mention it to any vampire or werewolf you run across. It'll ruin my killer reputation." Kendal kissed Piper now that she was smiling again. "And before you let the painting change your mind about making Oakgrove our home, you should know it was a gift from Tomas du'Pon. He brought it with them on their one and only visit. Charlie eventually hung it over the mantel, and I didn't remember it existed until I came back."

"Don't take what I'm about to say wrong. I love being in love, but it's making me a little crazy and a lot jealous. After all, I'm worried about a woman who's been dead for three hundred years. I'll need medication when the Viking goddess gets here."

"If it makes you feel better, I called ahead and had Charlie make the house more welcoming for you." She kissed Piper again before she started toward the road. "I never want you to feel out of place anywhere with me."

"My grandfather was wrong," Piper said before kissing Kendal. "I'm the lucky one."

"I'm glad you think so."

Charlie was waiting on the porch when they arrived, and Piper held him in a long embrace before she kissed his cheek. "Thank you for the big hint you dropped, Charlie. If you hadn't sent me to find Lenore, I'd still be in bed crying."

"Good people deserve to be in love, so I'm glad the prickly bear decided to wise up."

"Do you want me to demonstrate how I can stab you and you'd still survive?" Kendal asked Charlie when he opened his arms to her.

"Okay, I'll go with teddy bear," he joked as they went down for the bags. Since none of them needed sleep they went for a walk through the gardens on the way to the stables. "Hill accepted your offer and brought by a picture for you to look at."

"If it's a shot of her in her underwear so Piper will see what she's missing and leave me, we're not interested," she said, making Piper laugh.

"I deleted those. All that's left is some guy named Leonardo. He didn't give any other information about himself and offered her twenty-five grand for information on you." Charlie cut a yellow rosebud and handed it to Piper. "Her secret weapon to digging up dirt on Kendal was you, Piper."

"Did Hill send him packing?"

"She did, and she got footage of the guy to see if you recognized him," he told Kendal.

"I'll deal with that tomorrow," she said as she fed her horse Ruda an apple.

"What's Hill doing for you?" Piper asked.

"Since I was relocating here, I thought she'd be interested in being my head of security. She can upgrade the system here too."

"What are you planning to do?"

"I haven't decided, but maybe some kind of support business for places like Marmande. I could also do some consulting for you if you're nice enough to hire me, and if that doesn't work out, Charlie and I could start giving blindfolded fencing lessons."

They talked some more as they headed back to the main house, but Charlie turned toward home before they arrived. The house he'd shared with his family had been remodeled countless times, but he refused to leave it.

"Tell him it's okay to stay in the house now that we're back. I feel terrible that we're putting him out," Piper said.

"Charlie never stays anywhere except his home here, and I'm tired of arguing with him about moving. He likes to sleep where he and his family lived together, and I can't blame him."

"He's been alone since the night Henri went on a rampage?"

"He was in love with his wife, and it's taken him some time to get over it. But then it took me over three thousand years to find the right woman to settle down with, so I'm not rushing him."

She led Piper up to the master suite and opened the French doors to the veranda. It was cold outside, but not freezing; the breeze would make a fire comfortable.

"Who do you think Leonardo is?"

"I've met a few through the years, but no one by that name recently, so I'm not sure."

"Whoever he is, he didn't think much of Hill's scruples."

"Money and power are all some people understand, and they think everyone's the same." Piper pressed against her, and Kendal planned to hold her there until sunrise. "I'm sure it's nothing but someone trying to work an angle on Kendal Richoux."

"I hope you're right," Piper said, and shivered.

"Cold?"

"No. It's like someone walked over my grave," Piper said, emphasizing the old expression of foreboding with another shiver.

Kendal wanted a quiet life with Piper and peace, but sometimes those kinds of wishes were as fleeting as dew on the morning grass.

CHAPTER THREE

Hill walked out of Kendal's study after their meeting the next morning and smiled when she spotted Piper coming down the steps. Kendal had called Hill over earlier to discuss her new role as well as talk about the visit from Leonardo. While Hill was in Kendal's office Piper had stayed upstairs to rearrange their closet, since Molly had one of their staff packing Piper's belongings at her condo to bring over.

"You found all your answers?" Hill asked Piper.

"Even how she looks under her robe up close," she teased, and Kendal laughed.

"Good luck, Kendal, you're going to need it with this one," Hill teased back. "I've known Piper for years and she gives the word 'stubborn' its definition."

"She'd be boring if she was too agreeable, so I don't mind stubborn. Call me later and let me know what you think of the layout of those offices, and don't forget about Leonardo."

"You know who he is?" Piper asked.

"Not yet, but his picture made me curious as to why he's asking about me." She put her suit jacket on and offered Piper her hand for the walk to the front door. "Want to meet me in town later?"

"Trying to ditch me already?"

"I'm having lunch with my soon-to-be past," she said before she kissed her.

"Which one?" Piper asked softly so Hill wouldn't overhear them.

"The New York one, and I thought lunch would be better than a phone call this time. It might make for fewer headaches down the road."

"I'm sure he'll appreciate it."

Kendal took one of the cars in, and from Bruce Babbage's smile and welcome, she could tell he had the wrong impression. He was starting to babble and making a lot of hand gestures the way he did when he was excited. It'd be short-lived.

"I can't believe you called," Bruce said as he sat with Kendal in the Palace Café. As in most of their takeovers, she'd tapped Bruce to take the lead when she'd chosen Marmande as her excuse to travel to New Orleans. He'd sulked ever since she'd sent him home with a severe reprimand and no prize. Marmande was off-limits to him. "It's a good thing you got all this crap out of your system. The team's put together some great prospects, and if you're not ready to go full-time, I'll take the lead."

"Don't get ahead of me, Bruce. I called you because I didn't want to do this over the phone or have you hear it from someone else." She stopped so the waiters could serve lunch and refill their glasses. "I'm retiring and I've asked Michelle Butler to take over. Once the news breaks I don't want you to think you're losing your place. You'll have a job with me as long as you want one."

He sat on his hands as if trying to keep from lashing out at her, but from the way his eyes moved rapidly back and forth, he was frantic. It didn't happen often, since Bruce prided himself on control, but she knew him well enough to recognize all the signs.

"You can't do that." He pushed his plate away and spilled half the cream sauce from his fish on the tablecloth. "You owe me more than that."

She twirled a little of the spicy shrimp and pasta she'd ordered and let him burn some of his anger away. This meeting was a waste of good food, but she'd wanted to let Bruce down easy as a favor to his father, who she cared for, and for the loyalty he'd shown her at first. After a few deals, Bruce enjoyed the kill more than any other part of the job. He seemed to thrive on the misery of the owners whose companies were on the block.

"I asked you here as a courtesy, so calm down. That's always been your problem. You get your head full of steam over stuff you have no control over, and it pisses me off since all that bravado is usually aimed at me."

"So after everything I've done to build you up and make money for you, there's no discussion on this? Michelle's in charge and I'm supposed to fall in line?"

"You've built me up?" She laughed and took a sip of wine. "I brought you into the business because our fathers were friends, so take your revisionist history and sell it to someone who's interested. Despite your behavior today, you'll retain your position, but Michelle is a better fit for the top job."

He put his hands flat on the table and leaned in. "You're delusional if you think I'm taking this bullshit like a punk who doesn't deserve better."

Bruce had a coughing fit when Piper grabbed him by the collar and yanked him back into his seat. "The world is full of possibilities, Mr. Babbage, but you won't find a better deal than this," Piper said softly as she kept moving to Kendal's side and kissed her.

"She's right. If you can do better I won't hold you back," Kendal said to Bruce, but she kept her eyes on Piper's face. Her part was done, and she was glad she'd done it in person. After this, she wouldn't see Bruce again and wouldn't miss him even though he'd been in her life for years.

When he reached into his jacket she refocused on him. "I thought we had a good relationship, but I can't accept being fucked over." He threw the envelope at her with so much force it landed in her plate. "My contract says I've got to give you three months, but I figure we end this today. The sooner I'm done with you, the quicker I can start my own shop. Nothing in my contract, though, states I can't bid on the stuff I'm working on now. Maybe the lost revenue will prove to you how valuable I am."

Kendal stared at him for a long uncomfortable span before she extended her hand to him. The business would continue to make money without her, and her absence would allow the name Kendal Richoux to start to die away. This would soon be a chapter of her history, but Bruce was missing a crucial fact of her makeup. Time, and all the years she'd lived, would never dull her competitiveness.

"Best of luck to you, but think carefully about doing anything stupid. You're gone as of today, and you'll be locked out of everything before you make it to the street." She squeezed his hand when he tried to pull away. "You want your own business, do it, but not at my expense. For once take after your father and work for what you want."

She increased the pressure and brought him closer. "You're not strong enough to threaten me, so don't try it again, and don't ever throw anything at me." She briefly glanced down at the envelope in her plate. "You do and I'll cram it down your throat and pull it out the other end."

"Listen, you—"

"It's time for you to go," Piper said.

"I may not be fucking her, but I know more about her—"

That was all he was able to get out before Kendal stood and grabbed him by the throat. "You ungrateful little son of a bitch." She tensed her hand and smiled at the panic in his eyes. "You think you can talk to her like that?"

"Let him go, honey," Piper said as she placed her hand over her heart. Bruce's face was getting redder, but Kendal wasn't ready to release him. "We don't want the nice restaurant people to call the cops, so drop him."

Kendal hesitated a second longer before pushing him back hard enough to topple him over. He immediately started to cough and massage his neck. "Get out of my sight, but apologize to the lady before you go."

"I'm sorry, Ms. Marmande," Bruce said in a whisper. "I didn't mean any disrespect."

"Sure you did, but it's not worth getting upset over." Piper tugged Kendal toward the bathroom. "You okay?" Piper asked when she was sure they were alone.

"I feel like an idiot for subjecting anyone to that asshole, and he ruined my pasta," she said, but laughed as she lifted Piper up on the counter.

"If you're lucky we might find something else on the menu to satisfy your appetite." Piper kissed her hard as she wrapped her legs around her waist.

"I'd say you were a tease, but I know better. My loss for not coming on to you sooner."

"You came on to me plenty," Piper said, and stopped her hand from getting any higher than her knee. "This is one of Gran's favorite places, so behave yourself."

"I'll try."

"Speaking of Gran, she asked if we'd gotten our costumes for the ball yet. They both sound so excited about it. It's been ten years since they attended, and they can't wait to introduce you to this bit of the New Orleans carnival tradition next week."

"Should I burst their bubble and tell them I attended the first of these things?"

"And have them think I'm marrying some lunatic? No way, Monsieur St. Louis. Do you care who we go as?"

Kendal slapped Piper softly on the butt and walked her back to their table. The mess had been cleared away and the table had been reset. "Whatever you like."

"I think I've already had the pleasure of meeting the dashing Jacques St. Louis the first couple of times we got together. That afternoon you had me over for lunch under those oaks made me think of the stories you'd told about him." She stopped and laughed at Kendal's wink. "God, that makes me sound as crazy as you," Piper whispered in her ear.

"If you'd like to meet Jacques for real, it can easily be arranged. I even have his walking stick somewhere around the house."

"Perhaps some other time. Like I said, I think I know that part of you already. The 'gentleman' I'd like to go with is Antonio De Cristo."

"Should I be worried that Italians in tight pants and leather boots turn you on so much?"

Four new dishes were put on the table and the waiter didn't interrupt when Piper leaned closer and took her hand. "I'm thinking the only ass you need concern yourself that I might be interested in is yours. After staying in the house you had then, seeing the flowers you created and hearing Lenore tell me that story—I don't know. I just thought 'he' sounded incredibly sexy."

"You're sweet, and Antonio was important back then because of the Inquisition. Kicking a little religious ass was his thing."

"That's who I want to go with, and with any luck, we'll run into a pack of priests on the way and you can show off for me," Piper said before kissing her cheek.

"You got it, but I hope you're into facial hair. It was a pain to get on back then, but I had to fit in the best I could." Kendal stopped talking when Piper trailed her fingers over her neck and face.

"I'll take you any way I can get you."

CHAPTER FOUR

The King's Masquerade Ball was always held on King's Day to launch the carnival season in New Orleans. The city's society elite had started it years before, but now the mayor and his or her spouse were always the hosts. Kendal had attended the inaugural event with Angelina, and Tomas had come as their chaperone, but that night hadn't been as thrilling as the anticipation of having Piper on her arm.

She'd left Piper with her grandparents to get ready while she transformed herself into one of her alter egos from her past. The tight leather pants and white silk shirt brought back memories, and the seamstress Charlie had found got the cut of her black velvet jacket right. The only thing missing was the sword she'd carried as De Cristo, and she scratched around the mustache and goatee Charlie had helped her with as she went down to get it.

Charlie had polished the silver on the ornate piece and left it on the desk in the library, but she stopped dead as she began to remove it from its sheath. Someone was outside and it couldn't be Charlie, who'd called from the stables a minute before. She stepped out to the large porch in front with the naked blade in her hand and closed her eyes, but all she heard was the wind through the leaves, traffic, and the clop of horse hooves.

"What's wrong?" Charlie asked when he was close enough.

"Did you see anyone out here?"

"Just you looking like a badass from the past."

"You're a funny guy, and I'm getting funny in the head since I thought I heard something." She put the sword away and took the reins from him.

"You want me to take a walk and check the area?"

"And get all sweaty before you pick up your date, Prince Alar?"

"It's been decades since I've heard that name."

"With any luck, you'll hear it screamed plenty tonight, if your date has any sense."

"Yeah, right," he said as he ran his hand down Ruda's neck. "I'm skipping the horse and taking the BMW, so I'll see you later."

She watched him go but still concentrated on the trees behind her to try to pick up the anomaly she'd heard. Despite the overwhelming sense someone was watching, she tied Ruda to the stair railing so she could finish dressing. When they got back she'd take him for a ride around the property as a precaution.

She finished by tying her hair back with a black silk ribbon and fastening her cape in place. "This is a fashion item I don't miss," she said as she pulled the material back to mount Ruda. She got in the saddle without damaging the bouquet of daffodils she'd ordered and headed next door at a trot. With her last glance back from the gate she didn't spot anything or anyone that didn't belong, but it didn't mean the scene was as peaceful as it seemed.

❖

"Meet me at the oasis an hour past sunrise." Travis stood at the line of pay phones at the airport. He was taking a huge risk flying commercial with the package in his carry-on, but his large bribes had gotten him through security so far. It'd only get easier when he landed in Egypt, where he had contacts everywhere who always needed money.

"Did you find it?" Bailey asked.

"Rolla's map was pretty accurate once you deciphered it, so we'll see what happens tomorrow."

He hung up and shouldered his pack, curious as to how this experiment would turn out. Rolla wouldn't find out about it until it was too late, but Travis was sure he'd be fascinated with the results. He and Bailey were about to test the limits of the elixir like never before—at least, Bailey hadn't found any records of such a test in Rolla's library, so they were sure they were breaking new ground.

"Let's hope we don't lose our heads over it if it doesn't work," he said, and laughed when he patted the top of the bag.

❖

"Piper, either that's your date at the front of the drive or it's a ploy to make Kendal jealous." Molly pointed outside through Piper's window. "If you don't know who it is, and they're available, I'm dumping your grandfather if they agree to take me."

Mac laughed as he stepped behind his wife. "Hell, that costume's so authentic I might go with her."

"How can you be sure it's her?" Piper asked as she finished her makeup. She'd decided to get dressed at Riverbend so Kendal could surprise her with her transformation.

"No matter how many times we've met or whatever the circumstances, she always carries herself the way she's sitting in that saddle." Mac and Molly took turns hugging Piper. "I'm glad she's on our side, because if she wasn't, I think she would've gotten this house too, along with my toothbrush. Now I believe she'd give up everything she had to make sure you're okay."

"I know that, but what makes you so sure?" Piper asked.

"At first it was because she stood and fought Kenny Delaney for the sake of your honor. Don't get me wrong, I knew she helped us so you'd get to keep the company, but I think shutting Kenny up and dropping him in a hole was a motivation too. Besides, it's not every day someone gets their head flushed in the toilet at the Piquant."

"You heard about that?" She wished Kendal had taken a picture of the asshole when she'd finished with him in the bathroom.

"A friend of ours was arriving for an early dinner and saw Kenny on the way out, soaking wet. The staff never usually talks about any of their guests, but they made an exception for that rude son of a gun."

"Kendal and I had a talk about Kenny and why she'd come to our rescue, and it made me feel cared for. It's nice to have someone I can count on aside from you guys."

"That's what I see whenever Kendal looks at you. No matter what happens to us, you have someone who'll hold you through the bad times and, more importantly, help you enjoy the hell out of the good times. She loves you, my sweet girl, and that makes us both happy."

Piper waited until they'd left the room before opening the doors out to the veranda. Like Oakgrove, Riverbend had a large wraparound front porch and matching veranda on the second floor. At night the upper level of the house had a nice breeze from the river, but all she cared about now was that the design gave her a good view of Kendal riding toward her.

She twitched the fabric of her dress into place, glad she'd done so much research before she'd made her selection. The top of the midnight-blue dress was tight, showing a fair amount of what she hoped Kendal thought would be enticing cleavage, while the bottom flared out, leaving the shape of her hips a mystery.

"I forgot to ask one thing," Kendal said before the horse came to a stop.

"What?"

"Do you speak Italian?" Kendal smiled up at Piper. She hadn't been able to take her eyes off Piper and how she looked in that dress.

"No, but I'm sure you'll muddle through somehow and figure out how to be romantic in English."

Kendal laughed and shook her head. She'd never met anyone like Piper. No matter how many years or centuries they spent together, she was positive she'd never be bored. With a quick tug, the cape rippled behind her without tangling when she dismounted as gracefully as she could, then sent Ruda home to the groomer with a slap to his rump.

"Buonanotte, bella Piper," she said as she bowed deeply at the waist, holding the flowers up and behind her. "I hope you're well this evening." She lowered her voice to the timbre she'd used whenever she'd had to don a male façade.

"I'm fabulous, but I'd really like to see those pants up close. Can you come up here in them?"

It took less than a minute to make the climb, and Piper kissed her when she handed her the daffodils. "You're beautiful."

"Would I have interested you, Antonio?" Piper asked as she unbuttoned Kendal's jacket so she could slip her hand inside her shirt.

"Had you lived back then our history would be much longer than the months we've been together." She put her hand at the base of Piper's throat and slowly moved it down. "I've enjoyed my life, but I've never felt blessed for the thousands of days they've gifted me with until I met you."

"If Gran and Pops weren't downstairs waiting on us, we'd be late."

She offered Piper her arm after another kiss and gladly accepted the hugs Mac and Molly gave her when they made it down.

"You two should win best costume tonight," Mac said as he helped Molly put her coat on.

"The only prize I'm after is getting Piper to dance with me."

"Don't overdo the sappy," Piper said with a pinch to her side.

The limousine Kendal had ordered was waiting outside, and they allowed Mac and Molly the most comfortable seats. She unstrapped the sword from her waist and scanned the area again before getting in after Piper. She was positive someone was out there watching and waiting, but for what?

"I think you'll like this ball, Kendal," Molly said as Kendal opened the bottle of champagne she'd gotten from the cellar at Oakgrove and had the driver chill. "When we were younger, we never missed it."

"Sounds fun," she said as she handed out glasses. "Here's to a great time."

The rest of the ride was pleasant as they talked about nothing important. When they arrived, the ballroom was already crowded, and the Marmandes seemed to enjoy introducing her to a few of their friends on the way to their table.

"Would you care to dance, madam?" Kendal offered Molly her hand. The music had changed to an old-fashioned waltz that'd made Molly start to sway in time with the tune.

"I'd love to."

Molly was a great dancer, and as much fun as Kendal was having getting to know her through small talk, a flash of color dragged her attention away. As she and Molly neared Piper and Mac, Piper's expression signaled that she'd noticed the same thing. Their fun was about to be cut short.

❖

"So much for leaving her alone like they promised," Piper said as she watched Kendal and Gran.

"Did you say something?" Mac asked.

"Only that Gran is monopolizing my dance partner. Let's go cut in." She took his arm and his lead until they were close to Kendal and Gran.

"May we cut in?" Mac asked.

"Notice anything out of place?" Piper asked when Kendal held her and twirled her around the floor; she almost wanted to pretend she was ignorant of unwelcome guests.

"Besides you in this sexy dress?" Kendal glanced at the bandstand. "Yes, but it doesn't make sense."

"Why not?"

"Because while you might recognize Cleopatra over there, I'm sure you missed the four others she brought with her." Kendal held her closer as the music changed again to a ballad. "It seems like a summons they expect me to reject so they brought muscle, but that's not the usual style. Maybe you should take your grandparents back and let me deal with this."

When Piper tugged on Kendal's goatee to force her to look at her, she hoped the glue Kendal had used would hold. "I'm not a piece of fluff on your arm, and I'm never going to play that part. Do you understand me?"

"I don't think I've ever treated you like that."

Another tug made Kendal tense in her arms from what seemed to be annoyance. "That you just dismissed me makes me think so. What, if something hard or dangerous comes along I'm supposed to run and hide until you take care of it?"

She caressed Kendal's cheek and brought back her smile. "My friends bought white dresses and made their intentions known at the end of an aisle. I drank from a cup to bind my life to yours forever— literally. That makes me your wife in a way more binding than anyone here can imagine, so don't *ever* shut me out."

They'd stopped moving even though they were in the middle of the dance floor, and Kendal shielded her from the other dancers.

"I love you, and because you're mine, it's my job to protect you from the evils I know exist. With more time you'll realize the monsters aren't simply fairy tales to frighten small children, and I want to shield you from all that as long as I can." Kendal kissed her and held her so she could whisper in her ear. "Don't hate me because I do."

"I could never hate you, but I want you to promise me you won't ask me to leave your side. It's where I belong."

"You might want to wait before you ask me that. I don't mean any disrespect, but you don't know yet what that might mean." The way Kendal said it made her sound as if the admission had pained her.

"I just need to know that you want me in your life…all aspects of it, and that'll be good enough for me. You've walked alone long enough, Asra. You don't have to anymore. It's why you big silent types take wives. I should correct that assumption now, in case you thought it was because you were expecting me to do dishes or something," she teased, trying to get Kendal to smile again.

"I love you, Piper, and I'll promise you whatever you want." Kendal kissed her again before taking her hand and leading her to the back of the room through a series of doors to an outside patio.

"Antonio De Cristo, that was an interesting choice," a masked figure said.

"Are you here for a reason, or are you here to play guessing games with me?" Kendal asked.

"I'm not your enemy, Asra, try to remember that. In the coming days you'll need as many of us who care about you on your side as you can get. It's why I've assembled the group I did to deliver the Elders' message." Morgaine was dressed as Cleopatra but had skipped the black wig.

"I did my job and asked to be released from my commitment. My brother and that unnatural bitch that made him are both dead, and I've given them three thousand years of loyalty. What else do they want?"

"Remember, in your position you're not supposed to question. You are to follow and do the will of the Clan. It is the price of your gift, the same gift they know you've now shared with another," Lenore said. "I came to verify that Morgaine's done her job and given you the invitation. At the next full moon you are expected, Asra, and I beg you to comply. You may not gain release from your obligation to the Elders."

"And if she doesn't comply?" Piper asked.

"I'm sure she's told you what happens if the sun is taken away from us. It's the fate of those who disobey." Morgaine moved closer and lowered her voice. "We share a commitment to keep Asra whole, so accept my apology for intruding, but I have no choice. It looks as if you are doing well, though, and you found what you were searching for in Italy, Piper."

"I did, and thank you for your help, but I hope these Elders don't mind if she brings guests. She's not going alone."

Morgaine nodded and smiled, then opened her mouth in apparent shock. "Lenore, come and see."

Piper barely recognized Lenore in the gypsy costume she was wearing, but she managed a warm smile when she moved closer. Had Piper talked only to Morgaine, she probably wouldn't have been convinced of Kendal's epic story. Lenore had written Asra's story and retold it with such passion Piper couldn't help but believe it.

She was about to ask why Lenore had paled considerably, but when Lenore took her hands, her world went instantly black and silent. She started to go down, almost like a balloon that someone had stuck with a pin, and the last thing she remembered was Kendal grabbing her before she hit the ground.

"What did you do to her?" Kendal yelled as she cradled Piper gently. She'd been dazed in battle but never, unless by choice, lost complete consciousness. Seeing Piper limp in her arms scared her more than anything she'd ever faced.

"You know I'd never harm her, Asra, and you also know the legend as well as I do." Lenore dropped to her knees and ran her hand over Piper's head.

"Do you seriously think the prophecies were waiting for a sarcastic boatbuilder from New Orleans?" Kendal regretted the flip question as soon as it left her mouth when she felt the hard pinch to her thigh.

"And what the hell is wrong with being a boatbuilder from New Orleans?" Piper asked before she pinched her harder. "You think I'm sarcastic?"

"It's the reason I fell in love with you, so I never want to change that about you." Relief flooded through her so quickly she came close to collapsing next to Piper. "Are you all right?"

"You have a little explaining to do, but I'm fine. I know we haven't been together long enough for me to know all your expressions and what they mean, but you look scared. Are you all right?"

"I'm just worried about you, my love."

Piper tugged her closer as if wanting a little privacy. "That wasn't supposed to happen, was it?"

"No, it wasn't. Did it feel like you fainted?"

"It was more like a current ran up my arms when Lenore touched me."

Morgaine and Lenore moved closer, interrupting their whispered conversation. "Then what happened?" Morgaine asked.

"It was weird," Piper replied, her answer loud enough for all of them to hear, but her eyes never leaving Kendal's.

"Elaboration would be good," Morgaine said with a little impatience.

"I love you, but back off," Kendal warned her.

"It's all right," Piper said softly, smiling at her in gentle affection. "I promise I'm fine." She turned to face Morgaine and Lenore. "I know you probably have a logical explanation for what happened, but to answer your question, I had the most vivid dream ever. It seemed so real but it couldn't have been."

"Why do you think so?" Lenore asked with a huge smile.

"It was about Kendal, but from the way she was dressed, I shouldn't have a mental reference for that level of detail. You did a great job when you told me her story, but this was like a clip from a movie."

"How was I dressed?" Kendal asked.

"You looked almost like a savage, and you were getting off a large black horse covered in as much armor as you were."

Morgaine fell back until her butt hit the floor. "Oh, gods."

"Think, love, the sword at my side, what did it look like?" Kendal asked, fascinated with what Piper had said so far.

"It was a dream, baby, what does it matter?"

"Try to answer her question, Piper. Trust me, it's important." Lenore reached out to touch Piper again, but pulled back at the last moment.

"It was very different from the ones I've seen you carry, and it was the only thing out of place, considering how you looked."

"What does that mean?" Morgaine asked.

"While Kendal looked wild, the weapon looked delicate. The handle appeared to be white ivory and..." Piper closed her eyes as if to remember better.

Kendal finished the description for her. "The only other color on it was a yellow dragon coiled on the tip, and its eyes were—"

Piper looked at her in disbelief. "Two perfectly matched sapphires."

She nodded to let Piper know she was right. "What you saw was the Sea Serpent Sword, and it's still one of my favorites."

"Where is it now?" Morgaine asked. "Asra, where is it now?" she asked again when she didn't answer quickly enough.

"It's at Farthington House outside London." Her legs twitched with an overwhelming urge to pick Piper up and just bolt.

"You have another collection of swords in England?" Piper teased her as if trying to defuse the tension. "How many do you need?"

"I've walked through our closet, love, and gotten a look at all your accessories. Don't think about making fun of me," she said with a kiss to the tip of Piper's nose.

"What else did you see, Piper?" Lenore asked.

"Kendal's hair was longer and she wore it down. She was standing on a hillside as if waiting for something to happen." The tone of Piper's voice had taken on an almost trancelike quality, sucking them in even more. "Troops stood behind her looking in the same direction as she was, but I couldn't make out what they were studying."

"And the day, what did it look like?" Lenore asked softly in a way that didn't break Piper's concentration.

Kendal pictured the events. She remembered the nervous energy prickling her skin and the weight of the new gift strapped to her side. The rain that made her leather jerkin squeak with every movement had been falling for days, causing her horse to constantly shake his massive head to clear his eyes. In that time, those who knew her thought she was young for a warrior, but her fighting skills were legendary.

No one thought it wise to challenge Erik Wolver no matter how different *he* looked from the rest of the northern people. Her dark hair and skin stood out in the sea of fair redheads and blonds, but they'd befriended her and given her a place in their society.

"It was stormy," Piper said. "It seemed like everyone's mood was like the thunder booming around them, except Kendal's." In a gesture of what felt like curiosity Piper pulled on the ribbon holding her hair back as if to compare the reality with her dream. "Erik. That was the name you picked in that life, wasn't it?"

"Erik Wolver."

"But how would I know that? I don't really remember all the chapters Lenore read from your book, but I'm fairly certain I'd remember the picture of you dressed that way. There wasn't one."

Before Kendal answered, she hugged Piper tight. In her heart it was an act of farewell to the innocent Piper she'd met. "Your grandparents are inside waiting for us."

"I asked you a question."

Kendal moved to stand, helping Piper to her feet as soon as she did. "And I have every intention of answering it, with help, I'm sure." She glanced at Morgaine and Lenore. "To give you an answer that'll satisfy you, though, will take time." She smiled before she kissed Piper's pout. "You have eternity to contend with, love, so it's a good idea to start practicing patience."

"You aren't always so patient."

"With you, no man or woman would ever learn patience once they tasted…" She paused, searching for the right word. She cocked her head to the side when Piper arched her eyebrow. "A bite of the peach, as it were." In a move worthy of the gallant Antonio, she bowed over Piper's hand and kissed it. "You can't blame me for my impatience in that arena, dear lady. I have the longevity of a god, just not the willpower of one."

"You never will if I have anything to do with it. There's a whole lot about you to love, Asra, but your hunger has to be one of my favorites." After their kiss ended, Piper laughed when she noticed they were alone. "We'll be all right, won't we?"

"I won't lie and tell you the future will always be easy, but you have chosen to spend your life with a warrior. To me that means no matter what the challenge, I'll meet it head-on to keep you safe. So yes, we'll be all right."

"Then dance with me one more time before we have to think about whatever all this is about."

Kendal requested another waltz from the band leader and gave Piper her wish. They smiled at Molly and Mac as they passed the table, then kept their eyes on each other.

"I fell in love with you here, and that only grew when we were in Venice," Piper said as she moved her hand closer to her neck. "But right now I love you so much I can hardly breathe."

"It's a long story, but tonight you've found your place, and the Elders can't deny you anything."

"My place is with you. That's all that's important to me."

"Yes, and I didn't need an old prophecy to prove it to me."

CHAPTER FIVE

The ride back was quiet and Piper seemed content to just rest in Kendal's arms as the car sped along. They promised Mac and Molly they'd have lunch with them the next day as they walked them to their door, and then Piper fell into her arms for the short trip home. When they reached Oakgrove, Kendal walked Piper upstairs, where one of the maids Morgaine and Lenore had obviously brought with them helped Piper out of her costume. Any servant who attended an Elder usually came from a family who'd served the Clan for generations and was highly trusted.

"Will you be okay?" Kendal asked Piper.

"Go, I'll be down soon."

Morgaine and Lenore were waiting for her in the front parlor. "How much time do I have before they want to see me?"

"I told you, they're expecting you by the next full moon. They're angry, but I think in light of tonight's developments, they might change their minds about the lecture they'd planned to deliver."

"Rolla's never been one for lectures, so I'm sure he had more than talk in mind. What happened tonight will most probably make him want to destroy her." The aged brandy burned a little going down, but it tasted good after a night of champagne. "You know as well as anyone that a good number of them don't want to see change. The world is of their making, and they won't accept someone like Piper coming into it and trying to steer us in a different direction, if that's what she sees."

"Have faith that the life you've led up to now is good for something," Lenore said. "No matter how long some of us have lived, we've seen you consistently pick the good fight, even though at times it would've been more prudent to either sit it out or fight for an enemy that would've given you power. Talent like yours hasn't always been used for the betterment of mankind against evil that even the Elders were at times powerless to stop."

"Tell them I'll come, but I'll fight anyone who tries to harm Piper. This time I *will* pick any side to keep her whole."

"We promised to help you tell her the story, but I think it'll be easier and better if she hears all this from you. Go to her, Asra, she is waiting for answers." Lenore kissed Kendal's cheek before walking out. If there was one thing Oakgrove didn't lack, it was guest rooms, and Kendal knew Lenore was anxious to get to her books.

Morgaine, though, stayed behind, so Kendal stood and poured herself another drink. For months she'd put the past out of her mind, but a large part of it sat across from her, looking at her like their worlds would never be the same.

"Are you happy?" Morgaine asked.

"Don't do this."

"After all we've been through I have a right to know if you're happy." Morgaine got up and moved behind her.

She tensed when Morgaine placed her hands on her shoulders, but she didn't shrug them off. "My answer will only bring you pain, and because of what we've been through, I'll never wish to do that to you." She let her head fall forward as she took a deep breath, and Morgaine tightened her hold on her. "I love you. I have for so long now, and you'll always be a part of my life."

Kendal spoke softly, but Piper heard every word, and she pressed her hands to her lips to keep quiet. She was smart enough to know it'd take time to erase Morgaine from Kendal's mind and her heart, but she never expected to hear the truth so bluntly put as she eavesdropped outside the door.

"But our roles now are that of warrior and watcher. She owns my heart and I love her with all that I am. I see it every time she looks at me, and it makes me want to cry from the joy of it. I've lived all this time waiting for her to come into this world and complete the person I am. If something ever happens to her I don't care to see another sunrise, and I'll sleep the sleep of the dead."

"You can feel like that in so short a time?"

Kendal finally stood and stretched to her full height, causing Morgaine to let go of her and take a step back, which made Piper relax a little. "Morgaine, you and I both know the most important law of the universe."

"For everything that exists, something else exists to balance it."

"Correct. For the darkness there is light, for good to exist there must be evil, and for every person another must be born to complete who they are. It's the only way to achieve balance. Piper is my balance. She's the other half of my soul."

Piper finally noticed something about the room she hadn't been in since their arrival. The picture of Angelina over the main fireplace was gone, and in its place was a large landscape she'd admired from the house in Venice. Kendal had made every effort for her to feel at home, no matter where they were.

"My search is done, and she's my peace as well as my lover."

"I'm sorry to question what you've found, Asra."

"I think you've earned the right to question whatever you see fit," Piper said when she came into the room. "You'll always be welcomed wherever we are, Morgaine. I know the friendship you and Asra share is special, and I don't ever want her to forfeit that, especially since you've taken such care to keep her safe all these years. With time I hope we can become good friends as well."

"Thank you, Piper." Morgaine turned to Kendal and bowed her head. "You have chosen well, Captain. I'll leave you two alone."

"How long have you been standing there?" Kendal's voice held no hint of accusation, and to Piper she looked incredibly sexy. The old-style white shirt was slightly opened at the neck and she'd pulled it out of her leather pants. With her hair still down, Kendal looked like she belonged in the pages of a romance novel.

"Long enough to learn something about myself."

"What's that?" Kendal looked at her as if trying to figure out if she was wearing anything under her robe. The expression on her face now made Piper believe she'd guessed nothing.

"That knowing I belong to someone, and I mean completely belong to someone, doesn't mean I've lost a part of myself."

"Did you think you would?"

"My friends seem to always be making huge sacrifices once they fall in love, so yes, I thought so."

"You should know I belong to you just as completely," Kendal said, and took a step closer.

"Knowing that taught me something else." She took a step forward too.

"What's that?"

"That I've never wanted you to touch me more than I do at this very moment."

She loosened the tie of her robe but Kendal didn't come any closer. Passion between them hadn't been a problem, just a dance that Kendal always initiated. Tonight that would change.

"I thought you wanted to talk?"

"I do, but why always talk of eternity if you don't mean it?" She dropped her robe and smiled at the way Kendal was staring at her. "I want to talk to you, but I want you to touch me first. Will you do that for me?"

Kendal moved fast to scoop her up and carry her to the rug in front of the fireplace. The burning logs made popping noises, but Piper ignored them as she watched Kendal strip off her clothes. The anticipation of Kendal lying over her and giving her what she wanted made her wet.

How much she craved Kendal embarrassed her at times, but when Kendal touched her and found her this ready, it seemed to only fuel Kendal's passion. In turn, Kendal's body was perfect in her eyes, with only a few scars she'd gotten as a small child, but to Piper it was the elixir's way of reminding her lover of her humanity and a way to keep her grounded.

"Asra," she said. The name was becoming more familiar and easy to say.

"What, love?" Kendal came to her, covering her but keeping most of her weight off her by pressing her hands to the floor.

She spread her legs wider to bring Kendal closer. "I need you, but I want—"

The words died in her throat as Kendal held her weight up by only one arm, moving her other hand between Piper's legs. Kendal spread her open and instantly found her hard clit. Piper dragged her nails down Kendal's back until she reached her butt, then with her newfound strength, she reversed their positions.

What amazed Piper was that even though she was now straddling

Kendal, the sexual massage she was getting had never stopped. "I can't let you get too smug, Captain," she teased as she dipped her hand between Kendal's legs. "I love that you want to touch me so much, but I want you to crave me. Do you?" Kendal was wet so there wasn't a question of how much she knew she was wanted, but she wanted to hear the words.

"Crave you?" Kendal tilted her hips up so she could feel more of her, but the move also drove her fingers deeper into Piper. "Like a hungry man who hasn't eaten in years craves a feast." Kendal flattened her feet on the ground so she could move with more strength.

With every upward thrust her fingers drove farther into Piper, who returned the favor with a countering downward stroke. The urge to stop and enjoy what Kendal was doing to her overwhelmed her senses. The orgasm was beginning to build like she was on a wave starting to crest, and when it broke it'd wash through her like a storm. She fought it, wanting more than anything for them to reach the shore together.

"Come on, let me hear you," she whispered into Kendal's ear when she bent over her, letting their bodies come closer together. The move slowed them down a little, but Kendal seemed to want more and flipped their positions again.

Kendal moved up a bit so she wouldn't have to stretch to keep her hand in place, then started their movement again. Their skin made a slapping noise as they came together, and Kendal stopped and looked at her.

"Are you all right? I'm not hurting you, am I?"

The sex together had been intense but never anything like this, and it wasn't a good time for talk or worry. "Don't you dare stop," Piper said before she bit down on Kendal's nipple. "I want to feel you and I want you to finally stop holding back. Don't hold anything back." A sound close to a battle cry ripped from Kendal's chest, and Piper was sure everyone in the house heard it.

"Oh, God," she said as the intense pleasure made her shut her eyes. She didn't move her hand, but she'd lost the ability to concentrate on anything except the orgasm she was experiencing. Kendal kept her hips moving, which was enough to get her off because she tensed, then slumped over her.

The walls of Piper's sex clutched Kendal's fingers, then relaxed. She felt spent but her body seemed to want more. Kendal took a deep breath and moved to the side a little so she could breathe, but kept her hand in place. After a minute she reached behind them and grabbed the soft blanket off the sofa.

Piper hissed when Kendal withdrew, but snuggled closer. "You know something else?" she said in a raspy voice.

With gentle fingers Kendal combed back her hair and smiled down at her. "What?"

"I've never felt beautiful and desirable with anyone until I met you. I regret that you weren't my first so this would forever be my definition of how it should be with someone you love."

"That's because you never met anyone with the sense the gods gave a goat, if they couldn't see you for who you really are. But then, I should be thanking those same gods that you didn't. It was different in the old days, but now the law really doesn't allow me to slice up my competition, no matter how much I want to. Now I'm limited to toilets and my fists when it isn't Clan business."

"Flatterer," she said with a laugh.

"With you and for you, definitely," Kendal said, and tapped the end of her nose.

"I love you and I can't tell you that enough." She sighed and hugged Kendal closer. "Now that even my toenails are completely relaxed, tell me a story."

"Before we start, have you ever heard of a seer?"

"Is it something like a fortune-teller?"

"Not like the ones in the French Quarter with the cards and the crystals, but someone truly gifted with sight of the future."

"I'm a Catholic girl who went to private schools, so no. None of the nuns who preached about everything I did wrong said anything insightful about the future except that I'd probably end up teenaged and pregnant if I didn't start paying attention in class."

Kendal laughed and shook her a little. "You didn't tell me you were wild back then."

"I wasn't. Their sheltered existence didn't make for very original threats, so they lumped us all together when it came to behavior. The worst thing I ever did was wear red socks every once in a while to brighten up my day."

"You'll have to show me pictures later, but let me get back to my story." Kendal stopped to throw more logs on the fire and grab the cushions off the sofa. "Considering what you've seen already, you know the fairy tales you've heard all your life are based on some iota of truth. In time they get a little exaggerated, but you'll come to see, and have to accept, that some things are real even if it's hard to wrap your brain around them."

She let Kendal lie down, then moved over her so they could face each other while they talked. "If you tell me something is true, I'll believe you."

"Thanks, your faith in me means a lot." Kendal took a deep breath. "Let's review some things first so you'll have the facts to understand what happened. The immortals who exist are all ruled by the Elders of the Genesis Clan, and their ages and makeup are known only to their ranks. I've met a few in my lifetime, and of all those, I'd guess Morgaine and Lenore are two of the oldest and serve on Rolla's governing court."

"And Rolla is?"

"The old man is one of the oldest and is the leader of the Elders. Like Lenore, his passion is his library and being an archivist. He seldom leaves the library in the compound in Egypt."

"If he's as good as Lenore, he must be a wonderful writer. Listening to her read your story was one of the best experiences of my life."

"She's good enough to make me think she was talking about someone else in those pages." Kendal kissed Piper's forehead when she laid her head on her chest. "I was brought into the ranks to fight back the darkness. Morgaine trained my body, and when I was ready, she took me to Lenore to train my mind."

Egypt, 1302 BC

"No warrior, no matter how talented, can win every battle, Asra. At least not without a good amount of wit." Lenore walked around the large cavernous room lighting candles as she spoke. "You've been in the desert for years now, and Morgaine has honed you into something to fear in battle, but I hope you'll give me as much of your attention during our time together so you'll go out into the world with a balanced education."

"I promise to do my best." Asra was still looking down at the strange clothes she'd been given to wear. The leather hid a lot of her tanned skin and felt strange after wearing only a loincloth for so long.

"Even if my hips aren't as enticing to watch when I walk as Morgaine's, let's hope that's true," Lenore said teasingly as she took a seat across from her. One of the servants brought out a tray loaded with tea and sweet cakes once they were situated.

Despite her new longevity, Asra felt the heat of a blush at what Lenore had said. "I'll try to keep myself in check."

For months after that they covered the history of the world, centering on stories she'd never heard as a child. She'd never seen any of the creatures and spirits Lenore told her about in the place where she'd grown up. Her only experience with the horror of it was the day she'd come home to find her father and their entire household staff ripped to shreds. With Morgaine she'd learned the defensive moves to protect herself and ultimately defeat her enemies, but Lenore taught her what to look for and what made them tick. Every weakness and everything ever learned about any evil that could tilt the fate of mankind could be found in her library, and Lenore made her learn every bit of it until it was as engrained as any defensive maneuver.

Once they'd covered that aspect of her responsibilities, Lenore gave her lessons on the Genesis Clan and the Elders who ruled it. Their rules would dictate her actions, but it didn't bother her since her life wasn't much different than it had been as captain of the Pharaoh Hatshepsut's elite forces. As it was then, her job was to fight on command and destroy any target they sent her after.

"Did you enjoy your night off?" Lenore asked when she joined her in the library.

"It was a training exercise, so it was all right. It still amazes me to find these things living in a city and no one has a clue."

"Did you have any trouble?"

Asra walked around the large space until she was in front of the shelves loaded with books instead of scrolls. "Everything you said was true when it came to spotting them, and everything Morgaine taught me made it easy." She ran her finger down the row at eye level until she reached one with no title. It was more of a journal, and all the passages were signed Bruik, followed by his crest stamped in wax with the date.

Oakgrove, Present Day

"Who's Bruik?" Piper asked as she lifted her head. "That sounds more like a car than a person."

"You remind me so much of a younger me." Kendal laughed and pressed her fingers to Piper's lips. "I interrupted so much in all our lessons, I thought I'd drive poor Lenore insane, but in Bruik's journal you'll find the answers to your questions."

Egypt, 1302 BC

"Why doesn't this book have a name?" Asra held it up and waved it in Lenore's direction.

"It needs no name and it needs to go back on the shelf where you found it." It was the first time Lenore had reprimanded her; thus far she'd only encouraged her to learn to love the library as much as she did. No book or scroll had ever been off-limits.

"Why?"

"Bruik is an Elder, one of the first, and those are his thoughts."

She put it back but wasn't ready to let the conversation die. "If he wanted to keep his thoughts private, he wouldn't have given you his journal. If it's in a library, it's meant to be read."

"Morgaine was right about you."

Asra lay across the pillows by the roaring fire and held her hand up to help Lenore down beside her. "In what respect?"

"You are relentless once something intrigues you. If I don't give you the answer you seek, you'll talk circles around me until I tell you. Am I right? Or better yet, you'll sneak back in here the moment I turn my back on you."

"If you're sure I will, save yourself the trouble and tell me."

"Bruik's our seer, and when he has insight of the future, one of his servants brings it to me for recording. These are his thoughts," Lenore said as she took the book down, "or more precisely, his visions of the future, so they aren't entirely private. Only those who have some idea of what to do with them are given the privilege of reading them. You wouldn't want to know all the things that are going to happen, would you? The future would hold no surprises for you."

Asra had almost let Lenore off the hook, but her last comment caught her attention. "I've never asked you for anything since I got here."

"You've been my best student so far." Lenore put the book behind her as if to make her forget it. "But I'm sure you're getting ready to ask me for something, so what is it?"

"Are there any visions of me in there?"

"I can't tell you that."

Asra reached for Lenore's hand when she began to stand and move away. "You can't, or you won't? If our time together has taught you one thing about me, it's that you can trust me." She released Lenore's hand and cupped her cheek. "Tell me, and I'll never betray your confidence."

Lenore hesitated, but opened the book and flipped to the right section. "Before I read anything, you need to know that no matter the talent of the seer, no one has full access to the future with perfect clarity."

"Is this Bruik often wrong?"

"Not wrong, no," Lenore said with her hand over the page she'd opened the journal to. "More like incomplete. He can see things, but a lot of interpretation still has to take place to determine the true meaning."

"What did he write about me?" She hadn't been this excited about anything since her father gave her her first practice sword. Her brother had taunted her for days that it'd never happen because she was being sent away to learn the role of a traditional Egyptian maid. Her father's gift was a sign he believed she was meant for something more than that, and maybe that's what Bruik had seen.

"One of our own will find the sibling with the true heart, while darkness will take the other of the great warrior's children," Lenore read, and Asra didn't need any explanation of the first line.

"The slayer will spend years roaming the world, always searching for the good fight. At times she'll fight where she's sent, but she'll always take arms where she's needed if the cause is just."

"That's a good thing, right?" she asked, and Lenore nodded.

"Among us are those who see the world only for what they can gain, but the slayer's sights will always be on the good that can be achieved for those we're sworn to protect, and her fate will always follow that path."

Asra wiped the tears Lenore had started to shed, and her touch made Lenore cry harder. "That's good enough. Don't read any more if it's going to upset you this much."

"My tears aren't because of sadness." Lenore dried her face and smiled. "Of all the passages in here, I've always found yours to be the most beautiful and hopeful. Understand this was written long before even your father was born, and Morgaine and I have longed to meet you because of this vision."

"Why?"

"Our slayer will stay true to her course," Lenore kept reading, "but in her future she'll find one who'll first be thought a worthy adversary, but not one that means her harm. At that meeting balance will finally be found, and the gift of eternal life will be given at the defiance of the Clan. Once this comes to pass, another will awaken her and a new powerful seer will come forth."

"Another will awaken her. What does that mean?"

Lenore turned so she could see the next line. "Love will find her, but only the touch of another will awaken her potential of sight."

"When's this supposed to happen?" she asked, and noticed a little more. "How will I know?"

"From the first of our kind, the power of the sun and the life it gives shine brightest in our eyes. The power of the sun and sky is the key to the blue of the eyes that will forever chronicle time." Lenore touched below her eye, then laid her hand on her chest. "The elixir will not be the same for the one the slayer mixes it for. It will bring immortality, but her eyes will stay the color of beautiful green water, and only then will the slayer know who she has found."

"Who will she be?"

Lenore smiled and pointed to the last line before Bruik's signature. "She will be the slayer's reason for living."

❖

Piper kept her eyes closed and ran her hand slowly over Kendal's chest. For once, no matter how much her life had changed since meeting Kendal, she didn't believe the story. At first she didn't buy the whole immortality thing because her eye color had stayed the same and because the concept was plain crazy, but the sleep or lack of it had convinced her, even though she still had a kernel of doubt. This, though, was too much.

"Do you think it's just because the elixir didn't work on me?" That was the first time she'd voiced her greatest fear. To have Kendal live on without her and not knowing if fate would ever bring them together again preyed on her mind.

"I have every confidence you're no different from me, my love. At first I doubted Bruik's writings, but never that you'd share your life with me for as long as there are sunrises."

"What made you doubt?"

"The picture over the mantel's gone, but when I first came back I sensed a trace of Angelina's ghost here, and I'd put Bruik's visions to rest when I thought about how she died." Kendal held her as if she couldn't look at her for this part of the story. "Think about it. She was given the gift of immortality and kept her green eyes, but even if she'd lived out the night, I doubt she'd have been much help in the realm of prophecy. Her visions would've always centered around the evil her life had become."

"Would you have let her live if she'd asked you?"

"No," Kendal said without hesitation. "The moment she drank from Henri, Angelina was dead. I mean, she'd always look the same, but the most important part of her was gone. Her soul died the second Henri turned her, and no matter how hard she fought, she'd have given in to the darkness as easily as she did to the thirst."

"So in a way you felt as if she was the love you sought."

"No." Kendal finally made eye contact with her. "The way I interpreted Bruik's passage was exactly how he wrote it, but not how you probably understood it. Love would find her. That was the first part, and it was love I felt for her, but my brother mistook my feelings as being deeper than they were and, in his mind, stole her from me. The last part was that another would awaken her, and in my opinion, that happened too. Henri awakened Angelina, not me. His gift would have given her an eternal life just as if I'd mixed the elixir for her, and once the night was over and I'd cleaned up the mess he'd left behind, I never thought of his prophecy again. Bruik's vision had come to pass as far as I was concerned, and it'd simply end up as a chapter in Lenore's book.

It'd never be the love story she'd hoped for, and I felt more guilt than sadness at Angelina's loss."

"And now?"

"I have found my love, my balance, and my other half, just like he said. Tonight it was Lenore's touch that awoke the part of your mind that'll see far into the future, if that's your choice."

"And if I don't?"

Kendal kissed her forehead. "Then we'll be boatbuilders or winemakers, if that's what makes us happy, but I won't allow anyone to force you into a life you don't want."

"And if I do?"

Kendal laughed at her question. "Then I suppose you'll always know when I'm doing something I shouldn't."

"And you'll love me no matter my choice?"

"Until the day even *we* have no more tomorrows to look forward to, and even then I'm positive I'll love you beyond that."

They lay quietly after that and Piper thought of what the future might hold now. Whatever her choice, it wouldn't change Kendal's feelings toward her, but this would be so far outside what she was used to, it was hard to accept.

"Remember, no matter what you decide, or your path, I love you and will walk it beside you," Kendal said, as if reading her mind.

"Then I'm blessed with so much more than infinite birthdays."

CHAPTER SIX

L enore went to Morgaine's room at sunrise to invite her out for a morning walk. After the previous night's events, it was more important than ever to pull their forces together to protect Piper and Asra from the faction of dissenting Elders that was becoming more powerful by the day.

With her hand on the knob of Morgaine's room, she concentrated her hearing downstairs to see if Kendal and Piper were still talking. "I pray you forgive me for not telling you the rest of Bruik's vision, Asra, but it was for your own protection. Our job now is to go where Piper leads us before it is too late for all mankind."

❖

A few spears of sunlight had pierced the thick veil of fog outside Morgaine's window, and she thought it resembled their future. It'd be mostly dark, with the people under Oakgrove's roof representing the last bit of light. The house was quiet, but the peace was the last calm before the storm that now seemed inevitable, considering what had happened last night.

She sighed as she placed her hand on a cold pane of glass. Her body was incapable of fatigue, but her mind felt tired from all the different scenarios she'd thought of since Piper fainted. The vision of the past had changed her mission, and Rolla would not only have to understand, he'd have to accept it if they wanted any chance of success.

"Well?" she asked Lenore when she entered without knocking.

"From the sound of it, we might have trouble getting them to concentrate on anything other than finding a place to lie down."

She laughed, which made her relax a little. No matter how hard the challenge, it was nice having Lenore so close. "Considering how they interact, flat surfaces might not be necessary."

"Are you okay?" Lenore sat on the unmade bed.

"I may not scream contentment, but I'm happy for her. You must be thrilled since your long-awaited love story has come to pass."

"You know the rest of Bruik's words as well as I do, so save the flowers and candles for later." Lenore ran her fingers through her dark hair to try to comb it back. "He gave an outline, but his vision is incomplete."

"It does suck that he didn't give any hint to the end of this story," she said, and smiled.

"I guess he thought that was Piper's job."

"Let's go for a walk and leave them to their afterglow a little while longer. You can tell me what you found in that stack of books you insisted on bringing. After that you can help me recruit Charlie."

On the way down the stairs Lenore touched the frames that held paintings of Oakgrove's past residents, which made Morgaine look at their faces. She'd never gotten close to the house when Kendal lived here as Jacques, since Henri had trapped her less than a day after her arrival. Her stupidity had cost her seeing Kendal as the master of this house and the brief happiness it'd given her.

"Do you think Charlie will turn you down?" Lenore stopped at the large portrait that took up most of one wall in the foyer. The beautiful woman holding a baby flanked by two small boys had an engaging smile, and the brass plate at the bottom had the name *Celia St. Louis* engraved on it, along with the names of her sons. This was Charlie's family.

"Actually, I think Charlie will be packed and ready for anything once we talk to him. I just think it'll be polite to ask."

"You have learned a few things with age," Lenore said as they walked outside toward the gate.

"The only one who's acknowledged him up to now is Kendal, so I want to give him the respect he's owed. Did she tell you he was the one who killed Henri?"

"Her written account was as riveting as always, and I was surprised she'd given him the reward she'd wanted for so long."

"Really?" Morgaine asked as she held Lenore's hand while they climbed the steep incline of the levee.

"Let me finish," Lenore said as they sat on the bench that overlooked the Mississippi. "Then I thought of who Asra is, and it wasn't all that shocking that she let Charlie destroy Henri, especially when you see the painting of his wife and children."

"They faced Ora and her strongest creation and won, even if some of the elders had their doubts."

"It's time to start Charlie's book, so I'm glad you're planning to ask him to join us. He can fill in the details of his life before he came to Oakgrove." The wind picked up, so they moved closer together. "Who else are you asking? You and Kendal are talented warriors, but it'll take more than that to win this fight."

"Aside from the four who came with us, I don't trust anyone else yet. It's probably not enough, but we can't chance anyone leaking information that might give us an edge."

"Do you have a chance with seven?" Lenore asked softly.

"I don't know, but one of the seven is the slayer of Bruik's vision. Not that I need his prophecies to tell me Asra's heart, but he was right about one thing. She'd fight anyone and anything for those she loves, especially Piper Marmande." Morgaine kissed Lenore's cheek to reassure her. "She's so close to getting the life she's only dreamed of, and that'll make her hard to beat."

"Promise me you'll put as much into the fight as she will. Once we're done I want to show you the city I love. Henri stole that from me before, but I think you'd enjoy the place that's been my home for a long time."

"I'd like that." She kissed Lenore's cheek again. They'd been friends for ages, and like Asra, Lenore had taught her when she'd first come to the Clan. Lenore's lessons and help had been the main reason she'd achieved Elder status. "And I promise, what Bruik saw involves more than just Piper and Kendal. Rolla knows as well as we do the consequences of failure. Once we talk to Charlie we're going to have to contact Rolla and tell him what's going on."

"I'll be happy to take care of that, but because the message is coming from us, he's going to be skeptical. He knows how we both feel about Asra, so he'll see this as a ploy against his wish to punish her."

"We'll call him together, and if he ignores us, we'll know we really are on our own."

Lenore stood and held her hand out. "I hope he can convince the others, but some of them couldn't care less about the fate of mankind."

"Bruik's prophecy stems from what the Elders decided, and that alone should make them realize mankind isn't the only group in danger. If an old enemy really is awakened he'll turn his vengeance on them before he concerns himself with the world." Morgaine lifted Lenore's hand with her fingers when she stopped walking. "Rolla and the others should've listened to you back then. You were right about the evil that dwelled in our ranks."

"They buried the truth because no one wanted to admit their mistake."

"We'll know soon enough if they've learned anything from it." She started toward the house again, glad the fog had lifted a little.

"This really is a beautiful place," Lenore said as they stopped at the road for traffic.

"When she wrote me and told me about the land she'd purchased and what her plans were, I thought she'd finally gone crazy."

Lenore laughed and bumped shoulders with her. "Why?"

"Back then I thought she was wasting time and energy building something for no reason. Because of who we are, we can't stay in one place too long, so she'd only get to enjoy her effort for a short time." The mist and the early hour made it easy to imagine the house then.

"What do you think now?"

"She's wiser than I gave her credit for because she's enjoying the effort now. With careful planning, the house and lands passed to the St. Louis 'heirs' so she could come back when she was ready."

"I'm a woman who loves books, but I believe we can all find what Asra has in Piper. I don't want to spend eternity with the written word as my only passion."

"Where do you think you'll find this great love?"

"I, as well as you, will find it when we stop looking," Lenore said with a smile as she released Morgaine's hand and walked away.

❖

Kendal and Piper were still wrapped in their blanket on the cushions Kendal had thrown on the floor. The fire had gone out, but Piper was happy to lie in Kendal's arms lost in thought. One of the greatest aspects of being in a relationship with Kendal was her ability to let her be silent and not be intimidated by it. She hadn't been in many relationships before this, and that was why. Most people felt compelled to fill the air with nonsense when they had nothing important to say.

She heard Morgaine and Lenore outside but Kendal never moved, so she didn't worry they were suddenly needed to run off somewhere.

"What are you thinking so hard about?" Kendal finally asked after a few hours had passed.

"Where exactly do they expect you to go and meet these people?"

"The Elders' compound in Egypt is where Rolla likes to get his henchmen together," Kendal said, but didn't sound concerned.

"He's pissed because of me, right?"

"You have to understand Rolla and the others."

Piper moved so she was lying completely on Kendal so she could kiss her. Nothing she'd ever experienced made her worry more than this, not even the loss of the business. "What about them?"

"I've served the Elders so long because they do stand for justice and believe in the protection of mankind, but they're not perfect." Kendal combed Piper's hair back when she laid her head back down on her chest. "Neither am I, but my decision to give you that cup wasn't wrong."

"Obviously he and the others don't think so."

"They just don't like change, but they hate imbalance more than anything."

She could hear the beat of Kendal's heart and wondered what would happen if they were both locked in a cave somewhere. Would she have even this small comfort? "Do they think I've unbalanced something?"

"No, their worry will come from me fighting for someone else or, more importantly, against them. Imagine an army of things like Henri, and we sit the fight out."

That'd be a nightmare, actually, and why Piper was glad she no longer slept. The sight of Kendal with that sword sticking out of her chest and her falling to her knees would've dominated her dreamscape for months. "So we're going to Cairo?"

"Actually their compound is deep in the desert. Decades ago they decided to stay away from the big cities in a place where they could expand. It's where Rolla spends most of his time, even though Morgaine told me he's originally from Scotland." Kendal laughed and Piper joined in because she sounded so carefree. "I thought the heat alone would've sent him running back to the Highlands, but he loves it."

"And no one's ever seen a huge building in the desert?"

"It's all underground."

"I thought the sun is important to us now?"

"It is, and the lack of humidity there allows Rolla to read outside without his ancient texts falling apart." Kendal moved her hands to her back but her touch was soothing. "Of all the places that belong to the Clan, it's big enough so that all of us have rooms there. It's where I keep some of the pieces I was able to salvage from my father's home."

"When do we leave? I'd like to see all that."

"What happened last night makes me think we need to put the Elders on hold. I find it a strange coincidence that, of all the swords I own, you picked one out and were able to describe it in detail. Before Egypt, we need to go to London."

"How long do you think we'll be gone if we have to visit both places?"

"You can stay if you want. I'll be back as soon as I can."

Piper moved so fast she was surprised that she startled Kendal a little when she lifted her head and pressed their noses together. "Get the fact that I'm not letting you go anywhere without me. I just have to think of a story to tell my grandparents if it'll be more than a long weekend."

"I could always make it a quick trip for both things, and you can concentrate on what's happening at Marmande's."

Piper pressed her hands to Kendal's cheeks hard enough to make her look funny. "I don't think it's a good idea for us to separate. My grandparents are really my only concern, not going with you." She squeezed a little more and Kendal's mouth was a tight *O*. "Stop trying to ditch me."

Kendal didn't break Piper's hold and enjoyed her smile. The elixir had increased Piper's strength, so maybe she would eventually be interested in learning how to defend herself. Even if she retired from the Clan for a while, evil wouldn't take a vacation from them.

"I might have an idea," Kendal said as she rolled them over.

"Does it include me?"

The logical part of her mind screamed it'd be a huge complication to bring the Marmandes, but it might also be a mistake to leave them behind. "Call your grandparents and invite them to come to England with us. Tell them I have business there and outside Cairo. They can stay at Farthington if we end up going."

"You won't mind?"

"Nothing should happen in England except some sightseeing and some nights on the town. On the off chance they see something hard to explain, how will they handle that?"

Piper sat up and let the blanket fall away. "If I have enough time my grandparents will accept anything about me"—she reached out and tapped the end of Kendal's nose—"even you."

"Let's hope we always have the time to explain well enough that they won't need intense therapy." Kendal admired Piper's body as she rose and stood over her.

"Gran and Pops will roll with the punches, you'll see," Piper said as she offered her a hand up. "Now I'd like to see the sword room. Think we can sneak upstairs before anyone sees us so you can show it to me? A shower would be good."

Kendal stepped over their clothes and went to open the door. "I doubt we'll have to sneak anywhere." There lay two folded robes and a tray with a coffee service and a basket of croissants. "Our staff is as good at discretion as fulfilling needs." Piper came and looked. "So, sword room or shower?"

"Can't I have both?"

"Tell me why you're interested in the sword room and you can have whatever you want." She helped Piper put on the fresh robe.

"I'm as curious as you are about how I picked one from all the ones you own. Maybe if I'm surrounded in your collection I'll have another fainting spell so I can give you more answers."

"If you promise to stay conscious we can have breakfast in there and I'll finish my story."

❖

"Don't feed me a load of empty air, Morgaine. I gave you a task and I expect you to do it." Rolla wasn't screaming but she saw him start to breathe heavy. Their video link had taken longer since she'd asked him to empty the room he was in so they could tell him what Piper had seen.

"Bruik's prophecy about the slayer has been fulfilled," Lenore said as she squeezed Morgaine's knee.

"What other fanciful daydreams will you two come up with to save Asra? I realize you love her, but she must face the Elders for what she's done."

"My oath to you and the others is to chronicle history as it happens," Lenore said with heat, and Morgaine returned the favor of putting her hand on her thigh out of sight of the webcam. "I'll never mislead anyone, as has happened through time in different civilizations to glorify those who don't deserve it, simply because someone orders me to." Lenore pointed at the screen and Morgaine almost laughed. "I resent the implication that I'd go back on my word for friendship."

"It seems suspicious that Bruik's vision would come to be at the moment Asra needed salvation."

"You've already decided her punishment to be that drastic?" Morgaine asked. "Did you think it'd be that simple? That she'd follow one of your puppets to her grave like a tamed lion?" His inability to see reason made her decision to break ranks with the Clan, should it be necessary, much easier.

"Careful how you talk to me, Morgaine."

"Try your best to tear me down, but I'm going to send the others a message before they arrive for your lynching. That way when you're facing defeat, and nothing's standing between you and complete darkness, they and you will realize your inability to accept the truth brought about your destruction."

"Come now, the end is near. That's going to be your cry of panic to save your pet?"

"No, Rolla, it's going to be that Asra has found the green-eyed seer of Bruik's prophecy. Lenore woke her, and the first sight she had was of the Sea Serpent Sword and Erik Wolver."

"With no prompting?" Rolla fell back in his seat and closed his eyes.

"Lenore's touch made her fly back to that point in time." She glanced at Lenore before Rolla opened his eyes. "Even if Asra had prompted her as a way of deflecting problems from what she did for love, she was never told all of Bruik's vision. There was no way for her to have that sight as her first unless she's extremely lucky."

"I'll call everyone and tell them to prepare in case they're needed, and you explain to Asra the importance of getting her head straight when it comes to her job. At this moment it'd be the worst thing for her to quit and lose the backing of the Clan."

"She'll be ready—she has no choice."

❖

"What's that about?" Bailey asked Travis.

Travis had his ear pressed to the door, but the thick teak walls of Rolla's study made it impossible to hear anything. Rolla's obsession with recording everything that affected the Clan meant he could watch the video later. "It was Morgaine and Lenore, but he threw me out before they started talking."

"You didn't hear anything?"

"We'll have to wait until they're done. Just calm down." He moved them away from the door and lowered his voice. "Anything yet?"

"I checked again at sunset, and the cuts have completely healed, but nothing yet."

"Months sounds like a long time, but we've got a lot to do before we miss our window. I'm going to make your existence hell if this doesn't work."

"Bruik saw it all, so it shouldn't be long now. Have faith."

"It might be Bruik I bury right after you for all this crap he's gotten everyone in a panic about."

"If you didn't believe it you wouldn't have done all this," Bailey said, and appeared smug. "Admit it. You can't quit in case the prize really is as great as what Bruik saw."

"I'm not quitting, but we're already behind. It's not going to be easy."

"Only those who are willing to fight for the reward will win it."

Chapter Seven

After their shower Piper followed Kendal down to a room in the middle of the house. Kendal placed her hand on a green glass pane, and a door slid open to reveal a large room with only two chairs and a small table with more coffee and food.

The weapons that lined the walls fascinated Piper. They seemed well cared for, but she noticed the nicks and scratches in all of them as she walked around to see them up close. The swords were used not only in the practice rounds like she'd seen Kendal lay out with Charlie, but in real fights with real monsters like Henri.

"Before you came to find me, Lenore did a good job of telling you my story, but to me—these are what sums up my history. Every one of them has a story locked in the metal, and I can tell you every detail down to the moment I took possession of it." Kendal didn't stop her from walking around, but Kendal sat when she smelled the coffee she'd poured.

"We never talked about all this, but I did have a question. Why swords? I can see their purpose when Morgaine found you, but why now? There's got to be an easier way that's safer for you."

"Vampires and the others I've faced don't react to guns or modern weaponry. Silver bullets do work on werewolves, but they aren't like the unthinking creatures you see in the movies. Like wolves in the wild, they tend to live in a family setting resembling a pack, and they aren't a problem unless you go after them. I don't think we'll run into any of them soon, though, so don't worry."

"Werewolves are real?" The truth of what existed and what happened in the night without anyone knowing was truly amazing.

"Yes." Kendal wore the type of smile Piper figured she would see often, since it appeared to be her attempt to be reassuring.

"We'll get to that eventually. Right now tell me about the sword in my dream."

"What kind of world-history student were you?" Kendal asked, and laughed as if not to insult her. "I know you excelled at everything else."

"I did okay, but if I'm going to have a pop quiz about specifics, I might need a refresher." Piper folded her legs up and cradled her coffee cup against her chest.

"In 406 AD a great strategist and leader was born." Kendal stretched her legs out and picked up a muffin. "Even if not everyone can remember the specifics of his reign and life, the greatest king of the Huns is a familiar name."

"That's interesting, love, but what's it got to do with your sword?"

"Attila the Hun came this close to conquering the known world." Kendal held her index finger and thumb slightly apart. "The vision you had took place during his last campaign. The men riding with me would eventually come to be known as the Vikings, and they'd followed me to the place you saw after I'd fought beside them for months."

Northern Italy, AD 452

"Do you want to move on, brother?" Leif asked Erik Wolver as they stood together on a hill overlooking the Hun encampment.

Leif and the others knew her not as Asra but as Erik, a warrior on a quest to find a peaceful place to settle. They'd all been suspicious at first since all she had in common with them was light-colored eyes, but when the first raiders of the season had tried to ride into their village, they hadn't gotten past their new defender, who'd camped in the forest outside the clearing where they lived.

After that their king had wisely offered her a place among them and a band of men to travel with her when the Elders' message arrived. It'd taken them three months to reach this spot far from their home.

"Tell the others to make camp near the stream we found, but tell them to stay clear of the Romans and the Huns. This isn't our fight, and there's no sense losing any of our brothers over this."

Leif went off to do what she'd asked, but she stayed to study the layout of the camp. She climbed a tree for a better look and settled her sights on the large tent at the back, farthest away from the battlefield. Whoever was occupying it was hidden from view behind the closed flaps and a number of posted guards. The Elders had sent a detailed message of what she'd find and what she had to do about it, but so far she'd seen no evidence of their claims.

"The stories of the strength of his arm are true, but where is our lost lamb?" she said as she kept her eyes on the tent.

Attila, from what she'd read of him, had been born with a warrior's heart and a love of fighting, but he'd conquered too much too fast to have done it on his own. Someone must have helped him develop his talent for the art of war, and that was the Elders' concern since they believed it'd come from one of their own.

"Where are you, Julius?" She sat on a large branch and pressed her back to the trunk. Like her with her new friends, Julius would stick out among the warriors gathered around the hundreds of campfires enjoying the calm before battle.

The Elders seldom got involved in the affairs of men, preferring to be indulgent parents who allowed their children to make and learn from their mistakes. But at times, men with the ability to live forever mistook the elixir for a drink that created gods. Once they'd so anointed themselves, they craved nothing but power. She never understood what you were supposed to do with all that power once you had it, but men like Julius were often shortsighted in their thinking, if he was really down there whispering in Attila's ear.

She scanned the field again, and the lone man standing on another hill staring at the distance caught her attention. She didn't know Julius well, but she remembered him from the few gatherings of the Elders she'd attended. He had an arrogant way of speaking and standing that was hard to forget. The posture was the same, and when he turned back toward the Hun, she recognized him. "What the hell are you doing?" she murmured.

What did Julius hope to accomplish by helping Attila seize control of the world? Was it to make the Hun king his puppet once he'd reached that goal?

She jumped down, not surprised to see Leif close by. "Stay with the others and make sure they follow orders, and take my horse back with you." Leif didn't reach for the reins when she held them up, and he spread his feet a bit as if preparing for a fight. "What's wrong?"

"Take me with you. If you're planning to go anywhere near that, you'll need my help." He nodded toward the Huns and frowned. "You're a fierce fighter, but you'll need someone to watch your back down there."

"Go back with the others and don't worry about me. Believe me, I've had my fill of unnecessary battles, so I plan no harm to myself or to them. I'm only going to see a man about some information." She gripped Leif's shoulder before she headed for the tree line that circled the back of the camp and ended close to where Julius was standing. Once she was out of sight of her men, she started running, anxious to get on with why she was there.

"I wondered when they'd send someone," Julius said when she stood behind him, but still in the trees. He'd obviously sensed her, but his guards had not. "Do you remember this from your life before the Clan? Do you miss the excitement before a battle, and the anticipation of victory?"

"I fought for my pharaoh and for Egypt, but I never found the slaughter and loss of my men exciting."

"From here you can almost smell their fear," he said when she came to stand next to him and saw the Roman forces. "With our seven hundred thousand men, we outnumber them almost two to one, but even if the odds were reversed I'd still be confident of victory. I've never seen men fight with such cruel passion. This is the last battle before Rome bows at Attila's feet and the world is his."

"What's your stake in this?" she asked, but searched for the Roman commander's tent while she had this vantage point.

"Is that why you're here? You're going to stop me?"

"Why I'm here and what I'm planning to do depend on you, so answer my question. Why encourage the Hun to do all this for you?"

"The Elders you serve have turned into old men and women trapped forever in the bodies of their youth. While they sit and worry about the small problems like your brother, I'm shaping the world into a place of my making."

"And you thought the way to best achieve it was to let this

murdering savage rule through fear?" She asked to make him angry enough to make a mistake.

"It's of no consequence to you or the ancient ones," he said, and laughed as he walked behind her. When she didn't turn around he laughed harder. "My plans will be known to them only when I'm ready, and you aren't strong enough to stop me." She heard him remove his sword from its sheath. "Especially if you turn your back on your enemy. Didn't Morgaine teach you—"

"To never let my guard down," she said as she turned with her sword in hand and stopped his downward stroke aimed at her head. Some of the soldiers nearby looked when their weapons met, but none of them moved to interfere. "I'm nothing but a weakling in your eyes, but don't mistake that for *weakness*."

He bore down harder as if trying to move her. "You play the part of a man well, but don't mistake the fact that you aren't, and because you aren't, you'll never best a fighter of my caliber."

The arrogance she remembered made her give him what he wanted when she relaxed her hands quickly and stepped clear of the blow, but the sudden move made it easy to flick his sword out of his hand. "Go home to your books and your pets and leave the rule of power to fate," she said. "Man isn't perfect, but they don't need our help when it comes to their future and who they'll decide to follow. Our job is to fight to protect them from what they don't understand, and not for personal gain."

"You idiot—pretty words aren't what these sheep need," he said before he called his guards closer. "Are you good enough to defeat me and all of them?"

"I don't need to," she said as she sheathed her sword and smiled. "I'll take a lesson from you about interference, and then I'll come back for you."

Oakgrove, Present Day

Piper put her cup down and Kendal noticed it was still full, as if she'd forgotten about it because she was so engrossed in her story. "You got to meet Attila the Hun?"

"I saw him a few times, but we never formally met. No one ever knew exactly what happened to him, but I was one of the factors that led to his death." She stood and accepted a new tray from the servant at the door. "I would've been curious as to how far he would've gotten on his own merit, but Julius and his own agenda left me no choice but to interfere."

"Did I ever read about you and didn't realize it when I was in Gran's history class?" Piper poured their drinks this time.

"Sorry to disappoint you, but no. The only history books I'm acknowledged in are in Elder libraries. I've always fought only the things the Clan wants destroyed, so I didn't often get involved like I did in this case." She accepted her tea from Piper and added a large dollop of honey. "Every generation has to learn in their own way that the fighting is easy. Any army can defeat a weaker opponent, but the aftermath is the quagmire. The laurels heaped by history have always gone to those willing to fix what's broken with the people and places they've crushed."

"That's not always the case, though. Sometimes tyrants win and reshape the people they conquer into something they don't want to be, but have no choice but to follow."

"You're right, but that's the definition of what many religions call free will. Even when people have history to fall back on, they choose to repeat it, especially when they fight for the wrong side." She sighed and took a sip of her hot tea. "To win peace, you have to be completely different from what's known, but even then there's no guarantee people will follow a better path."

"At least it'll give us plenty to talk about for centuries, but right now I want to hear the rest of your story," Piper said.

Northern Italy, AD 452

Erik waited for sunset before entering the Roman camp and making her way to the commander's tent. The flames of the oil lamps fluttered when she pulled back the flap and entered by the back entrance, and the man she'd come to see jumped up in fright. He'd moved so fast his inkwell spilled over whatever he'd been writing, but he seemed more worried about her than that.

"Excuse my intrusion, but it's important we talk before you lead your men to their deaths in the morning." She sat on one of the benches where his section leaders probably sat when they were strategizing around the large table covered in maps and war plans.

"Who are you and how did you get in here?" he asked, still on his feet.

"I'm not an assassin. All I'm asking is for a few moments before you retire."

The Roman sat but moved his sword closer before he did. "You still haven't said who you are."

"I'm an interested bystander trying to even the odds a bit." She put her hands on the table to not present a threat and smiled. "The world will be a poorer place with the defeat of the Roman Empire, so I'd like to offer some advice to assure it doesn't happen."

"I'm Aspar Cirilius, and what gain are you after in this battle?" He moved to sit across from her.

"I'm Erik Wolver of the northern lands, and you could say I seek your favor, but I don't." She bowed her head in respect. "You have my word I'm here only to help you live out the day. Now," she looked him in the eye, "it's getting late and we've got a lot to discuss."

"Tell me one reason I should trust you."

"My greatest teacher told me to trust no one even if you consider them a friend, because no one can know what's in another man's heart."

Aspar laughed and slapped the table. "Your strategy is for me not to trust you? That's an interesting way of getting me to listen to you."

"All I can offer is my advice, but it's up to you to decide whether to listen. Only you know what's in your heart, and you haven't risen to your rank without the ability to know what's worth your time and what's false."

He placed his elbows on the edge of the table and rested his head in his hands. The vulnerable position meant he trusted her not to hurt him, so maybe this wouldn't be a waste of time.

"No matter what we've done, we haven't been able to slow the Hun down. Our task is to stop him before he reaches Rome, but I'm beginning to believe he does fight with the sword of Mars as well as with his favor."

She poured them both some wine and shook her head. "No man carries that much favor from any god, so let that fear go. All you need to know is that not every victory comes on the battlefield." She told him her plan, and Aspar listened intently and didn't stop her from moving some of his war models on his map to better position his men, the minor moves surprising him.

"Do you think it possible?" he asked.

"I do, and I wish you good fortune. May the gods smile upon you and your men, and may they grant you favor." She stood and grasped arms with him.

"Will I see you again?"

"Perhaps, but if not, take care and know I'll be watching your back." She left by the same route she'd taken on the way in, staying vigilant until she was safely away into the forest.

"You're wrong, warrior," she heard a woman say as the darkness closed in on her.

"About what?" The old woman was stooped and walked with a cane. Asra almost laughed that she'd gotten by her well-honed defenses—she didn't know the woman was there until she spoke.

"The favor of the gods. It doesn't happen often, but there are times when favor is granted willingly to someone like you, perhaps, or the Hun king as a reward for his battle skills."

She moved closer to see the woman's face clearly because her voice sounded so familiar. "Attila has enjoyed luck, not the blessing of any god. Trust me in that because there's no divine intervention afoot."

The old woman reached inside her cloak and removed something wrapped in what looked like rags. "What if I could give you a sword blessed by the gods?"

Asra laughed, but not loud enough to draw any unwanted attention. "If you speak the truth, why not keep it?"

"I'm no fighter, Erik the Wolf." The nickname had been given to her by the Viking king after their first hunt together. "The one who owns and wields this sword must also be pure of heart, and I'm not always that."

The woman's clothing and jewelry were common to the tribes who'd aligned themselves with the Romans. "It's not often I meet a woman honest enough to admit not being pure of heart, but you seem harmless enough. Tell me why you think that?"

She'd get back to how the woman knew her name once she answered.

"Most people don't have time to redeem the misdeeds of their youth, but you," the woman grabbed her by the wrist, "have all the time in the world to continue the good life you had before." She let her go and lifted her fingers to her brow. "Don't be frightened. I simply saw you in my dreams and thought you'd come to me sooner. I thank the gods for giving me enough life to lay eyes on you."

"Is that how you know so much about me? Your dreams are that vivid?"

"All I want is to give you a gift, not to bring you harm." She held her bundle up again. "If you accept, I ask for only one thing in return."

Asra helped the woman deeper into the forest, not wanting to be so close to the Roman guards. "I've learned many times that most gifts come with a price, so I don't expect this to be any different." Her new friend clung to her arm as if enjoying her company. "Have we met before this? Your voice sounds so familiar to me." The other strange thing was that for such a frail-looking woman, she had a strong grip.

"Who I am isn't important. All that matters is if you'll accept my gift." She handed her what Asra guessed was the blessed sword. "You'll never regret having it, you have my word."

"And what will you expect in return?"

"That you fight the good fight when called. As you told the Roman tonight, the world will be a better place without people like the Hun in it."

"And for that you'll give me a blessed sword to make the battles easier?"

"That's my bargain, but you must answer tonight."

"Keep your gift for someone more worthy. I need no gift for helping the Roman turn the fight in his favor. If the Hun chooses to fight tomorrow, it'll be the beginning of the end for him even if he lives out the day." She studied the woman's face in the moonlight and felt she was not what she seemed. The frail body was too strong, and her blue eyes had a vibrancy Asra could see even with the low light.

"Do you say that because the Visigoths are beyond that hill?" The woman pointed to where another army lay in wait out of even Julius's sight. "At sunrise they will gain much from the Romans, but at a huge sacrifice."

"That's probably true, but every soldier knows the risks." The witching hour was close, and she wanted to get back to her men before they came in search of her. "With your insight I should've sent you to speak to the Roman."

"It's why I offer you this gift. Your insight is better than even mine."

"Can I see you home?" She offered her arm, ready to be done with the conversation.

"Your answer is still no?"

"Keep it for the one you've searched for of pure heart."

"Go then." The woman came close and touched her cheek. "Your men wait and tomorrow will be long for all of us." The woman's hands were soft and warm, and they made her close her eyes and think how long it'd been since she'd been with anyone. "May the gods keep you safe for the years you must face alone." The woman's voice seemed to weave a spell she didn't want to break. "Keep your faith because the day will come when your seeking ends and your deeds are rewarded."

When Asra opened her eyes the woman was gone, and she almost believed she'd conjured her up. This wasn't the time for her mind to crack, so she laughed at her overactive imagination. The only thing to concentrate on of any importance was the battle to come and her responsibility to sit and watch. She'd only send her men into the fray if the Romans and their backup started to lose and they were needed to turn the tides of war in favor of the lesser evil.

Oakgrove, Present Day

"The lesser evil?" Piper asked.

"The Romans weren't as savage as Attila and his men, but they had a taste for battle that would've kept the world at war for generations. It was that and the excesses of their leaders, though, that led to the fall of the Empire and brought about the Dark Ages."

"Was the old woman real, or did you slip into la-la land from the stress?"

"You're hilarious," she said, but kissed Piper anyway. "Let me finish and you tell me."

Viking Camp, AD 452

"Get some rest, Leif, and tell the others to as well. Everyone in both camps is as tight as a bowstring, so I doubt we're of any concern to either of them."

She was so sure they weren't in any danger that she posted no guards, and after the men went to their tents, the night fell silent. She doused the lamp in her tent and sat on her bedroll with a cup of wine, content to wait for sunrise. All her strategy was played out, but she reviewed her plan again on the off chance she'd forgotten something.

As she brought her cup up for another sip, her tent flap opened and a woman stepped inside. It was dark, but even so, she knew this wasn't the old woman from earlier, though they were similar in height and build. When the woman relit the lamp and dropped her robe, Asra was amazed by her visitor's flawless, stunning beauty. She'd never seen any woman who rivaled or came close to such perfection.

"You don't act surprised to see me."

"This forest must be enchanted because this is my night for surprises, and none has been unpleasant," Asra said as the woman came closer and dropped to her knees. "I'm—"

The woman pressed her fingers to her mouth and smiled. "I know you well, Erik, so you need no words with me."

"May I know your name?"

"I need no name to give you everything you need and deserve."

Oakgrove, Present Day

Kendal laughed, expecting Piper's interruption and questions. "I'm going to stop there since I'm sitting in a room full of sharp pointy things and we just had this rug cleaned."

"It's good to know you're not one to kiss and tell, but you're going to have to tell me something, sunshine." Piper held Kendal's hand against her chest and bit her thumb. "Don't worry. I'm pretty good at reading between the lines."

"At first I thought it was some misguided attempt to exhaust me to the point I couldn't fight if needed, but it didn't make any sense. Julius knew better, and the Romans had nothing to fear from me."

"What was it then?"

Northern Italy, AD 452

The taste of dawn was in the air, and Asra stretched out next to the woman still in her tent. She kept her eyes closed and pretended to be asleep to see if the woman had any other plans. If she was an assassin she'd make her move soon; she was now in a kneeling position next to Asra but was dead still.

The woman started chanting in a language Asra didn't understand and moved her fingers methodically over Asra's lower abdomen right above her thigh. The sensation was magical and Asra kept her eyes closed to enjoy it, but after a few more moments, it stopped and the woman laid her hand over her heart.

"One day the story of the sword will be revealed to you, and until it comes to pass, you'll wear my mark. The sea serpent will only uncoil for its true master, and when it does it will change your life forever if you choose wisely." The woman kissed her again and whispered her final message close to her ear: "Take care and know I'll always look over you and those you love."

Oakgrove, Present Day

"For the second time in less than a day I opened my eyes and the woman was gone, and I felt almost drunk when I moved. That was why I missed the vivid detail of what she'd done, and I've always wished I'd focused sooner."

Piper stood and knelt between her legs. "Focused on what?"

"I left that out of the story because I thought no one would believe me, but when I opened my eyes I could've sworn I saw…" She let her voice fade away, still somewhat convinced the woman and all of it were caused by some form of madness.

Piper put her hands on Kendal's thighs and rubbed them softly. "Whatever you saw was real, so don't doubt yourself. I certainly don't."

Kendal pointed to the spot where the woman had concentrated her touch. "I saw a tattoo of a dragon right here, but it faded fast. I thought maybe she was a witch sent from one of the nearby tribes to curse me, but in my heart I couldn't believe that." She still thought of that encounter and the dragon the woman had somehow drawn, but nothing like it had happened again. "When I sat up the sword lay next to me, and the dragon coiled at the end of the pommel exactly matched my tattoo."

"And you never saw the woman again?"

She shook her head as she helped Piper to her feet. "She and the tattoo disappeared that morning, but the sword has been mine since then. It looked a little dainty, but I wore it the next day even though we didn't fight. With the extra help the Romans didn't exactly win, but they did stop Attila's advance, and since he died the next winter, the Hun threat died with him."

"How so?"

"He had sons, but none of them had enough support to rule outright, so Attila's empire crumbled when it fractured into different warring tribes. The only thing that's important to us about all this is that your vision showed the day after my visit from the mysterious woman."

Piper stood on her toes and softly bit her chin. "Lucky for you it was the day after."

She laughed, enjoying Piper's playful side. "Lucky how?"

"Erik Wolver would've had to explain her black eye this morning," Piper said before she kissed her. "Thanks for the story, and now that you've finished, we have something to do."

"Run up and try out the bed this time?"

Piper kissed her again and laughed. "What a one-track mind you have, which is something I'm grateful for, but hold that nasty thought."

She took Piper's hands and followed her out of the room. "Let's find Morgaine and Lenore and compare your story to what they know about this."

"You think they withheld something?" That had never happened, to her recollection.

"I might or might not be this great seer everyone's been waiting for, but I don't need a gift like that to know they did."

"Why are you so sure?"

"Call it women's intuition," Piper said as she closed the room back up. "Stories are never as easy as they met and they lived happily ever after. We've got some lumps coming and I want to know how bad it's going to be."

"I never thought of it that way."

"That's why you hooked up with the sarcastic boatbuilder from New Orleans."

"Well," she said, and wiggled her eyebrows.

"Such a one-track mind."

CHAPTER EIGHT

"A ll recovered from last night?" Molly asked when Kendal and Piper joined everyone in the front parlor.

"Hey, Gran." Piper kissed her grandparents as Morgaine smiled at Kendal from her seat. "We slept in since we had so much fun last night, so I hope we didn't keep you waiting long?"

"You know your grandfather. We were thirty minutes early, but it did give us a chance to meet some of Kendal's colleagues." The way Molly said it made Kendal glance at Morgaine and Lenore again to see what, if anything, they were up to. "And it gave me the chance to appreciate this most authentic copy of *The Ninth Wave*." Molly walked to the painting over the mantel. "I saw the original in St. Petersburg when we toured Russia. I forget the artist's name."

"Ivan Aivazovsky," Kendal said, and was glad for Molly's faulty attention to minute detail. The painting wasn't a copy and wasn't the one she thought, but it was one of Ivan's. "I'd tell you more about its history, but I'm sure someone in the family picked it up somewhere because they thought it'd look good up there."

Piper shook her head and laughed at the obvious lie, but art usually was cheap when the artist was young and starving, and you had the time to shop during the day while vampires slept. "Would you like a tour?"

Molly accepted Kendal's arm and asked numerous questions as they walked through the house. Piper took Mac's and followed, but Morgaine and Lenore disappeared outside. Kendal wanted to know if they'd contacted Rolla, and how it'd gone, but putting Piper's family at ease was a priority, especially if they accepted her invitation.

"Except for running water and electricity, everything in here seems to be original to the house." Molly ran her hand over the carvings on the desk in Kendal's study. "That's extraordinary. Even the wealthiest families lose pieces to marriage and inheritance eventually."

"Oakgrove's been lucky, then, that no one's thought to take anything away." Kendal opened the doors to the formal dining room. It was too cold to eat outside, and the staff Morgaine and Lenore had brought loved to show off for people who appreciated the effort. "Mrs. Marmande." She pulled out Molly's chair.

"I taught for years but still consider myself a student of history, so thank you for the tour. You have a wonderful delivery of the facts that'd be a wonder in the classroom. Once you get tired of the corporate world, you should think about an encore in education." Molly smiled at the young woman who served the seafood gumbo as their first course.

"I'd like you to return the favor and join us for a trip I have to take for business. Piper's agreed to join me, but we'd love for you both to come too."

Morgaine stared at Kendal as if she'd gone mad, but Lenore nodded and slapped her hands together as if she couldn't wait to get started.

"With the contracts we've got lined up, this might not be a good time for both Piper and me to leave town," Mac said, making Molly lose her smile.

"That's why we have a management team, Pops." Piper shook her finger at him. "Besides, I'm sure Kendal's country house has a phone and Internet service."

"Country home where?" Mac asked.

"Outside London, and there's room for everyone, so don't disappoint the Marmande girls," she said, and Mac nodded, but not enthusiastically. "Great, we'd like to leave tomorrow if you can swing it."

"We'll be ready, don't worry," Molly said, followed by a muffled thump, which Kendal guessed was Molly kicking Mac under the table.

"Tomorrow's fine." Mac smiled.

The rest of lunch was uneventful and leisurely, but once they were done, the Marmandes left to pack with a promise they'd be ready by ten the next morning. Morgaine was right behind Kendal with her hands on her hips as she closed the door.

"Do you think that's wise?"

"You can argue with me later about anything else, but they're coming. We don't know who to trust, and they'll be in danger as soon as every enemy I've made figures out what Piper means to me. I won't leave them here with no idea of how to defend themselves."

"We're going to pick up a sword, not search for all the hidden vampire lairs in England."

"What haven't you and Lenore said about all this?" Kendal asked when Lenore joined them.

"I'm still researching and have some other materials being delivered to Farthington," Lenore said as she held both her and Morgaine's hands. "Once I know everything, you will, but I want to be sure so we don't make any mistakes."

"So you don't know any more than what you've said about the sword or Piper?" Considering what Piper had said, her suspicion of being kept in the dark was starting to grow.

"Kendal," Lenore placed her hands on her chest and looked up at her, "Morgaine and I will never hurt you or Piper for any reason. We knew the moment Piper came to us after you left that if we put you back together, you'd give her the elixir if she agreed. We knew, and we were prepared to fight whoever tried to punish you because we thought you deserved love and happiness. Please don't start to doubt our commitment and loyalty to both of you."

"Doubt in you has nothing to do with my question." Kendal covered Lenore's hands with hers. "But if you're not telling me something, I need to know, especially if it has to do with Piper."

"Can you wait until I have all the facts?"

"I have no choice," she said, but smiled. "I trust you both, and I'm grateful you understood what Piper means to me."

"You love fiercely, and we might need that passion in the coming days," Morgaine said. "Lenore woke Piper, but the prophecy come to life might've woken something else too."

❖

"If this was going to work, it should've by now." Travis paced around the body lying naked in the sand.

"Everything's healed and his body's filled out, so give it a few more days. You can't expect instant results if he's been asleep for over fifteen hundred years." Bailey rubbed oil along the now-muscular body.

Travis watched, amazed at the transformation. When they'd brought their prize here he'd resembled one of the mummies from the museum in Cairo, but the elixir had done its job and brought his body back to its original state. The power of the sun would really bring eternal life, of that he had no doubts now.

"He's breathing, but it could take months for him to wake up. If his brain was as shriveled as his dick, he might not be of any use to us."

"So much time with Rolla should've taught you to curb your crudeness, but if it's all you understand, his dick seems fine to me." Bailey slathered it with oil. The daily ritual had made the leathery skin start to appear healthy.

"Take a good look and remember what he looked like when we found him, because it'll give you a picture of what'll happen to us if Rolla finds out."

"You've been good to Rolla." Bailey lovingly stroked the man's penis. "He'll forgive you anything with time."

"If you think that, you weren't paying attention to the story you read me. When I was a soldier this was considered treason." Travis was about to head back and give Bailey up when a gasp came from the man, and he suddenly sat up and quickly drew his hands to his throat. When he made it to his feet, he was panting but was in a defensive position, as if to ward off any more harm.

"Master." Bailey dropped his hands and bowed his head. "You've come back to me."

"Asra." The raspy voice made it hard to understand him, but Travis got the name.

"She still lives and serves the Elders, but there are signs the prophecy has begun."

"Who is this?"

"Tell him to speak in a language I understand," Travis said, his hand on the pommel of his sword. He wasn't about to lose control of Bailey now.

"He just wants to know who you are," Bailey said, but his eyes never left the man's body.

"I am Julius, Elder of the Genesis Clan," Julius said in French.

"Travis," he said, and threw Julius a bag with clothes. "Are you okay to travel?"

"After so much sleep I'm well rested enough for anything, so lead the way."

Travis had to laugh at the humor, and that Julius was this sharp this soon meant they might actually have a chance to pull this off. "Bailey will take care of you and get you to safety. I'll meet both of you as soon as I put Rolla at ease."

He started back to the compound and saw Bailey and Julius kiss when he glanced back. Bailey's devotion to the fallen Elder might become a problem, but he had no choice but to return to Rolla. They needed more information before they could snatch the prize Julius had tried to get with Attila's help.

"You'll get to see the reality of it, Julius, but I'll be the one wielding the power."

❖

Their plane arrived two days later with an extra unexpected guest, since Hill had accepted Kendal's invitation after their follow-up meeting about the now-missing Leonardo. "Sit for a moment while I take care of these." Kendal held up everyone's passport.

"Don't we have to go through customs?" Mac looked out the window to the private hangar they'd taxied into.

"They'll come inside if that's necessary, but no sense all of us standing out in the cold." She took the stairs quickly and handed the stack of documents to the deputy, whose allegiance was first to the Elders and then to the British government.

"Will you be in the country long, Lord Wallace?" the man asked as he stamped her British passport with the appropriate documentation.

"About a week." She took back each one as he finished with it.

"Call me directly if you have any problems. Ming arranged transportation to the house whenever you're ready."

The 1933 Rolls-Royce Phantom that sat near the door gleaming like it'd just been driven off the lot was one of her favorites, but the limo accommodated only two people comfortably. She and Piper could enjoy the ride and talk while the others traveled in the newer cars Ming had sent. She would have offered the prize of her British collection to the Marmandes, but Lord Wallace wanted to take Lady Wallace home in style.

"What a beauty," Mac said when they all deplaned.

"I thought Piper would enjoy a bit of old England before I have to attend to my business." The staff loaded the bags, but she and Piper took off before they finished so she could talk to Farthington House's butler, Ming, before their guests arrived.

The Phantom was old, but it was in perfect mechanical condition and kept up with traffic with no problem. As they left London, she pointed out things of interest as they made their way to Kent.

"Where's the house?" Piper asked when they turned and passed through the large gates.

"It came with a bit of land, so patience, my love. You wouldn't want your grandparents to think I can't provide for you," she said as a joke. "These fields have never looked the same since the families I brought from Oakgrove moved on, but for years they were happy to call this home. Most of the homes they built around the acreage still stand, while others make for interesting ruins."

Ten miles in, the house came into view and Piper let out a long whistle. "When you said country house, this isn't what I pictured."

Farthington had fifteen bedrooms for guests, a grand ballroom, and enough art on its walls to fill a museum. Ming and three of his staff stood outside ready to greet them. The Li family had come to work here in the mid-1800s, and every generation since had not only kept her secrets but stayed in her employ. Farthington was more their home than hers.

"Welcome home, Lord Wallace. I hope your flight was satisfactory," Ming said in Chinese.

"Thank you for making all the arrangements. Your choice of cars almost makes up for all this rain and cold weather." She answered him in Chinese and returned his bow. "I hope you don't mind English for the rest of our stay."

"Certainly not," he said with a perfect British accent.

"Then let me introduce you to Piper Marmande, the new lady of Farthington." She put her arm around Piper as Ming kissed her hand.

"It's my pleasure to meet you, Lady Wallace. The staff and I look forward to serving you."

"Piper, Ming is the butler and manager of the estate," she said when Piper didn't let Ming's hand go.

"Thank you for the welcome," Piper said when Ming straightened up.

"Is everyone ready for the mob we've got coming?"

"Their rooms are ready, and we have a variety of meals planned we hope will be to everyone's liking. We put all the books that arrived for Lenore in the grand library, along with a few letters from the Elders for Lenore, and some for you."

"Thanks, I'll go through them later." The other cars were close and more staff members had come out with umbrellas for the light rain that'd replaced the mist.

"Will you require anything other than what we talked about for this evening?"

"No, but remember one important thing." Ming came closer as the cars stopped. "It's Kendal Richoux who's here for a visit."

"Lord Wallace?" Piper whispered. "How do you remember all these names?"

"Years of practice," she said as she held the large umbrella over both of them. "You'll get the hang of it."

Piper nodded and stood smiling as her grandparents got out with Hill. One of the things she'd planned to do before dinner was to find out what was bothering her grandfather. He'd clammed up after the lunch at Oakgrove, and no amount of asking had made him talk.

"This is a beautiful place," Molly said when she switched places with Piper.

"It's prettier in the spring and summer when everything's in bloom." Kendal pointed to the gardens where a few men were still working despite the weather. "Mr. Li the butler tries to add bulbs every year, so they're putting them in now."

"What kind?" Molly asked as she walked with Kendal to where the men were planting. "Maybe I'll steal a few for Riverbend."

"I can see your bug is still alive and well," Piper said to Mac as she slowed him down to let Kendal and her grandmother get ahead of them.

"What are you talking about?"

"The bug that's crawled up your—"

"That's enough of that, young lady. I'm just worried about you and all this."

Finally some progress. "All of this what?"

"The house, the diplomatic greeting, the money—it doesn't add up to what I thought Kendal was about." He didn't sound angry, but she could tell he wasn't happy either. "I thought she came from humble beginnings."

"All of us have something to prove when it's our turn to make our mark in the world, and Kendal isn't any different. She did that, but if she'd failed I guess there was family money to fall back on," she said, and wiggled her eyebrows, getting him to laugh. "How much she is or isn't worth doesn't change who she is."

"Does that mean she has a contingency plan for everything, including her personal life?"

"I don't care what her business plans are, but her personal life is all sewn up."

He stopped them when Molly stopped to talk to a gardener and accepted a bag from him that Kendal carried for her. "We haven't really talked alone since you got back, so I want to make sure you're all right. Are you sure about all this?"

"I thought you liked her and you trusted me. My judgment hasn't disappeared because I fell in love."

"If we didn't know about all this, what else don't we know about her?" he asked as he lifted his arm up as if to point at something, then just dropped it.

"You're right that we haven't had a chance to talk except for our car ride home, but let me set you straight." She led him away from the others. "I know about every house she owns, all the assets in her portfolio, and how many pairs of underwear are in her suitcase. I also know that she's successful, ambitious in an honorable way, and loves me and my family. That she had her legal team draw up papers while we were in Venice that gave me half of everything she owns wasn't necessary, but it proved to me that I was more important than her possessions."

"Is everything okay?" Kendal asked, but didn't come closer.

Piper glanced at Kendal and winked. "We're fine. Pops just isn't a plant person."

"You own half this place?" he asked as he stared at the house.

"This place, Oakgrove, and a few more. I picked well because I found someone I'm crazy about and it's mutual, and the fact she's made me filthy rich doesn't really matter. It might count for something when I take Gran shopping in London, but that's not why I'm deliriously happy."

"That's good enough for me, then. I was only worried because that's my job, and I wanted to make sure my replacement is up for the task."

"She is, believe me."

They joined Kendal and Molly as they finished their talk with the garden crew and they all followed Kendal to a side entrance that led to the grand library. Mac moved to the fireplace to warm his hands and glanced down to the book Lenore had been engrossed in since they'd taken off.

"Did you enjoy the grounds, Mr. Marmande?" Lenore smiled up at him.

"It's a beautiful place. We may need a crowbar to get Molly to leave once Kendal's done. As much as I love anything that floats is how much my wife loves flowers." The writing on the pages didn't look like any language he'd ever seen. "What do you do for Kendal?"

"I'm a librarian, but I also do research for her."

"What's Morgaine do?"

"I'm a security expert," Morgaine said from next to Lenore. "Lenore's the brains and I'm the muscle."

He took off his coat and sat in the wingback chair close to them. "Don't take this wrong, but are there any men on her payroll besides Charlie?"

"Feel free to ask her." Morgaine pointed in Kendal's direction. She was helping Piper and Molly take off their coats. "Whatever you want to know, she's usually forthcoming."

"Usually?"

"When it's about her personal life, she's not too loose with the facts, especially if she thinks it's none of your business."

Both women seemed devoted to Kendal, and that they were both beautiful made Mac wonder if that'd be a problem for Piper in the future. He had attractive people on his payroll, but they didn't stay over.

"Thanks for the advice. I think I'll follow it." Before he could ask to talk to Kendal, Ming and a maid brought in tea for everyone.

As they sat and talked, Kendal answered a lot of his questions in the conversation without prompting, as if she'd overheard first him and Piper, then him and her employees. They continued their tour of the inside of the house and ended at the door to their room.

"This could be your twin," he said when he noticed the painting in the hallway. The young man in the painting standing next to a large white horse was dressed casually in riding pants, boots, and a white shirt opened at the collar.

"That's actually Lord Henry Wallace, the first owner of the house," Kendal said.

"I mean, he could be your twin."

"Good genes was my father's opinion," Kendal said as she opened the bedroom door. "You two have time for a nap before dinner, if you like."

"Do you have time for a private talk later?" He ignored Piper and Molly's frowns. "I have some questions about Marmande and wanted your input." *And a few other things*, he thought, but didn't say that out loud to save himself a few slaps to the head.

"I've got a few calls to make after dinner, but I can have Ming set us up in the solarium for breakfast in the morning."

"You've got a date."

"If you two are done, I need Kendal to show me something," Piper said as she pushed Kendal toward the stairs. "Were you finished, Pops?"

"She's all yours, sweet girl."

"And I've got the papers to prove it," Piper said, and laughed.

"Let's hope you're right."

"Macarthur Marmande, get your ass in here now," Molly said sternly.

"At least she's got enough money to give me a proper burial if I'm wrong to worry."

❖

"Is he still giving you a hard time?" Piper asked Kendal whey they reached the landing.

"You can't blame him, can you?" Kendal took Piper's hand and glanced up to make sure they were alone. "All this and how fast we left after being gone for so long has him in overdrive. Add Morgaine and Lenore, and he's got no choice but to start to ask questions. It would've been better to stay in London, but my apartment's not that big, and we'll need the ton of books Lenore brought with her. Besides, I hate hotels, especially for long stays."

"If you don't mind talking to him, Pops will be okay. Macarthur Marmande sees things in black and white. He's just an old-fashioned guy."

"Not as old-fashioned as me. I've just aged well."

"I was talking about the beautiful women running around here. He's worried you might have a roving eye, and if you do, he'll make you black and blue."

"You've got no problems there. I need them here to help us find out more about what you saw, not because of anything else. You understand that, right?"

Piper backed her against a wood panel and pressed her body against Kendal's. "I understand, but did they both have to be so good-looking?"

"They came before me, so maybe Rolla and his pals had an appreciation for beautiful women." She kissed Piper and put her arms around her. "The only appreciation I have is for you, and you're all I need. Now that I've reached my sap quotient for the day, would you like to see my sword?"

Piper laughed and pulled away so they could start walking. "That would've been a cheap pickup line if it'd been anyone else."

"Cheap?" Kendal keyed in the code, then placed her hand on the glass panel. "Cheap would be me asking if you want to see my etchings, but I actually have some of those too."

The door slid open and Piper walked in first. It was similar to the room in Oakgrove, but much larger with the wall cases of swords, though broken with niches with mannequins wearing armor. The history locked away in here was amazing, but not as amazing as the fact that one person had made it all.

"Have you used all these?"

"Mostly all. A number of them are simply collectible pieces I've picked up through the years." Kendal walked along in front of her and touched a few of the blades. "Like I said, most of the creatures I've faced can only be destroyed by piercing them through the heart with wood or a blade with the essence of wood incorporated into the metal. When I first got to New Orleans, the majority of Henri's newer recruits didn't seem to know how to fight because they were all unarmed. Only the older ones knew how to protect themselves."

"That's still so surreal to me."

"It was to me at first too, but then in time, modern warfare became surreal. When I've watched footage of it on television, I've wondered how war would change if you had to face your opponent with only this amount of space between you." Kendal removed a sword and thrust it into the empty air in front of her.

Piper slid her hand down Kendal's arm to her wrist. "As sexy as you look when you do that, I want to see the Sea Serpent Sword." A strange current in this room was making her tingle in a way she'd never experienced, and it seemed to emanate from the middle of the opposite wall. "Wait, don't say anything." She thought it important to find it herself.

The mannequin she walked to wore a layer of chainmail over what seemed to be thick leather, and the metal over the chest was woven in a pattern that formed a dragon. The dragon's tail was uncoiled, and its mouth was open as if ready to devour something with the stream of flames. She reached out to touch it as she saw the same dragon stamped on the metal of the gauntlets and boot greaves. As well made as all that was, it didn't compare to the prize laid carefully across its hands—the sword from her vision.

This was the Sea Serpent Sword.

"Why call it a sea serpent when it's a dragon?"

"The woman who gave it to me named it. Out of respect for her and the beautiful gift, I never thought to change it."

"It's a sword, honey, not exactly something I'd call beautiful." She ran her fingers along the pommel, which was so real she was almost afraid the dragon would come to life and bite her. "Not exactly a sexy gift either. I'll most likely shop for lingerie to model for you for Valentine's Day rather than get you something like this."

"Don't form an opinion too soon because there are swords, and then there is this sword," Kendal said as she leaned against the table close to her.

"Okay." She dragged out the word. "What do you mean?"

Kendal pulled a sword from the barrel next to the cleared space in the room. "These are all practice pieces that are as good as the ones on the wall, but they're missing the bits of wood I need to make them effective in the field." Kendal started to warm up and stretch. "Come see."

Kendal moved her in front, so close their bodies still touched, and put her hand over Piper's on the sword. "I'm going to teach you a basic warm-up exercise, and then I want you to do it by yourself." They started slowly and Piper lost herself in the serenity the movements evoked in her. By the third time, Kendal stepped away and handed her the sword. "It doesn't have to be perfect, but try to repeat the routine."

"How was that?" she asked when she was done. "Did I miss something?" She started again, but Kendal stopped her and took the sword from her.

"That was great. You're a fast learner." Kendal removed the Sea Serpent Sword from the display. "I want you to do it again with this one." Kendal held it by the blade and presented it to her with a bow.

Piper was less tentative and could feel the difference even though she'd never held a sword before today. "I don't know enough about all this to explain, but this one feels more balanced. Does that make sense?"

"Perfect sense, and it's perfectly balanced. The only way to understand it is to actually use it."

She handed it back to Kendal and sat to watch her go through the same routine, but in its entirety. At the end the revolutions were so fast the blade almost disappeared, and she could see Kendal's years of training in action.

"I never thought something so deadly could be so sexy," she said when Kendal finished and stood with the sword at her side. Whatever had made her tingle when they'd walked in was getting stronger, but now all she craved was Kendal's hands on her.

She stood and Kendal walked to her as if under the same spell, and before Kendal could lay the sword down, she put her hand over Kendal's. The sensation Piper felt was instant and intense, and from the way Kendal's pupils dilated, she didn't need to ask if she'd felt the current that'd come from the sword. Whatever had happened wasn't painful, but the best word she could come up with was lust. She hoped Kendal experienced the same thing when she grabbed her by the hair and pulled her head down to reach her lips.

"I think we need to go upstairs now," Piper said when their kiss ended, but that wasn't enough. "We should, but I don't think I can wait that long." She put her hands on Kendal's belt, so desperate she couldn't get it undone.

Her skin burned like a brush fire started by a bolt of lightning, and the only way to put it out was to press it to Kendal's. As soon as the sword dropped from Kendal's fingers, Piper wrapped her legs around her hips and hung on as Kendal carried her to the table. When Kendal put her down, she pushed her hands under Piper's skirt, and it was almost too much.

"Oh, God." She brought Kendal closer with her legs. "I want to touch you, but I need you inside me now." When Kendal put a small amount of space between them she wanted to be embarrassed because of the wet spot she'd left on Kendal's pants, but the throbbing between her legs had become the center of her need.

Kendal put her other hand under Piper's skirt and ripped her panties off, and from her expression she appeared to want this as much as Piper did. She opened her mouth to ask Kendal to move faster, but Kendal kissed her—hard. Kendal's tongue went into her mouth as Kendal buried her fingers deep. She put her feet behind Kendal's legs, and the orgasm she wanted more than air started immediately.

"Fuck," she said in a long groan, "don't stop." Her command sped Kendal's strokes and slammed Kendal's thumb into her hard clit, the sensation making her want it to last, but she could no more hold back coming than she could the scream she let out when she did.

As soon as the spasms stopped she ripped Kendal's shirt open and bit down on her nipple. Kendal hissed—from pleasure, since she didn't pull away and held her head in place.

"I'm going to suck you until you come for me." Piper finished with Kendal's belt and unzipped her pants, letting them fall to her ankles. When she rubbed her feet down Kendal's legs, Kendal wrapped her hand firmly around the back of Piper's hair and tugged her head back so she could kiss her. The act of possession and Kendal's tongue in her mouth made Piper want Kendal's fingers inside her again, but Kendal's needs were paramount.

When she dropped to her knees, she buried her face between Kendal's legs and found the rock-hard clit with her tongue. She smiled around it when Kendal grabbed her hair again with one hand and hung on to the table with the other. It was always such a thrill to make Kendal this crazy, but this was new. The sword had somehow lowered any wall, no matter how slight, between them, and all that was left was this raw, unquenchable desire.

She sucked Kendal in, but if she didn't get relief her skin would burn off, so she put her hand between her own legs to stanch the pounding. It was like she'd been sexually starved until Kendal had come along, and now they'd reached a new peak.

"Wait," she said when Kendal lifted her to her feet.

There wasn't another word between them when Kendal turned her around, bent her over the table, and pressed up against her ass. Piper reached behind her and squeezed Kendal's butt cheek when Kendal put her fingers in place for her to ride to another orgasm even better than the first.

The only sound in the room was skin slapping against skin, and Kendal's grunts in her ear were making Piper crazy. It was incredible, and when Kendal paused and whispered, "I love you," she let go and gave in. Kendal, and everything she'd brought into her life, would take an eternity to enjoy.

If she'd never given thanks for drinking the elixir, she would've now. She was finally alive.

CHAPTER NINE

"They've been in there awhile," Morgaine said as she paced to the door of the library and glanced down the hall. "Should I go check?"

Lenore snapped her book closed and smiled at Morgaine's anxiety. "They and the sword are okay for now, so come sit." She patted the spot next to her.

"Okay for now? What's that supposed to mean?"

"Every time I read this book," she held up an old leather-bound book Rolla had sent along with the others, "I find something I missed." She ran her fingertips over the pressed dragon on the cover. "Whatever the sword's secrets are, they'll stay locked up for some time yet."

"I'd have thought you'd have memorized it by now. That thing looks like it's only got ten pages."

"It's more than that, and it's in an ancient dialect so I'm having trouble getting through it."

"You're ancient, Lenore, so how bad could it be?" Morgaine sat next to her and laughed.

"Even you and I weren't around when Atlantis was thriving. We can control time, but not the forces that drove that civilization to the bottom of the ocean. I'm not a hundred percent sure, but I think an Atlantean wrote the book."

"Why would they have knowledge of the sword?"

"It doesn't mention that, and Rolla didn't say in his letter how he came by the book."

"So how long before you memorize it?" Morgaine asked sweetly but sarcastically.

"The Marmandes think we're part of a harem, Charlie's out in the stables taking inventory, and our hosts are busy, so relax. It's also raining outside, and I hate getting wet if I don't absolutely have to."

Morgaine gave her a huge smile. "That's your problem, bookworm," she said as she released the clip at the back of Lenore's hair so it'd come out of the ponytail.

"What's my problem?" For the first time in their long friendship, she felt like Morgaine finally saw her.

"You should learn to distinguish between getting wet because you have to, and getting wet because you *want* to."

"I can see it might be a valuable lesson."

"It is," Morgaine said, and ran her fingers through her hair to comb it out. "Especially with the right teacher."

❖

"I'm not comfortable," Julius said in Latin, not caring that Travis couldn't understand him. "If there's a need for travel, I'd like to do it in my own clothing."

Bailey buttoned Julius's shirt slowly, as if not wanting to upset him any further. "We need to get out of Egypt, so you have to put all this on."

The pants hadn't been so bad and he was pleased with the fit, but the shirt he found binding at the collar and sleeves. He was still in shock from the strange vehicle that'd transported them to the hotel in Cairo. The world had certainly changed while he rotted away in a cave, and he'd found nothing familiar in the fast, crowded, and noisy city. Nothing seemed the same at all, and that alone set him on edge.

"Your documents will be ready soon, and they'll be the best money can buy, but it's not a good idea to stand out." Bailey stood behind him and held up the suit jacket for him.

"What news of Asra?" It was as if something was restricting him when he put the jacket on and Bailey fastened the tie around his neck.

"I've got William checking on it to confirm, but his last report said Asra left New Orleans for London. She has an estate outside the city, and since Lenore and Morgaine are with her, maybe she's gotten a clue about the sword," Travis said in French.

"Those two bitches will eventually be a problem, so try your best to find a solution before we lose our opportunity." Bailey had given him a choice between shoes and boots, so he slipped on the boots, hoping to regain some sense of the man he'd been.

All those years of dark dreams and nothingness had made him almost wish never to be found, since he thought he'd be insane if restored. When he'd opened his eyes, though, all he could think of was revenge. No one who'd passed judgment on him would be spared. Once he was done with Asra, he'd return here to start Rolla's suffering, which would last as long as he'd been in that cave.

"They'll be easy to deal with, so stop obsessing." Travis sat by the window and cracked the walnuts he'd brought with him one by one. The noise was as unnerving as the man himself. "Is this special sword in the house?" Travis asked Bailey.

"The Sea Serpent Sword hasn't been seen since the great injustice." Bailey caressed his shoulders as he spoke. "We don't know why they're in London, but we need to find out before we waste time we can't afford."

"She's probably dropping off the bitch she's sleeping with and her family while she deals with whatever Rolla's pissed about," Travis said.

"Pissed?" Julius asked.

"Angry," Bailey said with compassion. Julius truly was a babe in a vastly scary world if he couldn't understand the simplest of phrases.

"Travis, eventually I'll come to see the gifts you possess that made Rolla give you the elixir, but aside from a large penis I'm blind as to why, so let me explain…again." His attention waned for a moment when the box with moving pictures showed a glimpse of a war before it returned to the talking man. "I've been asleep for centuries, though I remember everything about the prophecy, but now, with her access to the archives, Lenore is most probably more knowledgeable about the sword and its prophecy than I am. Consider too how Lenore and Morgaine feel about Asra, and you don't need anyone to tell you they'll do anything to stop it from happening. All of them are too weak to bring the prophecy to life."

"You deciphered the prophecy by accident, so don't delude yourself into thinking you're a genius. We got this far. Don't lose your head now." Travis laughed loudly. "After all, you just got it back."

"Would you like me to show you the Clan's ultimate punishment?"

He moved faster than Travis to the sword on the bed. "Either respect me or get out," he said with the weapon pressed against Travis's neck.

The sight of the blade against Travis's skin brought it all back in vivid detail. Since Julius had woken, he'd had trouble remembering.

Genesis Clan's Compound in Egypt, AD 453

"The Hun is dead," Asra said as she moved around behind Julius, out of his sight.

"His many sons will avenge him." Julius tried to relax because whenever he flexed against the ropes Asra had tied him with, they tightened and stayed taut even when he stopped. His hands and forearms were numb, but once Rolla arrived, he'd have her insolent head on a platter.

"He and you didn't have enough time with them, and your puppet loved the power too much to share. With Attila gone, none of his people or his family will be able to pull the tribes together like he did." She poured herself a cup of wine and sat across from him, staring at him as if she was studying something important. "Strength in war comes only in numbers, and that advantage is gone, along with your chance to anoint yourself a god."

He cocked his head back and gazed at the ceiling of the great meeting room and the series of paintings Rolla had commissioned that told their history. How many times had he sat in here in a seat of honor for their discussions and debates? That would have to count for something, in his opinion, as the others decided his fate.

"Will this be the highlight of your life—humiliating me, I mean?" He kept his body loose but barked the question at her. "You're nothing but a well-trained dog who strives only to please his master."

"The rest of my life will be a bore if the most exciting thing I accomplish is capturing you." She laughed and stared at him over the rim of her cup. She was starting to irritate him, but he'd never give her the satisfaction of showing weakness. "That was as hard as relieving myself in the morning."

"Not this, idiot. I meant you'll live only to serve people like me forever. Is that all you want for as long as there are sunrises?"

"First, why would you care?" She put her cup down and leaned forward closer to him. "You should've learned from your recent activities that for any army to be effective, we must all play a role. Those who don't have an interest in doing so become farmers and such." He flinched when she stood but accepted her offer of wine when she held the cup to his lips. "Can I ask something of you?"

Perhaps escape wasn't out of his grasp yet, if she softened toward him. "Ask whatever you wish."

"What did you hope to gain with Attila?" She sat once he'd drained the cup.

"To rule the world," he said, relaxing again because of how irresistibly easy this had suddenly become. With Asra's reputation he'd expected more than this simple-minded question.

"Then what?"

He focused his attention again to see if she was only toying with him while they waited for the others. "What do you mean by that?"

"I can't make the question any simpler." She moved her head from side to side, and he heard a crack each time. "When I found you I rode with a force of men from the north with superb fighting skills. With my sword and ability, I could've talked their entire nation into following me, as well as gotten others to join me on a path of conquest, if that's what I wanted. I'd never need someone like the Hun to fight for me," she said sarcastically, as if to insult him even further. "If world domination is what you wanted, you should've unsheathed that ornate sword you're fond of and earned it. For the sake of my question let's say you had beaten the masses until they worshipped at your feet. What's left to challenge you after that?"

"To mold the world into the vision of perfection should be the Clan's goal, not only mine. What good is having all this knowledge surrounding us for eternity if we don't use it for that?" He closed his eyes to slits, but that only made her smile. "Instead, we hide away like frightened women while the world is in chaos."

The doors opened behind him but Asra didn't get up. He'd had enough of her smart mouth and simple ideas. Even the tunic and leather britches she wore were simple, and to consider her a warrior was laughable. No warrior went anywhere without his sword, and the only one between them was his.

"If the world can only be perfect with your vision, then thank the gods I'm blind to it."

Asra finally stood, so he tried to turn enough to see who was behind them. "Are you here to beg forgiveness, Rolla?" He was pushed to the head of the table as the Elders took their places. Rolla, Morgaine, Lenore, Zanga, and Nalic were the seniors entrusted to judge those who went beyond the scope the Clan placed on all immortals. The only member not voting today would be Julius himself, but he wasn't too concerned since so far the harshest punishment had been confinement to the compound in Egypt to serve the Elders. He could handle that, since it'd keep him close to the archives.

"We're here to tell you our decision, and forgiveness has nothing to do with the verdict." Rolla briefly glanced back when Asra moved to stand at his right side. "Your actions have put a blight on our existence and have possibly changed fate for generations to come."

"You have no right to make judgment until I'm heard. Have you all forgotten I'm part of this group?"

"It's you who's forgotten himself, Julius. You came to us as Harg, and we welcomed you to our clan," Zanga said. "You disregarded all that in your quest for power."

"You are no brethren of mine. From the first day, I was superior to every one of you, and I won't rest until I repay you for this humiliation." The door opened again and Bailey squeezed through, his face wet with tears. Bailey had been the only one he'd missed in his years away from this place, but it had been too dangerous to bring him when he'd started his travels to meet Attila. Bailey had stayed close to Rolla but had sworn allegiance to him. No matter what happened with the panel, Bailey would be his salvation.

"Your chosen name in this life is Julius, but he will cease to be as of now," Rolla said as he read from the scroll he'd unfurled.

"What are you babbling about, Rolla?"

"Harg of the Highlands, the Clan finds you guilty of interference, and your sentence is sleep." Rolla looked up at him, then Bailey. "If those loyal to you wish to free you from the darkness that awaits you, their search will be long and unfruitful."

He tugged at his bindings again, not caring about the pain. "What do you mean?"

"Your head will be severed at the neck," Rolla said as he waved in Asra's direction. She walked to the corner and returned with a sword, and Julius almost forgot his sentence when he realized what it was. His need to rule the known world was more than about power; it was also to find the sword in Asra's hand. Time had run out, and he'd face the darkness without knowing how this bitch had acquired his prize.

"Your head will lie in darkness where the sun rises, and your body where the sun sets," Rolla said.

His last real thought was how beautiful the sword was as Asra held it with both hands and swung it at his head.

Then everything went dark.

❖

When Julius had felt the sun on his face again he'd been grateful to Bailey for not breaking his promise. To assure their success, Bailey had waited until the year of the dragon's awakening, but they still had a lot left to accomplish before they could perform the ritual.

"Do whatever it takes, but hit Asra and the others as soon as possible," Julius repeated as he put his sword away.

"You've been a husk all this time, and you can't wait a few more months?" Travis asked.

"If you can't speak to me with respect," he said, having to think of the English words but wanting the practice, "then get out of my sight. When I have the sword you'll be a sheep like the rest."

"Without me you don't have a chance, so enough with the grandiose threats. If I leave you'll have Bailey, and that's it. If winning is contingent on who can suck a dick better than anyone else, then he's your man. But if not, give it a rest." Travis stood as if daring him to make a move toward him, which he didn't. "Yeah, I didn't think so. I don't take orders from you—try to remember that."

Travis walked out and slammed the door, and the only sound once he'd gone was the talking box. It was too late to replace Travis, but Bailey was tempted to try.

"What's his problem?"

"He was invaluable in helping me find you, but he did it for his own reasons, I think," Bailey said as he laid his head on Julius's chest.

"Everyone has his own agenda, my love," he said, wanting to keep Bailey happy for now.

"Mine is to be with you, that's all. I never wanted you to leave to join the Hun, but you did because the sword was the most important thing to you. I beg you to forget it now, and we can find a quiet place to settle and be happy together."

"I want that too," he said, trying to sound sincere, "but Rolla and the others will never allow it. The only hope we have of never being separated again is to finish this."

"I'm afraid I'll lose you again."

"Our time is finally here, and no one will keep me from my destiny or you."

CHAPTER TEN

"That was different," Piper said, and laughed. Kendal was pressed against her back and they were both still breathing heavily.

"Did I hurt you?" Kendal kissed the back of Piper's neck before releasing her so she could straighten up.

"If this is the result of showing me your collection, I might own more swords than you do." When Kendal didn't laugh, she turned and put her arms around her waist. "What's wrong?"

"I don't know what came over me." Kendal's shirt was still on, but every button was missing, and her pants were pooled around one ankle.

"I love that you love me, but that you really want me doesn't upset me. I'll speak up if I'm not comfortable with something." She moved Kendal back an arm's length and smiled. "By the look of you, it's you who needs to be afraid. I'm not sure what came over me either, but if we concentrate we might be able to figure it out so we can try again."

This time Kendal did laugh as she kicked off the only shoe she had on, along with her pants, so she could bend to pick up the sword they'd carelessly dropped when the overwhelming feelings had come over them. Kendal started to place it on the nearest empty pegs, but Piper almost called her back to see if the same sensations would happen again. Kendal must've had the same thought because she held it a little longer before she put it up.

"It was the sword, wasn't it?" Piper asked as she studied Kendal's expression.

"I'd have to say yes, but as long as I've had this, I've never experienced that before. It must have been a combination of the sword and the girl." Kendal unbuttoned her cuffs and rolled up her sleeves. "Want to try an experiment?"

"Is that a line I'm going to be hearing for years to come?" She hoisted herself back on the table and crooked her finger in Kendal's direction. "Because I've been falling for your lines since the day we met."

"Is that a complaint?"

She fanned her fingers across her chest. "Me, complain?" she said in her best Southern accent. "I sometimes wonder now how I lasted as long as I did against that devastating charm of yours, but I've never been happier."

"Which brings me back to my question," Kendal said as she picked up the sword again and faced her.

"Whatever you want, Asra, just ask me." She opened her arms so Kendal would hold her. "Just ask me, baby."

"I've never been one to pray to the gods, but because they sent you into my life it may be time to start." Kendal placed the sword next to Piper, who felt the same strong energy as before even though she wasn't touching it.

She tried to ignore it for now as Kendal held her. The steady sound of Kendal's heartbeat beneath her ear assured her Kendal wasn't worked up about anything, so whatever she had in mind wasn't worrying her. "I think I know what you're thinking about." She ran her hand under the open shirt along the muscles of Kendal's back. "Only this time I can't promise I won't leave any hickeys if the same thing happens." She kissed the spot over Kendal's heart before she placed her hand on the hilt of the sword.

"Maybe I should put my pants back on before we do this," Kendal said as her hand hovered over Piper's. Their closeness made the air around her almost vibrate.

"Chicken," she said, and laughed, but she was being carried away again, only this time passion didn't seem like the direction they were headed. Kendal laughed with her, and together they took deep breaths.

"Ready?" Kendal asked.

"With you here, I'm ready for anything." Kendal's hand dropped at the words and neither of them lost eye contact this time, but instantly Kendal knew this was different. It wasn't a repeat of Piper's first vision since she hadn't lost consciousness, but her focus seemed to have flown off somewhere she couldn't follow.

Now all she could do was stand and support Piper until whatever she was seeing in her mind's eye was complete. The waiting, though, made it seem like an eternity, but she restrained herself from shaking Piper and allowed her to wake gently. When she did, Piper sucked in a deep breath and closed her eyes, as if whatever she'd seen had scared her. She pressed her cheek against Kendal's chest again, holding on to her as if to prove she hadn't disappeared.

"I saw a place with a lot of rooms, and I think some of them belonged to you." Piper pulled her nearer and closed her eyes. "It felt old, and a lot of the rooms were filled with rolls of paper and books, while others held art and statues. I couldn't tell where it is, but it seemed desolate, and the people who stared at me as I moved around there looked at me and asked when you were coming. You're expected, and they're angry you haven't come."

"It's the Clan's compound in Egypt I told you about." She tried to fill in some of the gaps for Piper so she'd relax.

"I sensed a lot of anger, some of it directed at you, but also a building panic. If what I saw was the place we were going, at first they wanted you to come back to face your punishment, but now their focus has changed."

"Could you tell what they're worried about?"

"I saw a lot of confusion and fear, love. Something's happened that they didn't expect and they don't know how to deal with it, but they don't know how to ask you for help. If you do go back, some of them will set a trap for you because they want you out of the way so you won't interfere with something important to them."

"Is it something you saw, or something you feel?" Kendal tipped Piper's head back, wanting to see her face. This time around Piper didn't seem as anxious to talk about her vision after she'd come out of her trancelike state.

"I saw only the place, but the rest was just a feeling. There's every chance I imagined that part, but it seemed so real. Like I said, some of the people living there want whatever they're freaked out about to happen, and the rest know that would be disastrous."

Piper pressed her palm to the side of Kendal's face. "What are we going to do?"

"We have to take this one step at a time, so we begin with where we are and what we have." Kendal stopped and kissed Piper before she went on. "And we have to collect more information." The past week was like a puzzle missing pieces, so while Kendal could make out the final picture, the real art would be found in the fine details.

"Think the two with their ears probably pressed to the door know more than they're telling us?"

"Only one way to find out," Kendal said, then kissed Piper one more time before she moved around to collect her clothing. She left her shirt open, but put her pants and shoes back on before she scooped Piper off the table and walked across the room.

"Hold up, Lord Wallace," Piper said, and pulled her hair. "If you think I'm going to take the chance of running into my grandparents in this condition, you're insane."

"Your grandfather seems to have started a list of things wrong with me, so I'm not about to add sexual deviant to my growing number of sins. If you hang on I promise we won't run into anyone until we've showered and I find a shirt that actually closes." She pressed down on the corner of one of the display cases and a small door slid open.

"If you have a secret passage at your disposal, you should've skipped getting dressed again. The sooner we shower, the quicker we can talk to Lenore and the Viking goddess."

"I never take these things without wearing shoes since I hate stepping on any stray bugs."

Piper looked up to the hidden staircase and laughed. "You fight things that nightmares are made of and you're afraid of stepping on a bug?"

"Fear is your word, sweet pea." She started up the passage that'd lead them to the master suite. "I'm not afraid of them. I just find them gross underfoot. Some hang-ups are a little tougher than others to overcome, no matter how many years you're given. It's one of the things I'm still working on, so no teasing or I'll make you carry me upstairs and we'll see how much you like squishy stuff under your feet."

They took a shower together and went down to dinner. Everyone had changed and seemed to be in better spirits after the long flight, since they were all laughing and having drinks in one of the larger sitting rooms. Piper joined Mac and Molly, and she smiled when Hill approached with an extra glass in her hand.

"Aside from enjoying a free vacation, do you need me to do anything for you while we're here?" Hill asked her.

"There might be, but this isn't the time to talk about it." Kendal stopped to take a sip of the scotch Ming had poured for her and allowed Hill to deliver.

"If it's a matter of trust, I offered to sign a confidentiality agreement, but you turned me down."

"It's not that I don't trust you." She led Hill away from the others so their conversation would stay somewhat private. "Piper trusts you and, more importantly, has known you for years and has a deep respect for you. I would've offered you a job eventually, but you're here because of her impassioned defense of your honor and sense of righteousness. I want you to be here, but I've always been a very private person, and that's going to be a hard habit to break."

"Hopefully you'll see that no matter what, I'll do a good job for you because I don't want to sit around all day fishing for things to occupy my time. I don't do well when I'm bored out of my mind." Hill accepted another drink from the server and took a seat across from her.

"My business is strange at times," she said, and tried to think of the best way to ease Hill into the work Piper seemed to think she'd be right for. Lenore and Morgaine were great at research, but they wouldn't always be around full-time so it'd be nice to have someone with Hill's skills to do that for them when needed.

"Strange how? Like human trafficking or something similar?"

"Human trafficking? That's where your imagination skittered off to first?" Kendal laughed. "More like..." Ming came in again and announced dinner was served. "Let's save it until tomorrow and I'll explain, but I can assure you I'm not buying or selling anyone for profit. Even my ancestors had a definite distaste for that sort of thing when it was legal."

The staff served a great meal and afterward everyone retired to the library. Piper smiled as Kendal did her best to make her grandparents and Hill feel as if they were welcome and wanted. After another round of after-dinner drinks, the older couple and Hill had no choice but to retire, if they wanted to start fresh in the morning. Before Lenore and Morgaine could escape, Kendal closed the door, locked it, and pointed to the sofa across from where Piper sat.

She sat and smiled, waiting to see if they'd crack, but Morgaine feigned a bored expression while Lenore stared into the fire. "Is there something you two would like to get off your chest? Some burning piece of information you just can't wait to tell me," she said, and took Piper's hand.

Lenore finally looked at her and took a deep breath, as if to prepare herself for a cross-examination. "Nothing comes to mind."

"How about you, Blondie?" Piper asked Morgaine.

"Excuse me?" Morgaine said, with heat.

"Cut the bullshit, both of you," she said, aggravated as well. "Something unusual is going on, and it's important enough that Rolla and his buddies were willing to forgive me with no questions asked. At least that's your story."

"Until we know more, there's no sense in getting everyone worked up," Lenore said.

"I'm already worked up, and if you and the others want my help, start talking, and I mean now. To encourage you I'll start by telling you that something happened to us this afternoon."

"Actually, two somethings," Piper said, and shrugged when Kendal gazed at her.

"Okay, two things happened, and I think you may know a little about that," she added.

"What exactly?" Lenore leaned forward like a child waiting for a treat.

"We need to make a deal here before we begin," Piper said with her hands up.

Kendal had to laugh at the different responses that proposal got from her two old friends. Piper seemed to drive Morgaine mad, but Lenore seemed completely charmed by her. That both of them had any reaction at all to the woman she loved made her feel better about the future and whatever they had to face. If something were to happen to her, both Lenore and Morgaine would make sure Piper came through it safely.

"What do you want?" Morgaine asked.

"We both want the same thing," Kendal said as she put her arm around Piper. "From the time you recruited me, the three of us have been through a lot together, so it surprises and saddens me now that you've kept me in the dark. Why all the evasiveness?"

"Do you think that's what we're doing?" Lenore asked.

"I agree with Piper that you're not telling us something, and from our first lesson together you told me the most important thing in any fight, besides the skills Morgaine so carefully taught me, was information." Kendal's words made Lenore appear almost ashamed. "Now that it seems to count for something, you've purposely cut me out as if you don't trust me. Do you have some reservation about me or Piper?"

Lenore took a breath to answer, but Morgaine put her hand on her knee and started talking. "Lenore and I are truly happy for what you have found in each other, and you must believe we're here to protect you both. Please accept our apologies. Piper's right. We haven't told you everything, but we simply don't know all the answers."

"Then let's share what we all know and start from there," Piper said.

Morgaine stood, took Piper's hand, and bowed her head over it. "I give you my word and the promise of my sword to fight for you and Asra in the days to come."

"I know that, aside from me, you two love Asra the most, so thank you for including me in your circle," Piper responded.

"Let's be honest with each other, then," Morgaine said with a smile.

"This afternoon we went into the sword room so Piper could see the Sea Serpent," Kendal said.

"Did you have any kind of reaction when you were in there together?" Lenore asked again, appearing excited.

"That might be putting it mildly," Piper said, and laughed as she blushed.

Kendal laughed as well, since she figured Piper wouldn't be comfortable having to discuss their sex life with anyone, but there was no other way to explain what had happened.

"Let's begin by saying that Piper picked the sword without any help from me, so we can trust the vision she had the night Lenore touched her." She kissed the top of Piper's head. "After that we had two very different experiences when we touched it together."

"I don't mean to pry into your private lives, but was one of the reactions of a passionate nature?" Lenore asked in a way that made her sound like she was trying to navigate a minefield.

"If it had gotten any more passionate I would've lost consciousness again," Piper said, and her blush became more pronounced. Both Lenore and Morgaine nodded as if they already knew that part, but stayed quiet.

"That was the first thing, but the second time we tried it…" Kendal told them about Piper's vision.

Lenore nodded again, then closed her eyes for a moment. "Asra, before we begin this conversation I want to ask your forgiveness for something I did a very long time ago."

"Forgiveness for what?"

"When you asked about Bruik's vision about you, I told you only a part of what he'd seen because I didn't think you should have to carry that worry for so long." Lenore's eyes were filled with tears, and Kendal could tell the lie of omission truly pained her. "Believe me, I did it only because I thought I was helping you."

"Whatever else he saw, I assume the distant future he predicted is upon us, so you don't need my forgiveness because you did nothing wrong." She stood and gave Lenore a kiss on the cheek to calm her.

"Thank you, and you're right again. Bruik, as you know, had a vision that, at that time, was a long way off, but the signs indicate that the time is indeed now. From our first communication with Rolla after Piper's first vision, he's reached the same conclusion." Lenore retrieved the book Kendal recognized as the one she'd been reading for days. "The one thing Bruik didn't see was the sword, but he did see Piper, so we'll have to assume she'll have to fill in all the gaps for us. Since Piper's first sight was of the Sea Serpent, I believe it definitely has something to do with whatever happens."

"Let's start with the story of that sword," Piper said. "Every time we ask, something interrupts, so before the sky starts falling, tell us."

Lenore held up the book and opened the cover to show them the picture inside. It was an excellent sketch of the sword, but the dragon on the hilt was uncoiled and alive. "According to legend this weapon is blessed by the gods," she said, but then shook her head. "I take that back. It's blessed by only one in particular."

"Which?" Kendal asked.

"Aphrodite or Venus, depending on your background and citizenship." Lenore turned to the next page and the sketch of a beautiful woman holding the blade across her hands. "It was the only time she commissioned something that could be used in war, but she had her reasons."

"Lenore told me that Rolla has had this book for years, but never believed the legend it contained because no one ever thought the sword to be real. And since you never mentioned it in your reports to Lenore, neither did we until Piper's vision," Morgaine said.

"But every time I reread this it mentions that the true owner is somehow marked by the goddess." Lenore flipped through the pages of the old text with care, obviously trying to find that passage.

Kendal put her hand on the spot on her upper thigh. "Marked how?"

"It states here that the dragon will one day awaken, but only if it's in the hands of the goddess's chosen one."

"If it does awaken, then what?" she asked.

"I can't answer that because that's all this says. The dragon will awaken, but nothing else," Lenore said, but Kendal could tell Lenore's eyes were on her hand.

"What happens if the chosen one isn't holding it?" Piper asked, pressing closer to her.

"When Aphrodite had her husband, Hephaestus, cast the sword, she had to make a pact with her brother, Ares, under order from their father. Zeus dictated that if siblings dabbled in things neither knew well, the sword had to be balanced."

"Balanced how?" Piper asked.

Kendal smiled since she could guess the meaning. "Most of the lessons I received when I became a slayer revolved around the fact that all things in life are balanced," she said to Piper, and Lenore nodded. "For every bit of good, there is something equally bad, and so on. In the true nature of things, we can't have one without the other, so if the sword is really of Ares and Aphrodite's making, it contains the power of both love and war."

"The power it contains, and how it's used, depends solely on the person who awakens the dragon," Lenore said.

"Does the book say when?" she asked.

Lenore flipped through a few more sections and started reading. "The legend starts with a couple in ancient Greece. They fell in love, but their families had been sworn enemies for generations, so they thought a future together would be impossible."

"When I first heard this it sounded like a million other stories bards told during that era," Morgaine said.

"It reminds me of *Romeo and Juliet*," Piper said.

"A lot of the classics come from legends like this," Lenore said before she began reading from the book. "With a very bleak outlook for happiness, the two young women ran off one night in search of a place or time when their love would be accepted. They traveled for weeks to reach the shore where they found shelter and consummated their relationship. It wasn't long before word came that both families were close to finding them, and if they succeeded, the young women would be ripped apart forever. That night they made love one last time and sacrificed themselves to Aphrodite."

"I've never known the goddess of love to encourage human sacrifices," Kendal said, remembering the temples back then. "Her altars were always covered in flowers and fruits."

"Before they died, they asked for the goddess's blessing so in death their spirits would be intertwined and they'd be together again in another life."

A tear rolled down Piper's cheek when Lenore finished, and Kendal wiped it away. "Thank God I found you and my family accepted you. It's sad they saw death as their only option."

"Their sacrifice touched the goddess, so she chose to honor the love they had for each other by granting their prayer, and she bound their spirits as one. From that, Aphrodite also created, with Hephaestus's help, a mystical creature we came to know as the dragon."

"The goddess of love created dragons?" Kendal laughed at the absurdity.

"Dragons are supposedly loyal creatures with pure hearts," Morgaine said. "In my life I've seen only one, but among the folklore of my people they were once commonplace. The stories said they were a problem only when provoked or when their lairs were disturbed, because they were fiercely protective of their young."

"Why would anyone do that?" Piper asked.

"Their eggs were made of pure gold, and sometimes greed overrides sense," Lenore said. "Originally the dragon symbolized the goddess's concept of true love. To Aphrodite, love was fierce and could use its power to defeat hate and evil, but like the sword, the dragon has Ares's blood as well."

"Dragons don't exist anymore, so why does all this matter?" Kendal asked as Piper reached for her hand.

"Your time as slayer came after they were dealt with, but they most certainly exist," Morgaine said. "Once their true nature was corrupted by man, the Clan members that came before me had no choice but to stop their rampage."

Kendal understood what Piper must be going through. It had been a long time since a children's story had been proved to be real. "What happened to them?"

"After a lot of effort to preserve them, the Clan put them into indefinite hibernation." Morgaine had a faraway expression, but after a sigh she refocused. "The dragons suffered a fate they didn't really deserve, but the Clan did what they felt was right at the time."

"They're still in hibernation?" she asked.

"The spell that was cast over them locked them away forever," Lenore said.

"Does the sword have anything to do with that?" Piper asked.

"The book says that when the dragon wakes, and if it's by someone who wants to conquer the world, they'll be unstoppable." Lenore had her finger on a line on the last page.

"And the right time is?" Kendal asked.

"I can't be exactly sure." Lenore opened her journal to a chart of something. "I wrote out all the clues in here and assume the sacrifice occurred close to the witching hour on what came to be known as All Hallows' Eve."

"Since I'm not familiar with all these cryptic clues, when is that exactly?" Piper asked.

"Midnight on Halloween," Kendal said, and smiled when Piper laughed.

"You're joking, right?" Piper glanced at all three of them and laughed again. "Is this an elaborate joke to initiate me into the immortals' club? That's the corniest thing I've ever heard."

"Piper, every story you've ever read comes about from a certain truth," Lenore said. She appeared stunned by Piper's reaction.

"Kendal's told me that every time she informs me that something like werewolves are real, so I get that, but come on. This is a bit over-the-top."

Kendal held up her hand for quiet so she could offer a better explanation. "The most important thing to accept is that on certain days, certain barriers are easier to breach."

"What barriers?" Piper asked, then snorted when Kendal pinched her nose. "Okay, I'll shut up and let you finish."

"Halloween was, for a long time, much more than kids in cute costumes and candy. And if you're someone up to no good, you know that at the stroke of midnight the barriers between good and evil become nonexistent. It's why some organized religions picked the following minute as All Saints' Day. In a way it was the equivalent of drawing a line in the sand for their followers to pick a side. If the book is right about the sword, it makes sense that its fate would be decided in the one instant no side has an advantage."

Piper looked at her and nodded her understanding before she kissed her. "Gran's right, you'd make a great teacher."

"Thanks," she said, and kissed Piper again. "This is only a crisis if someone else knows about the sword, and I used it only briefly before locking it away here. Has anyone shown interest in this legend?" she asked Lenore.

"In Piper's vision she felt that someone close to the Elders in Egypt—I don't know who—wants to trap you, so obviously they've heard of the legend and its prophecy. We have less than ten months to find out." Lenore closed her books and looked at Piper. "It's not a lot of time, but we need to figure out how to hone your gift so we can get as much information from your visions as possible."

"Surprisingly, Seeing the Future Through Visions class wasn't offered at Tulane, so how do you plan to teach me that?" Piper asked, and Kendal laughed at her humor.

"I'm sure you'll do fine," Lenore said with confidence.

"The best thing is to not worry about it," Morgaine added.

"Thanks for the pep talk." Piper looked up at Kendal. "Do you think we'll be okay? I just found you, and you promised forever."

"We might encounter a few headaches along the way, but we'll get through this together."

"What choice do we have, huh?" Piper said, and Kendal knew she hadn't bought her evasive answer.

"What choice indeed?"

CHAPTER ELEVEN

The next morning Piper looked out at the grounds from the balcony attached to the master bedroom and noticed a large spot near the back of the house where trees had been planted in a perfect circle around a patch where the grass was still green. In the center of that Kendal stood with Ming, Charlie, Morgaine, and two others she didn't recognize. With the gray light of dawn outlining them, they went through a series of exercises that reminded her of a ballet. The others were in perfect synch with Kendal, but she didn't pay close attention to them.

Kendal wore the gi pants she seemed to be fond of, but unlike the last time Piper saw her like this, the only other thing she wore was a sports bra. She seemed oblivious to the cold and dampness of the morning, since they didn't impede the fluidity of her movements. The sword she used resembled the Sea Serpent, but it was another katana like the one she'd used in New Orleans. They all thought it best to keep the real thing locked away until they knew more of what it was capable of.

Piper held her large coffee mug with both hands and was glad for the blanket Kendal had wrapped her in before she'd gone down. They'd talked a lot more the previous night, but her worry that she'd fail to help them through this was making her colder than the English weather.

"Look at her and clear your mind," Lenore said softly when she joined Piper. "Concentrate only on what you feel for her."

"That'll do it?"

"We all have a center." Lenore placed her fingers in the middle of her chest. "It's the place where we feel nothing can harm us. For her," she pointed to Kendal, "she's always found it in her skills." Lenore must've seen the disappointment in her face. "Don't take that to mean she loves the battles more than you. That's far from the truth now."

"How so?"

"She got lost in the skills to find her center before you, and now she must maintain them to protect her center. Do you understand?"

"Center is what we find in each other."

"Exactly, because you can see in every one of her moves the desire to be the best. It's the only way to win what she wants most."

Piper studied Kendal again and envied her ability to totally concentrate. "She's already won my love, so she has nothing left to prove, if you mean me."

"But she will whenever the need arises, so learn from what you see. If you let go of the doubt and worry, your mind will open and you'll find every answer before the question even forms."

Piper laughed as she put her cup down to reach for Lenore's hand. "Nothing like a little pressure to make me relax."

"Think of it this way," Lenore said, holding Piper's hand between hers. "You can never have another vision, and we'll still be fine. You own her heart, but I've known her longer. I've seen her come out the victor long after everyone thought the fight was over, so look," she pointed to Kendal again, "and clear your mind."

Piper let her thoughts wander as she watched Kendal move from one position to the next as if she were gliding on a cloud because of the pants. Even from this distance she could see the muscles in Kendal's back, and when she turned and pointed her sword at the others, Piper closed her eyes and had the sensation of flying off to another place. This time, though, the trip was to the future.

Kendal stood with the Sea Serpent Sword in her hand, and the stones of the dragon's eyes glowed vibrant green, as if an electric current ran through Kendal's hand. The moment for the dragon to wake was here, and Kendal planned to send the power back to the gods who'd made it, but a man fought her for it. When he took it the stones glowed red, and the change made him laugh.

"Come here and we'll finish this together," the man said to Piper, and she was pushed from behind. Closer to this stranger she could sense the magnitude of the power that flowed through him from the sword. It truly felt like an instrument of the gods.

"Asra," she said, confused as to why Asra wasn't helping her.

"She's lost to you now," he said, and pointed the tip of the sword as if forcing her to look.

Two men held Asra down and a third drove his sword into her chest with savage strokes, making her drop to her knees, completely weakened. The sight was worse than the night Henri and Ora had done the same.

"You're mine," the man said as he reached for her and ripped her shirt open.

Piper's eyes opened and she took deep breaths to keep from crying because the fear was so overwhelming. It might've been a vision but it'd been so real, down to the copper smell of Kendal's blood.

"Try to let it go, but not to the point you forget," Lenore said, but she sounded miles away.

"All this stuff I see, will it happen?"

"I can't answer that, Piper, but I wish I could. From my experience with the seers in the Clan, the things you see are the future as it will happen if nothing changes it. If one little thing we do changes fate, then you might have another vision of the same thing and it'll be completely different. It could be that you're different from the others and whatever you see is unchangeable, but even Bruik, the Clan's best seer, doesn't have complete domination of the future."

Piper told Lenore everything she'd envisioned but kept her eyes on Kendal, comforted that she was healthy and strong and disarming everyone she faced. "I wish I could describe the men who attacked us, but I didn't see any faces clearly and they used no names."

"Nothing was distinguishable about them?"

"All I know for sure is they want to destroy her to the point that we won't be able to salvage what's left even with the help of the elixir."

"Luckily we know for sure now that whatever is coming definitely has to do with the sword, so all we have to do is figure out a way to change what you saw to keep it from happening."

Piper's head didn't hurt, but she rubbed her temples as if it did. "Do I tell her what I saw just now?"

"If it were her having the visions, would you want to know?"

"That was a stupid question, so forget I asked it." Even if she could keep this from Kendal, she wouldn't want to. "Do you have any idea who hates her enough to destroy her?"

"Asra has made plenty of enemies through the years, but she destroyed most of them."

"So no one comes to mind?" she asked. Having to study every year of Kendal's life for the answer would make their quest impossible.

"It's either someone or something that slipped through the cracks of time, or someone loyal to someone she destroyed, who sees this as an opportunity to seek revenge."

Piper sighed and stood. "I'm afraid we'll run out of time before we know for sure, and if we do, it'll end in disaster."

"Trust her and trust yourself, Piper. It's the only way to win."

"Trust in each other isn't the problem." She smiled at Lenore for her always-upbeat outlook on things. "I'm not that old compared to you all, but sometimes, no matter how hard we try, the right side doesn't always win."

She was surprised to see Hill come out and join the others, happily accepting a sword from Charlie. Kendal seemed to be giving her pointers as she engaged her, and they were both laughing. The scene didn't make Piper feel like something wicked was waiting to destroy them and the world as they knew it, but she was happy that Hill had found a new set of friends who would understand her as well as she did.

"Even I know it's impossible not to worry, but look at how willing they all are to fight for her. That she has you to fight for, combined with that kind of loyalty, will make this all okay."

"No matter what, I'll stand or fall at her side. I need no visions to be certain about that."

❖

Kendal hurried upstairs to shower so she could keep her date with Mac and from the landing saw Lenore leaving the master bedroom. Lenore walked quickly to her room, so Kendal took the last set of stairs two at a time. When she entered the room Piper stood next to the bed with an expression that was hard to read.

"Is everything all right? I saw Lenore rushing to her room." Kendal stripped off her sports bra. It was cold outside, but they'd moved around enough for her to sweat.

"Are you still having breakfast with Pops?"

"I was planning to, unless he cancels or you need me for

something." She took her pants off next but Piper never moved. Whatever she and Lenore had discussed had bothered Piper enough to knock the playfulness out of her. "You didn't answer my question. Is everything all right?"

"I sat with Lenore this morning and had another vision," Piper said, then told her what she'd seen. "Whoever this is wants more than just the sword, and it made me feel dirty."

"Let me call downstairs and tell Mac we'll make it lunch."

"No." Piper finally moved toward her and leaned against her. "I want to write down everything I saw while it's still fresh in my mind. If I have another one of these flashes of the future, maybe we can chart a way to change what I saw this morning. So don't keep Pops waiting. If he calms down again, it'll be one less thing for me to worry about."

"Are you sure? I can stay really quiet while you do that, if you need me close by."

"I'll always need you close by, but I need my grandfather to like you too, and that wins out this time." Piper led her to the shower and helped her clean herself, then get dressed.

Ming led Kendal to the estate's sunroom where Mac sat reading the paper and having coffee. "Would you like me to serve now, ma'am?" Ming asked.

"Please, then have everyone clear out and close the door." While the servants placed everything on the table, Kendal took the time to fix herself a cup of coffee as well. Once they were alone, she looked at Mac and smiled. "Good morning. I apologize for keeping you waiting a few minutes. I was going over something with Piper."

Mac stared her down as if trying to decide the best way to start taking pieces out of her hide. "Can we cut through the bullshit?" he asked.

"I'd be happy to do that if you'll answer something for me," she said, realizing Mac was an old-fashioned guy who was used to the simple approach. People like that hadn't done as well in the modern world because they expected everyone to be as honest as they were, making them easy targets at times.

"Like I said, no bullshit, so shoot."

"I gave you my word that I love your granddaughter and promised to take care of her, so what's changed that I've lost your blessing? Granted, you never really came out and gave it to me, but I thought you approved of our relationship." She scooped up some lemon curd and put it on her scone, giving him a chance to think of an answer.

"When we met I had a certain impression of you and where you came from, and all this doesn't fit into that. Piper has already gone through that dance with that jackass Kenny, and I don't want a repeat of that for her." He placed his fists on the table but didn't come across as angry. "I love Piper with all I am, and I want more than anything to trust you with my little girl."

"Mr. Marmande, I owe you another apology."

"For what?" He lowered his hands and leaned back in his seat as if she'd surprised him.

"I should've called you before I made certain promises to Piper, to get that blessing from you, but I love her so much it made me rush."

"I get the feeling you've never had to do the in-law thing. Hell, I didn't do all that great either when it was my turn, so no need for apologies."

She reached across the table and offered him her hand. "It matters to me that you know there'll never be a day in our life together that I won't take Piper's welfare as seriously as you have. I love her and she will be safe with me."

"In the end, all we have is our families, and I really thought mine would've been filled with grandkids, my son, and his wife. God didn't grant me that, so I hope you understand my concerns when it comes to Piper."

"I'll go through this with you as many times as it takes to convince you I'm the right choice for her, so don't worry about it." He shook her hand and finally let the smile she was used to seeing on his face appear. "If it'll make you feel better, I'll have my attorneys send over the paperwork we signed in Venice. We entered into this with the belief it's going to be forever, so there was no need to protect assets from each other."

"And have Molly mount my head in the trophy room I got a look at last night? No, thank you." He appeared to have suddenly gotten his appetite back when he started putting salt on everything like he was going to finish it all. "My wife won't ask you, but if you two start talking babies soon, she'll be in heaven."

She laughed at the notion but was grateful Mac seemed fine. "I'll have to run that one by Piper before I make any commitments."

"I'd love to see a little Marmande-Richoux running the business one day."

"Speaking of business, mine might keep us in the area longer than I thought, but I want you and Molly to stay with us if you like." She got up to warm their coffee and grab another scone. "You're both welcome, and since Piper tells me that you left someone you trust in charge of the business, think of Farthington as home for as long as you wish."

"Then we might be here until the flowers start to bloom, if Molly has a say."

"I'm sure the gardeners will appreciate her input." They finished eating, and then she excused herself to make a few calls.

It was time to start changing the first of Piper's visions to see what would come of it. If a trip to the Elder compound was a trap, they'd stay clear of the place, but Kendal still wanted to give Rolla the respect *he* thought he deserved. In her office she retrieved a blank scroll and got out her fountain pen to write the note in ancient Greek, since it was still Rolla's favorite language.

The invitation was short and to the point, but it got her thoughts across. She signed her name after she'd reread it a few times, then rolled it closed. From the top drawer she pulled a stick of wax and the signet ring she'd worn when the world knew her simply as Asra of the House of Raad. The crest imprinted in gold made her think of her father. Even after all this time she felt a connection to him, and she wondered how much he would've loved getting to know Piper.

After the candle had melted enough of the wax to press the document closed, she called for Ming. "Yes, Lord Wallace?" Ming asked from the doorway.

She held the parchment out to him. "Please have Winston deliver this for me and tell him not to linger in Egypt. I want him back in a couple of days, not because I want to ruin his fun, but because I want him out of harm's way. Your son is getting good with the sword, but he's no match for the henchmen the Elders have at their disposal."

"I shall make it so."

"The message is for Rolla, and for his hands alone."

Ming bowed, the parchment pressed against his chest. "I'll make sure he leaves today."

Kendal stood and bowed to him in respect before he left the room, grateful for people like Ming in her life. Time was important, but now she had no choice but to wait.

"Hopefully you choose wisely, Rolla, because you won't like the consequences of going against me or Piper."

❖

At dinner that night, Mac and Molly announced their decision to stay, saying they were looking forward to spending time exploring the area and getting to know Kendal better. For the next week, Kendal continued her workouts with a variety of opponents, and Piper tried her best to sharpen her sight.

Seven days after that Piper sat on the veranda outside their bedroom to watch Kendal's usual morning workout when a man she'd never seen before entered the circle that she now knew had been planted in homage to Morgaine's roots. She couldn't hear what they were saying, but the visitor handed Kendal what looked like a scroll.

While Kendal read whatever it was, the man seemed to be focusing on her sword that she'd handed Morgaine to hold. He nodded at whatever Kendal said next, but before he left he tried to reach out and touch her sword, and Kendal grabbed his wrist. As soon as the man was out of sight, Kendal gazed up at her and started for the house.

"Trouble?" she asked when she heard Kendal's footsteps behind her.

Kendal had told her to expect a response, but it might take time. If the man this morning was from Rolla, Piper was surprised it hadn't been weeks, considering the archaic forms of communication the Elders preferred. In an age of cell phones and e-mail, they didn't even use the mail, as if to retain some of the things they liked from their ancient pasts no matter what century they were in.

"It's another invitation, only this time," Kendal sat next to her and cracked open a bottle of juice, "I've been given a warning not to turn it down."

"Was it from Rolla and the others?" She accepted the bottle and took a long sip. The strawberry-and-mango mix was one of Kendal's favorites.

"Rolla wants to meet me alone, but the old man never travels by himself. When he says a meeting with just the two of us, it usually means him and at least three guards, unless he's locked away in that maze in Egypt."

"When do we go?" Piper ran her hand along Kendal's forearm.

"I've never thought I'd hear that phrase again, since the last person to say it to me was my father," Kendal said wistfully. "I've always faced every fight I've had up to now alone. It's nice to know I don't have to anymore. We're going to take him up on his offer since he's coming to us."

"I'm not sure how useful I'll be in a fight, but I'm glad I'm here with you." She touched Kendal's face. "I love you."

"I love you too, but if you want to stay behind that's okay too." Kendal pressed closer to her and wrapped her arms around her waist. With a gentleness she never showed on the practice field, Kendal kissed her until Piper felt the first stirrings of desire.

"Did you get knocked in the head when I wasn't looking? That's the only way to explain you wanting to go anywhere without me."

"I'm not telling you that you have to stay behind, just giving you an option." Kendal kissed her again and lifted her so she was lying on top of her on the chaise they shared.

"I want all my options to include you."

"Will you make a deal with me?" Kendal asked with a smile.

"Now there's my charmer. I'll make you any deal you want, as soon as you give me what I want." Piper ran her finger along Kendal's bottom lip. "Take me inside before we start talking about Rolla and his collection of misfits."

"Did you have a vision about Rolla's little helpers, because that's a good description for them."

"I had some visions while I watched you this morning, but they were of a more personal nature. Make love to me, baby."

No other words were needed for the moment.

CHAPTER TWELVE

They lay in bed together a few hours later, under the canopy of the antique bed fitted with crisp sheets, and enjoyed the silence of the house. Other people were inside and on the grounds, but in this room, they were almost in a peaceful cocoon.

"What'd you do with Hill? I haven't seen her in a few days," Piper said as she stretched before curling around Kendal again.

"I sent her to London to meet some friends of mine who work for Scotland Yard. With their help and the picture she got of Leonardo, she may be able to find some leads."

"You think this guy might have something to do with all this?"

Kendal scratched Piper's back in a slow circle, enjoying how she shivered every so often. "I don't know anything about him except that he wanted information about me. At first I thought we could put it off, but we can't afford to leave anything undone, considering what we could be facing."

"Do you think we'll ever be able to share our secrets with Hill?"

"Not yet, but not because I think she'll sell our story to the news or some rag." She rolled them over and fit herself between Piper's legs. "Hill deserves to stay innocent as long as she can, because once I tell her what she needs to know to be effective as our security chief, she's going to have to make a huge commitment."

"Can I do something for you?" Piper asked when she rocked their hips together. "I've suddenly lost interest in where anyone is and who does or doesn't work for us."

"Would you like to go on a date with me tonight?" The way Piper came up to meet her made her want more.

"I may have to go into the city early if you want to do something like the opera, since I don't have the clothes for that." Piper moaned in her ear when she sucked on her nipple.

Kendal let go and stared at how hard it'd gotten before she continued their conversation, as if they were enjoying afternoon tea together. "Not quite what I have in mind, but if you really want to go I'll be happy to take you some other night." She sucked in Piper's other nipple and almost lost contact when Piper's hips came up with more force.

"Are we talking jeans and a sweater?" Piper asked, and she sounded a little stressed.

Before Kendal came up she'd requested the staff to prepare the vehicle she wanted to use, and they'd promised to have it waxed and gassed. "Still a little off the mark, but don't worry. I'll help you dress appropriately for the evening."

"How about helping me right now?" Piper asked as she almost unbalanced her off the bed when she grabbed Kendal's hand and put it between her legs. Piper was wet and she felt hot, making Kendal want more.

She wet her fingers by sliding them up and down Piper's sex before she pressed down hard on her clit. The pressure made Piper groan and move as if to get more stimulation. "I love making you crazy."

Piper opened her eyes and glanced between her legs before she met Kendal's eyes. "I want you inside me." After their experience with the sword, Piper had seemingly become more comfortable with telling her what she wanted. A few times she'd wondered if the sword itself had somehow placed a spell on Piper, but Lenore had told her not to worry about that.

Now wasn't the time to be concerned about it as her fingers filled Piper and made her hiss in what looked to be total satisfaction. Earlier they'd been frantic for each other, so Kendal held herself up with one hand and slowly pumped her other hand in and out of Piper's sex, wanting the buildup to be gradual.

Piper must have wanted more than that because she encouraged her onto her back so she could straddle her hips and continued the slow movements, but with their mouths together. "Do you feel me?" Piper sat up enough to bring her breasts into view.

"I feel every bit of you, and I love that you share this part of yourself with me."

"Do I belong to you, Asra?" Piper asked as she stopped her hips at the point that would keep her fingers buried deep.

"I don't want to own you."

"I asked if I belong to you, so answer me," Piper said, then kissed her hard.

"You belong to me and no other," she said honestly, and hoped she didn't sound offensive.

"Remember that in the coming months."

There had been no other visions, but the one Piper had that morning with Lenore had stayed with Kendal. "I won't forget, and I promise to kill any bastard stupid enough to touch what's mine. No vision of the future will keep me from protecting you."

Piper sat up and moved her hips at a faster pace so it didn't take long for her to come.

Kendal was disappointed Piper got up immediately afterward, but she took her hand when Piper led her to the bathroom and sat her on the bench in the shower. "Tonight and whatever comes after, we'll do together," Piper said from her knees before she put her mouth on her. She used her tongue first and was as patient in getting her worked up as Kendal had been.

When they were done, Ming brought up a small snack and the package she'd ordered for Piper. She laid it out when Piper was in the bathroom drying her hair, then went outside to see if the staff had finished preparing their ride.

"She's got to be kidding," Piper said from inside, making Kendal laugh as she walked back into their room. The clothing she'd picked was out of the norm for Piper and, if she had to guess, something Piper never imagined herself wearing.

"She isn't kidding," Kendal said in a low voice as she admired Piper in her underwear. "But if you don't feel comfortable with my choice you can pick something else."

Piper was certain the elixir helped her hold her breath as long as she did when she looked at Kendal leaning against the door frame. Kendal wore a thick black leather belt to hold up the leather pants that fit nicely over her boots. The tight leather vest was far from Kendal's usual crisp white shirt, but Piper loved how sexy it made her look. Kendal's corporate persona had been stashed for the evening and replaced by this dangerous-looking replica who was making her heart pump faster.

After seeing the way Kendal was dressed, the outfit she'd chosen for her made sense, if she wanted to look like they were together wherever they were going. "Why do my pants have laces on the sides?" When she put them on, a good portion of her skin was on display from her ankles to her thigh.

"You have nicer legs than I do." Kendal walked to the closet and came out with a leather jacket and two daggers she slid into the sides of her boots. "To me you're the most important thing in the world, but if everyone else walks away with the impression you're nothing but a piece of fluff, I think that's best."

"Excuse me?" She put her hands on her hips and thought Kendal had lost her mind.

"Tonight isn't all about dress-up, love. We're going into London to see Rolla, and since he can order a hundred warriors with fighting abilities that rival mine, I'll be okay if the men with him think you're nothing but a plaything to me. I know better, and so do you, but I don't want them to consider you a threat." Kendal came closer and put her arms around Piper, who relaxed her stance. "And if they don't see you as a threat, you'll be free to study Rolla and his misfits and see if you pick up on anything."

"This is going to cost you, Richoux." She moved her hands around Kendal's hips and slid her fingers into the top of her pants. When Kendal bent her head, she kissed the spot above her chin close to her lips.

"What's it going to cost me?"

She glanced at the bed, then back at Kendal. "I'll think of something."

"Come on, vixen." Kendal kissed her one more time before going to the closet again and stepping out with a long black leather coat that resembled the one Piper had seen her hunt in.

"Honey, you've already picked out a coat," she said, and pointed to the short but thick waist-length coat Kendal had thrown on the bed.

"This is for you, Lady Wallace." Kendal held the coat up with a flourish for her to put on. "It's chilly out, so you'll need this for the ride in."

"Whatever you say," she said as Kendal twitched the coat into place.

They came down together holding hands. The only ones waiting were Lenore and Morgaine, who were dressed a little more conservatively. Kendal and Morgaine had argued earlier, and Morgaine had won that round when Piper had agreed they should join them in case Rolla had brought more men with him than Kendal planned for.

"Remember, you stay in the office out of sight unless I call for you," Kendal said as they walked outside.

Piper was about to ask why Kendal had put on a clear pair of glasses, then noticed the big BMW motorcycle parked next to a black sports car. The amount of leather they were wearing meant they were taking the bike.

"We remember," Lenore said, and rolled her eyes at both Morgaine and Kendal, but only so Piper would notice.

It took them an hour with traffic to make it into London, and Piper was surprised when they stopped next to what looked like a popular club. From what she'd heard of Rolla—or the old man, as Kendal and the others called him—meeting him somewhere full of partiers wasn't what she had in mind.

"Did you have a sudden urge to dance before we meet with this guy?" she asked as Kendal put the kickstand down. After a quick scan of the street she saw the Porsche Morgaine had driven in was already parked and vacant.

"A wise woman told me the meeting I was going to have with Rolla was a trap, and even though this is a different meeting, I tailored it to give us the advantage." Kendal kissed her forehead and took her hand. "If there are traps to set, why shouldn't they be ours?"

"Since I'm not a military strategist either, could you say that again so I'll understand it?"

"The club is one of the holdings in the Wallace portfolio. People think you put Lord in front of someone's name and it equals stuffy. I may be many things…"

"But stuffy is definitely not one of them." Piper pinched Kendal's side. She watched as Kendal slid a magnetic key card through the appropriate slot on the wall, making the embellished glass doors open.

The pounding beat coming from the speakers was loud enough

that Piper felt each note reverberating through her body. For once, she felt like the coolest kid in the place as she made her way in on Kendal's arm. It was still early in terms of people starting their evening, but a lot of people were already crowding the crystal-lined bar and the dance floor. In an instant one of the waitresses came up and took both their coats, smiling up at Kendal in a way that made Piper want to punch her in the throat.

"Welcome back, Lord Wallace," the woman said loudly, and her smile was so wide it appeared freakish. She then turned to Piper and gave a slightly weaker courteous one. "And, Lady Wallace, welcome as well and congratulations."

"Thank you." Piper raised her voice a little to be heard over the music. She smiled when the title the woman had addressed her by registered. Kendal kept her hand on her backside as she guided her toward the bar.

"Dance with me?" Kendal asked.

She shook her head and tried to take a seat at the bar. "I'm not really a good—" Kendal pulled her gently into the group of dancers already on the floor.

Memories of the sword room came back when Kendal turned her around and pressed their bodies together front to back. When she felt how Kendal's fingers skimmed along the laces at the sides of her pants, and how she was grinding into her, she almost forgot why they were there. She snapped out of her stupor when Kendal whispered in her ear.

"See the thick-bodied guy sitting on the banquette toward the back of the room?" She nodded and followed Kendal's lead on the dance floor. "The great Rolla."

The old man was anything but. A thick strand of light-brown hair hung down his forehead, covering a little of the familiar blue eyes, and he fit in with his jeans and velvet jacket. He had a strong, handsome face, and if she'd had to guess, he was no older than thirty. His body was solid but he wasn't overweight, and his hands were lying flat on the table on the sides of one of the club's cobalt-blue glasses. He was watching them with the same interest she had in him, and every so often he picked up his drink and took a sip.

"I thought you said he was old."

"Believe me, he's not young, especially in dog years." Kendal was joking with her. "Let's get this over with. Keep an eye out for the idiot sitting about twenty feet from him."

"Which idiot?"

"The guy in the suede shirt." Kendal turned them slightly on the dance floor so she could get a good look at the blond eyeing them with his head cocked to one side. "We haven't met yet, but I'm guessing that would be Travis. Morgaine had nothing nice to say about him." The women walked off the dance floor.

"It's comforting that despite the passing of time, you don't change much, do you?" Rolla said, staring at Piper. He didn't raise his voice to force her closer. "Get rid of her since we've got a lot to talk about."

"She's not a reporter, Rolla." Kendal pulled a chair out for Piper. Without asking, she possessively put her hand on Piper's shoulder and guided her down onto it. "Besides, you brought friends to the party, so I should be allowed at least one."

"Do you feel any remorse for what you've done? Things have changed and I have no choice but to grant you forgiveness, but I don't like being defied." He picked up the glass and took another sip of his drink.

Kendal sat next to Piper and put her arm around her. "I've denied myself long enough, and I couldn't anymore."

"Yet you've brought this plaything with you instead of this great love you're willing to throw everything away for."

"You've given yourself to the Clan, as have I," she said, and he nodded. "In all that time, haven't you ever wanted more?"

"We all do," Rolla said, and held his hand palm up to her. When Kendal accepted, he walked her to the empty corner behind them. "She's lovely, so I partially understand why you defied our laws, and it doesn't hurt that she's a prophecy come to life."

"Thank you for my reprieve," she said sincerely. Morgaine had always been the one she answered to, but she'd worked directly for Rolla numerous times in the past. She'd always found him fair-minded and kind. "I suppose it's too late to ask for your forgiveness, but I regret only doing what I did without your blessing."

"You've always exceeded my expectations, so had you asked, I believe I would've given it to you. That you didn't angered me enough to want to punish you, but I care about you too much to have been too harsh." He whispered in her ear to keep their talk private, and she smiled when she saw his ink-stained fingers. Another thousand years of scrubbing would never get the stains out. "Now that we've gotten that out of the way, will you help us? A majority of the Elders know the legend, but there's a split amongst us."

"Half want the power and half want to stop it?"

"If that were true I wouldn't be so worried," he said, and sighed. "Half want the dragon to wake and the other half believe it to be a fairy tale with no merit. Those nonbelievers aren't motivated to stop something they think is impossible."

"Do they all know about Piper?" Kendal glanced back to see that Travis had moved closer to Piper.

"Only I know that, and I'll keep it that way because I don't know who to trust, and the numbers unhappy with my rule grow by the day."

She squeezed his hand and smiled at him. In years Rolla was old, but he still resembled a cherub. "The day they replace you with someone who tries to impose a hard line as to world affairs is the day I walk away. I've served you faithfully because I believe in you."

"That's comforting as well," he said, and smiled. "So shall we finish this charade so we can get back to finding our Judas and his allies?"

"Have you found anything new on who might have knowledge of the sword?"

"I'll send word through Lenore when I do."

She moved back to Piper quickly when Travis lifted his hand to touch her. Before he could, she'd pulled a dagger from her boot and slammed his head to the table. "Who told you it's okay to touch other people's property?"

"Let me up, bitch," Travis said as he pushed against her hand.

She pressed the tip to the side of his mouth hard enough to cut through his bottom lip. "Stick to fights where you have a chance."

"Travis, go back to your seat," Rolla said, finally raising his voice. "Asra, let him go and stay out of my sight until I decide what to do with you. I forbid you to lift a sword to anyone until we've dealt with your insolence."

"Remember what I said," she said loudly, pointing the dagger at

Rolla as if she were about to fling it at his head. "My allegiance to you is held only by a thin thread, so don't make me angry. I'll join the first group who offers me the chance to bring you down."

"Your loyalty or lack of it will be known by the others," he said, and winked so no one with him would see.

"Now what?" Piper asked when they stepped on the dance floor again.

"We wait and see if someone approaches me for the sword. Even if they don't, they'll think Rolla is in a weaker position because of the dissension in his ranks."

"Is he still mad at you?"

"I'm not perfect, but he doesn't doubt my loyalty to him and the Clan." She held Piper and swayed to the beat. "He also knows the dragon's time is coming, and it mustn't be allowed to spread its wings."

"I'll be home in just a few minutes." The young woman juggled her phone as she put her briefcase in the trunk of her car. "After a week of overtime, I think the boss has finally noticed me." She put the sack of groceries down next and stooped to pick up the keys she'd dropped. "I love you too, and I'll see you in a bit." After she finished her call she seemed genuinely scared and surprised when she noticed the woman standing in front of her.

"Excuse me." She tried to go around the stranger with her keys held out as if she planned to stab her with them.

Vadoma used her strength to pin the woman to her car and quickly punctured her neck, moaning when the hot gush of blood filled her mouth. The woman struggled against her but had no chance at escape, and the fight left her a few moments later. Vadoma drank her fill and disengaged before death.

She hadn't been terribly thirsty, but the damp cold was more bearable with the woman's blood in her belly. One of her fledglings wiped her mouth for her as the others placed the woman in her own trunk. All of them owed their immortality to Vadoma, and after her spells and hard work, they'd all gained tremendous strength when she'd harnessed her cousin Ora's power at her destruction. She was now the oldest, so the crown of queen had passed to her, as well as all of Ora's knowledge, and she planned to use both wisely.

Ora had tried for centuries, with Henri's help, to destroy the Genesis Clan and their slayers, and their ignorance and arrogance had cost them their existence. The only way to succeed in getting the Clan to leave them in peace was to help them destroy themselves. She'd thought the opportunity was years in the future, but the chance was here and she planned to take it.

"Are you sure about this, mistress?"

"Make sure the others are positioned around the grounds." Vadoma bound her thick red hair with a leather thong, irritated with it and the wind. "I'm anxious to meet this fallen Elder Julius, but not so much so that I'll fall into some pathetic attempt at a trap. He also doesn't sound like he's at full strength, so we'll be fine even if he brings a few protectors."

"But why go at all?" He had to quicken his pace to keep up with her.

"His offer sounded too interesting to ignore. After all, it's not often an Elder of the famed Clan calls with such tempting enticements." She scaled the wall surrounding the Tower of London with little effort and jumped down onto the grounds. This place, considering its history, seemed perfect for their talk.

"I'm glad you came," the man she figured was Julius said. He stood on the spot where Anne Boleyn had lost her head to the executioner's axe. "From the way you move and the number of followers keeping watch, the rumors are true. You have managed to harness Ora's power as well as inherit her title."

"I'm sure you're not here out of curiosity as to how I came to be the queen, so tell me what you want." Vadoma used the title seriously, but she was sure her jeans and casual sweater made her look like anything but royalty. "And tell your little pet to come out from his hiding place." She stared at the dark side of the tower until a smallish man stepped out. "Who are you?"

"Bailey, mistress," he said as he walked to Julius's side.

"An Elder and an Elder archivist. I'm a lucky woman to have captured the eye of such important men." She laughed. "Tell me, Bailey, what have you written about me so far in those scrolls you all love so much?"

"You have a gift for magic, or so say the stories among your people. You were given the gift by your cousin Ora herself to fulfill a request made to her by her uncle, your father. I couldn't find much on your father except that he and Ora's father were brothers. Before you were turned, you were a powerful witch revered by your tribe, and the Elders think with a few more centuries your power will surpass your cousin's."

"Such flattery might make me send them a tribute," she said, and sat near Julius. "But you should change the tense of the last sentence."

"What do you mean?" Bailey asked.

"I am still powerful in the dark arts, and I detest the word *witch*."

"Unless you need more fan mail read to you, can we get down to business?" Julius asked.

"You called me." She crossed her legs, unconcerned by the other smallish man near the wall. Julius so far wasn't impressive, considering the company he traveled with. "Tell me what you want."

"I wanted to see you before we moved on." Julius sat next to her and she stared into his pale-blue eyes, as fascinated with them as the first time she'd seen the same color on a member of the Clan.

To her what the Clan considered their greatest achievement was their biggest weakness. It was the one aspect of yourself you couldn't hide—the eyes. No Clan member could ever hide in plain sight.

"For what? Are you slumming?"

"I needed to see what Asra created."

"The slayer has nothing to do with me." She was close to leaving, not finding Julius worth her time.

"You're wrong." Julius moved closer, and she morphed a little to keep him back. "Asra destroyed Ora and in turn created you."

"Do you intend to talk about nothing all night or what your archivist called me about?"

"Can you do what we asked?" Julius asked, and moved even closer.

"I can do more than you asked, but why would I?" She trusted her fledglings, but the sound of someone coming over the wall concerned her. "You must think I'm stupid, because no Elder would allow me to exist for long, no matter what I do for you."

The soft thump of someone's feet hitting the ground made her stand and completely transform, and that change brought forth half her followers. "You dare to set a trap?" She was close to draining him. It wouldn't kill him, but she'd rip out his throat to teach him a lesson.

"Wait," Julius said, his hands out in front of him as if to placate her. "His name is Travis and he's with us."

"He's a slayer," she said, taking a step toward him. "Do you think the Clan members are the only ones who research their enemies?"

"He is a slayer, but he wants the same thing we do."

"Just spell it out before I take a piece of you that'll take a month of sunny days to heal."

"If we combine forces they'll never see it coming, and we both get what we want. Once we destroy the Elders and Asra, you'll have peace and I'll have my revenge for the betrayal they carried out against me."

She came close enough to run her tongue across his throat and almost laughed at his shiver. "Okay, but I'll hunt you for eternity if you turn on me once you get what you're after."

"I could warn you of the same thing."

"You could, but remember which of us asked for help. I already know you're in the weaker position, and so will Asra." She circled him as she taunted him, and he stiffened as tight as a board. "Threaten me and I'll stand back and watch Asra bury you."

"I'll have Bailey call you when we're ready," he said, as if he couldn't wait to flee.

"Remember, Julius, someone like Asra might worry me, but you and those weaklings will fall easily if you're lying." He turned before he reached the wall and stared at her before he nodded.

"Are you sure you want to make an enemy of the slayer, mistress?" her most trusted follower Boldo said.

"Even without this bargain we must bring her down. Ora was family and deserves to be avenged. Without Asra, we will also have peace."

"And these others?"

"Send a few of our day protectors to keep watch over them. Julius speaks pretty words, but he's not to be trusted."

CHAPTER THIRTEEN

Kendal, Piper, and their houseguests spent the rest of the summer in London and their routine didn't change, but neither did Piper's vision of the night the dragon awoke. It was the only sight of the future she had repeatedly, and Kendal always lost the sword to a man who made the gems glow red.

Piper worked to try to expand her gift, but the only new vision came from the night they met Rolla, and while the other times the sight came while she meditated, this one had come from watching Rolla whisper to Kendal.

Before Travis had disrupted her, Piper had seen a rolling black cloud over Rolla that would consume him and plunge him into darkness. While she watched it coming for Rolla it grew and totally enveloped him, fueled completely by hate. That was all, though; no other hint as to its origin and who fed it.

At the beginning of September, Piper was frantic to see something other than Kendal on her knees bleeding, those red glowing eyes and the man's infuriating laugh. Adding to her stress, Lenore's and Rolla's research hadn't found anything that would at least give them an idea of who to prepare for. She had nothing to convince her the vision could be changed.

"Not one thing will stop this, will it?" Piper asked Lenore as they shared tea together and watched Kendal and the others go through their workout.

"You know what is the most important lesson I've learned in a very long life?" Lenore looked her in the eye with her always-open expression.

Piper shook her head, glad for the conversation since it put off having to relive the vision of Kendal's demise one more time. Granted she, as Kendal did in her fairy circle, as she called it, exercised her special talent every morning, always hoping for a different result. "Do you mind sharing it with me?"

"Life is too long to ever give up hope," Lenore said, and smiled at the twist in her words. "Almost everyone at one time or other has thought life too short. This isn't the first time and it won't be the last that darkness threatens not only our ranks, but the world. And you have to believe that the threat and its outcome do not simply lie at your feet. You aren't to blame for this, Piper, and you have to set your sights with that belief in your heart."

"Let's try again, then." She closed her eyes and took a series of deep breaths before she looked down at Kendal as she taught Hill some new moves. A curtain seemed to fall on her sight and she shifted to a different scene.

The three mysterious men weren't waiting this time, though, but a group of vampires like she'd seen Kendal fight at Oakgrove. Hordes of them stood around a woman, but Piper could see only her red hair. Unlike her recurring vision, in which she could do nothing but observe, this time she asked what they wanted and the woman answered.

"I saw a group of vampires, but they're not interested in the sword. All they want is Kendal," she said when she returned to normal. "When I wanted to see something different, that's not what I had in mind. We already have enough problems."

"You're right, but your sights are expanding." Lenore stood to get Morgaine's attention. "This situation might be easier dealt with than the others, since we have the two best slayers in the house."

Lenore told Morgaine about the new vision so she could arrange better security around Piper and Kendal. "You don't want to get Kendal up here for this?"

"It's better if you tell her alone," Morgaine said.

"Because?" she said, dragging out the word so Morgaine would elaborate.

"She loves you, and her presence in your life will feed your abilities. Bruik's vision of you mentions that indirectly. Maybe we haven't been giving you both the opportunity to share the energy you generate together." When the sound of clashing metal stopped, Morgaine glanced to the yard. "While you do that we'll track down information on the new covens formed after Ora."

"Vampires still exist?" Piper asked, figuring Kendal had eradicated them all in New Orleans.

"Unfortunately they're like cockroaches. Not even nuclear warfare will kill them all. Ora was simply the strongest, the oldest, and the biggest headache." Morgaine took her hand and held it. "Rolla will have information on this, so we can prepare. I'm also certain that you're growing stronger, and I'm glad you're here with us and with Asra."

"Let's hope I can come through."

"You already have," Lenore and Morgaine said together.

❖

Julius lay on his stomach next to Bailey and marveled at the high-powered binoculars Bailey had given him. It was as if he'd been transported to where Lenore and Morgaine were talking to the beautiful blond woman. He couldn't hear them, but it seemed they were comforting her about something.

"Who is she?" he asked in a whisper, even though they were far from where Asra practiced.

"Piper Marmande is from New Orleans and someone Asra met on her recent trip back. Lenore hasn't finished recording the full account, but from the rumors that filtered back to Rolla, Asra started a relationship with her after destroying Ora and Henri."

"So she's a new plaything."

"Travis did hear from Rolla himself that she was almost a twin of some woman from Asra's past." Bailey appeared to look from Piper to the practice circle.

Travis had been gone for weeks to keep Rolla happy and to warn them of any travel the old man planned. They'd been in Egypt most of the summer, and so far Rolla had shown no signs of suspicion.

"Who are the older people and the woman with Asra?"

"The couple is Miss Marmande's grandparents, who raised her, and the woman is Hill Hickman, a friend of Miss Marmande."

"What are they doing here?"

Piper stood up and leaned on the stone wall that surrounded the balcony. She was stunning as the sun broke through the clouds momentarily.

"I really don't know for sure, but I guess it's because Asra likes them. This isn't much different than what she's done in the past. She finds playthings, like you said, and spends time with them."

"We have a starting point, then," he said, and turned his face to the sun. He needed it to return to full strength. "Even if she plans to discard them eventually, I'll help her do that. It'll be my first favor for what she did to me."

The swordplay started again, so he watched to see if Asra had gotten any better during his time away. She faced off against a large black man and laughed as he engaged. Her style was the same, only smoother and quicker, as if she'd learned to economize her movements, and it didn't take long for the man to lose his sword.

"I'll take it all from you. All this time and you're still nothing but the Clan's whore." He spoke no louder than before, but she stopped the man before he struck her sword and seemed to look directly at Julius through the lenses. "Impossible," he said, but she started walking in their direction and then ran.

"What?" Bailey said, and his voice carried in the wind. Julius grabbed him and ran deeper into the woods to the road where they'd parked their vehicle. He didn't look back, almost afraid he'd see her with her sword ready to strike his head from his shoulders.

"Not yet. I'm too close."

❖

Kendal ran with Charlie, Hill, and Ming trying to keep up.

"What's wrong?" Charlie asked when Kendal stopped and studied the ground.

"We had visitors." She pointed to the tracks in the muddy ground that led to the woods. Whoever it was had left in a hurry and was fast enough to be long gone.

"Something wicked is getting closer, my friend."

"It'll find nothing but pain here," Charlie said as Ming and Hill finally caught up.

"Did you run track or something?" Hill asked, holding her side.

"All this fresh damp air made me crave a sprint. Sorry I scared all of you."

"Are you sure that's all? You ran like you were chasing someone," Hill said, as Kendal walked them all back. "Do you want me to set up some surveillance equipment out here?"

"The house has all the security necessary." She liked Hill's enthusiasm.

"If it has any kind of alarm I haven't seen any sign of it."

She smiled at Charlie and Ming, who knew the house was protected by a number of spells that kept out a majority of the things that roamed at night. The only way for them to enter was to be invited in, and no one was about to make that mistake.

"It's low-tech since we don't get a lot of intruders. There's a shotgun in every room. If anyone breaks in, feel free to open fire."

❖

"You want to go where?" Piper asked as she watched Kendal get dressed after her shower.

"We haven't been out of the house in days, and I don't want your grandparents to get suspicious about anything. They're starting to ask questions since all of us are reading our way through those stacks in the library and nothing else." Kendal moved closer and put her arms around Piper. She'd listened carefully to why Kendal had run off with the others earlier, but it couldn't have anything to do with her vision. Vampires didn't prowl during the day.

"You did understand what I said about what I saw today?" She looked up at Kendal, and the weight she felt like she was carrying around lightened when Kendal smiled, then kissed her. No matter what she saw, Kendal never appeared overly worried.

"I understood, and I think Morgaine's right. Your gift is growing, and you'll get us close to the answers."

"How can you be so sure?"

"I want you to try something new and then I'll answer that." Kendal finished buttoning her shirt and led her back to the bedroom.

"If you tell me to relax like Lenore keeps telling me, I'm going to pinch you," she threatened with a laugh. "And I might throw her off that balcony if I hear that one more time while all this gruesomeness is going through my head."

"I do plan to relax you, but before that I want to take you and your grandparents out to lunch and to look at some beautiful art to help you wipe away some of the ugliness you've been seeing lately. When I'm in a rut, a change of scenery helps me clear any blocks that prevent me from seeing something I missed."

While Kendal put her shoes on, Piper stood behind her and kissed her neck. "Are you a little worried? I'd feel better if I'm not the only one who's freaked out about all this. If this loop that keeps playing over in my head is right, I'm going to lose you soon, and it's making me nuts."

"I don't want to sound like I'm not listening to you and don't care what you're going through, but I've always tried not to build up anything I'm facing more than I have to."

"So you use some kind of yoga you learned along the way to ignore the fear?" she asked as she slipped into Kendal's lap. All the exercise had knocked a few pounds off Kendal and had started to make the muscles across her shoulders and arms more pronounced.

"Yoga does keep me limber, but I'm not sure it's ever made me ignore anything," Kendal said. "It's human nature to fear what we don't know, but this time I know I'm not alone, so all I can do is wait and prepare." Piper felt adored as Kendal looked at her and held her like she wanted to keep her safe. "No matter what, I'll have you by my side."

"The thought of never seeing you again, or that someone would put you somewhere I'd never be able to find you…that terrifies me."

Kendal kissed above each of Piper's eyes before she kissed her lips long enough to make her put her arms around her. Piper felt the tears form at the possibility of never having this again. If Kendal lost this fight it would be a slow death to know she was out there somewhere waiting for her, but finding her would be like finding one certain raindrop in a storm. The world was a big place with plenty of hiding spots.

"I'm not saying this to make you crazy with more stress, but think of who you are now, and what gifts you've been given. If you don't believe in your sight, then believe in the man who wrote about it so very long ago." Kendal wiped Piper's cheeks with her fingers and kissed her again. "I plan to walk with you for the rest of time, and I'll enjoy every step because it's you I'm with. If anyone ever separates us, then I have every faith in you to find me if it's me in the darkness."

"You think it'd be that easy?"

"As easy as it is to love you. That requires no thought, no work, and no hesitation because it's engrained so deep, nothing will ever erase it."

❖

Mac and Molly appeared happy to be heading into town with them, even though they'd taken to country life like they'd been born to it. They were both tan and looked more fit from all the long walks they took every day, and the stable hands were happy to have them both come by for rides often.

Kendal knew Mac spent a few hours on a video chat with the managers at Marmande conducting business from her office, and he seemed content with the progress they were making on all the projects they had going. It was a blessing; in the future if they had to travel, he'd realize he didn't have to be there every second to keep an eye on things.

After their talk, Piper seemed more relaxed as well and was content to sit pressed against Kendal as they drove into London. None of them seemed interested in small talk, so they gazed out the windows and watched the world go by in a blur.

After lunch they entered the National Gallery and let Mac and Molly go their own way, having agreed on a meeting point a few hours later. Kendal led Piper to one of the galleries and walked slowly along the portraits and landscapes to make Piper concentrate on the colors and beauty instead of the images in her head. This was the only way she could think of to break the cycle that'd taken over Piper's imagination, knowing it was only dragging her down into a despair that would swallow her whole.

"There's one more painting in this room I wanted you to see," Kendal said as she guided Piper to the bench in front of it.

"This one looks so sad but beautiful." Piper looked at the old man fixing a tattered net as he sat next to a fishing boat. Whoever had painted it had used muted colors for the sea and sky, but they seemed to match the man's outlook and mood, and she knew that without knowing anything about the artist or the canvas.

"I sat for more than one afternoon and watched as the artist worked on this. He had a good eye for detail and the patience not to rush his work." Kendal sat slightly behind Piper so she could hold her and whisper in her ear. It was like she was supporting her but not giving her a view of anything but the painting. "He was always waiting there with his easel and his paints, happy for whatever time the fisherman gave him."

As she stared at the painting, Piper again saw the room fade away as if she'd developed tunnel vision. It led to the past this time, and in her bones she knew something she'd fought so hard to find was waiting for her. "Kendal…" She said the name but Kendal was so far away, even though she could feel her right behind her.

"Close your eyes and take deep breaths. Let it come to you, don't chase it."

"They want to harm Gran and Pops." The sight of the fangs sinking into their necks made her want to throw up. "I'm not just going to lose you." She turned slightly and pressed her face to Kendal's neck and cried. The vision had to have come because the old man in the painting reminded her of Mac, but the scene in her mind had been so real as he slumped lifeless and pale to the floor.

"Piper, look at me, sweetheart." Kendal pulled her away just far enough to gaze into her eyes. "The only way you'll lose Mac or Molly will be years from now after they've lived a long and peaceful life. We can change the images you see."

"You don't know that."

"Have you seen the clan's compound again?"

"No, but what does that matter now?" All she wanted to do was to run through this place and find her grandparents and flee. Maybe if they got far enough away from all this she could keep them safe.

"That was your first vision after your gifts were awakened and you saw the trap they'd intended to set for me. We changed that by meeting with Rolla in London, and that vision hasn't come to you again because he came to us as a friend, not a judge. We altered our movements, and because we did, we changed the outcome, so yes, I'm sure nothing you see is certain if we work together to change it." Kendal placed her hands on the sides of Piper's neck and almost forced her to focus on her face. "Once that happened your visions changed, and each one has let us glimpse a possibility, not the outcome. I'm as certain of that as I am in the love I have for you."

Piper nodded and focused on the painting again, ready to continue. "He loved the sea, didn't he?"

"The painter or the old man?"

"The old man." As she relaxed, her mind seemed to widen its view and she stood on the sand watching him work, trying to ignore the young man so interested in his craft that he wanted to preserve it in paint. "He's been fishing all day and already sold his catch, so he's getting ready for tomorrow. The painter, though, is just now getting started, and he'll be here until he loses the light."

She closed her eyes when the wind picked up, bringing the smell of the salt water with it. This spot could've been anywhere and she couldn't sense any danger around her, but it was nice to feel Kendal pressed up behind her. It was like she'd taken this journey back with her. "Miguel loved two things. He loved the sea and he loved that boat." Kendal's soft voice made her open her eyes and watch Miguel's quick sure hands as he mended the net.

"He loved three things actually, honey, because he loved you as well, or at least who you were back then." Piper smiled at the faint footsteps Kendal had left over the tapestry of time, touching so many lives along the way.

When he glanced up at her from his net, Piper knew instantly that Miguel loved his boat and the water it glided over, but he had no family left except for the young woman who helped him pull up his nets every day and helped him clean his catch in the afternoons.

"What happened to his family? You're the only thing holding the madness at losing them at bay."

"He lost them to an outbreak of the plague, and his guilt that he'd survived when they didn't ate at him like a shark devouring a wounded fish. His three sons and his wife were all he had, aside from his boat, and when they died, I kept him from taking his boat out and drowning himself."

Piper heard the sad affection in Kendal's voice for the broken soul she'd cared for. The painting might have been done in muted colors, but the sun was shining now and it was warm on her face and it stirred the seagulls into a lazy flight over the water. Miguel's fingers, though old, worked the nets like a fine weaver making a tapestry, and he laughed at the teasing he was getting.

"Tell me, Mari, do you believe in God?" Miguel asked in Spanish, but Piper understood him perfectly.

"I've seen the devil too many times not to." This voice she knew instantly, and she turned to look at the end of the dock where a barefoot Kendal sat on a crate watching the young man put paint on the canvas. Her skin was darker, from all the sun, Piper imagined, but the smile was always the same. "Now smile pretty so you don't look like a crab when he's done."

Miguel never glanced up from his work but he laughed at Kendal's joke. Once they were done Piper knew they'd head to his small house for a plate of fish stew, then a drink at the tavern near the dock. As if she could read his mind, she also knew he admired Kendal as well because she never complained about the hard work and always paid for their drinks no matter how much he protested.

His biggest fear was she would grow tired of his sadness and move on, and then he'd truly be alone, but that never came to pass, and he never questioned why she never changed while he grew feeble and so old that all he could do was sit and watch as she did all the work on the boat. On the day he was buried next to his family, Kendal was the only mourner there, but she'd ensured that even in death he hadn't been alone.

He worked the last knot into place and brought his knife out to cut the thread so they could get home to their meal. When he lifted his head he hesitated, turned in her direction, and looked right at Piper. "Thank her for me and tell her she was right. My family, they were waiting for me, and paradise is an endless sea of calm water and blue skies."

"I'll tell her."

He nodded and stood to join the woman he knew as Mari. The artist was busy packing up his supplies and talking to her. Miguel turned again before he got too far away and put his finger up to get Piper's attention. "Can I ask just you to do one more thing for me?"

"Anything."

"Tell her it's Julius. He's waiting for the right time, but he'll stop at nothing to repay her for what wrongs he thinks she committed against him, and he'll use the sword and the dragon to do it."

Piper did her best to keep her feet on that beach and the connection she had to Miguel. "How do you know all this?"

"This is my way of repaying her for all she did for an old, sad man, Piper," he said with a bright smile, and waved to her. "It makes me happy that she's finally found you, but you must be ready and accept who you are to her and what position you have in her life. The dragon is about to awaken from its watery home and show its true power."

"Will she win?"

"There is time, but you must use it wisely and find the key."

"The key to what?" she screamed, but he was gone, locked forever in the painting that came back into view. She still had a slew of unanswered questions, but she looked at Kendal, glad to have found another piece of the puzzle.

"Julius."

CHAPTER FOURTEEN

Julius." Kendal said the name, and it sounded strange to hear it after so many years. She knew immediately who Piper was talking about since she hadn't known many with the same name in her lifetime. "That's impossible."

"If he's the Julius from the story you told me of when you got the Sea Serpent Sword, it would be impossible, considering the ending, but that's not what Miguel told me." Piper pointed to the painting. "I saw you back on that dock with him, and he talked to me." Piper explained her vision and her conversation with Miguel.

"I believe you, and it sends us in two different directions after the two very different things you've seen here. The vampires I could almost understand, but Julius makes no sense." She held Piper while her mind raced. "The way Rolla carried out the punishment would make it impossible for anyone to find him unless everyone involved got together to free him. That means I would've had to have been one of the people, and you know that's not true."

Piper pressed their lips together before she whispered, "Where'd you put the pieces?"

"The body was Rolla's responsibility, and he charged me with the head, so you see what I'm saying. Both of us would've had to have told someone." She thought of something that made her pause, but surely Rolla hadn't been that stupid.

"What's wrong?" Piper asked as if she'd picked up on where her thoughts had gone.

"Part of the deal Rolla and I made when I carried out the judgment for him was we'd tell each other where we'd placed Julius. I don't think he'd be foolish enough to tell anyone, but he has this obsession about writing everything down." She cocked her head back and stared at the ceiling as she thought of something else. "Back then I didn't really believe the sword was blessed by the gods, so I brought it with me and used it. The way he looked at it as I swung it at his head…"

"You think he recognized it?"

"For someone who was milliseconds from losing his head, Julius looked like a man in love. I never understood the expression until now. He not only recognized it, but he knew exactly what it was capable of. I'm sure of it."

"Can we find out if he's still in place?" Piper pulled her up so they could go.

"There's only one way."

"How?" Piper asked as they headed to the spot where they had to meet the Marmandes.

"I have to see Rolla again, but this time I have to go alone." She pressed her fingers to Piper's lips to keep her quiet. "This isn't an issue of trust, so don't say anything like that."

"I don't distrust Rolla, but do you remember the first vision I had about them? Rolla isn't the only Elder, and he seems to be in a small group, along with Morgaine and Lenore, who actually wants to stop this. I don't know who the others are, but they seem tired of living in the shadows of history. If that's true I don't want to let you out of my sight if I can help it, so stop asking me to."

"You're right. Let me see what I can find out—I don't want to chance the phone." She took Piper's hand and finally felt the fear of the unknown Piper had saddled herself with for weeks. If this had something to do with Julius and he'd found a way to escape his dark prisons, not even Henri and Ora would match his hatred for her and his need to destroy everyone she loved.

Piper took a deep breath and let it out slowly, as if she was about to say something important. "You've lived long enough to know the best way to handle all the people involved in this. If you need to see Rolla alone, please do. I won't be thrilled about it, but it might be the fastest way for us to deal with it. Right now I want to get everything that'll keep us apart out of the way."

"The most important thing right now is to find out if Julius is back and somehow planning something. If he managed to escape, he's going to come at me or Rolla first with all the rage that's built over the years, if he was able to feel anything at all."

"Now you know what's been on my mind since all this started. If someone out there hates you that much, it terrifies me as to what they'll do to you." Piper wrapped her arm around Kendal's waist and put her hand in her jacket pocket. "All this time you've given me won't mean anything without you. If whoever is lurking out there wins, and they take you away from me, that would be my definition of a nightmare I'll be stuck in forever."

Kendal ducked into a quiet spot and phoned Ming to ask him to make a call for her. While they waited she rested her chin on Piper's head as she held her and hoped for the best. A few minutes later she answered the call and conversed in Russian. It didn't matter now if Julius's head was discovered and removed from its hiding place; she just needed confirmation it was where she'd left it. An old friend Kendal trusted was off to look for the box she'd buried deep in a cave where winter winds always blew outside.

"Depending on the weather it should take a couple of days for him to call back and let us know if the head is where I left it. If it's not, then we'll have another clue as to who and possibly what this dragon business is about, but now we have to work on how it's possible Julius would know anything about it."

❖

"We'll have to come back here," Molly said. The Marmandes were ready for dinner after the hours they'd spent in the gallery, and they ordered drinks while they waited for their table. Piper smiled at her and kissed Kendal, who excused herself to greet the old friend who sat alone at the center table in the dining room.

With their time getting short, Rolla was already close and didn't mind coming out to talk to her, and while their talk was private, it was happening in Piper's line of sight.

"What did she see exactly?" Rolla asked, and Kendal told him about Piper's vision that afternoon. He sat back in his chair and pushed the plate of lamb chops away from him. "Do you think it's possible?"

"You remember him as much as I do." She took a sip of the whiskey she'd ordered. "Julius was never content with the life you offered him, only with the immortality aspect of it. He thought himself a god with a right to rule. Who was the man who cried over his body once the judgment was past?"

"Bailey," Rolla said softly, and shook his head. "He's been a junior archivist since Julius has been gone, and he's been content with his position. I don't think he's capable of this."

"He was the only one I can remember who seemed upset with what happened and has had total access to the archives. Do you know what was written about this sword and the dragon trapped in the hilt? There had to be something besides the book Lenore's memorized by now. She still hasn't found anything useful in the history it contains."

"There might've been one or two more details, but like you, I never took the story literally since very few objects found in our long history have actually been touched by the gods. That a woman would've come to you and gifted you with a sword blessed by Greek gods seemed too fanciful to believe."

"Considering you sent all the books you had on the subject to Lenore, the others that existed are gone or missing. You need to send for Bailey and have him brought to Farthington. Morgaine and I'll have a talk with him and convince him to tell us what he knows." She nodded to the waiter when he brought her another drink, then pushed Rolla's plate closer to him so he'd finish.

He stared at it but didn't pick up his utensils again. "Bailey's been missing since you arrived here and hasn't contacted us."

"I'm about to pay for this because I'm the one who carried out the punishment. That I was ordered to do so isn't something he's going to remember, but I won't be his only target." She put her hands on the table and looked at Travis and how intently he was again staring at Piper and her family. "Find out if Julius's body is still where you placed it. If it's not, make sure the others know that once he takes care of me and ensures that he has destroyed everyone I hold dear, he'll come for them."

Rolla inhaled deeply before answering, as if trying to put off the inevitable. "The body is gone from where I buried it, and if you find out the head is also missing we can be assured that Julius is back among us."

It was like Rolla had sucker-punched her in the stomach. What had started as something she didn't totally believe had turned into a true nightmarish threat. "How long do you think before he's back to full strength?"

"I don't know."

"Has anyone else come back after so much time in total darkness?"

"The elixir has never been tested for this length of time, and it could be he can't be brought back after being separated at the neck so long."

"How would someone have known where to look?" She finished her drink, and the smoky flavor washed away the bitter taste the subject had left in her mouth. "We were the only ones who knew the locations. You didn't write a scroll about it, did you?"

He defended himself. "It didn't give the exact location. I thought it was important for the others to know his story so they would never meddle in the lives of mankind like that again. The scroll only gave clues as to where he could be found."

"And someone close to you followed them right to the hidden treasure. I'd have to guess it was your little archivist, who's been pining for his lover for a very long time." Obviously Julius hadn't lost a step as he served his sentence, and they had to make up fifteen hundred years of research in less than two months. "Do you think anyone else is working with them? From what I remember of this Bailey, he wasn't the type of man who did well by himself."

"I'll call the other Elders of the judgment panel together and start our own investigation." He offered his arm and she clasped it like warriors did at one time. "We will give you the same loyalty now that you gave us then. You and yours won't be abandoned now, Asra. You have my word."

"What I need is Bruik. Can you have him brought to us? If anything, he can maybe help Piper refine her gifts."

"That's a promise I'm more than willing to make to you, old friend. Remember to be careful until then." When Rolla stood, Travis jumped to his feet and came closer. Kendal stared at them until they were out the door, not surprised that Travis looked back at her the entire time. Something about Travis made her think he held some hatred for her that had nothing to do with the first night they'd met.

Kendal and the Marmandes finished dinner with no other interruptions, then enjoyed the ride home in silence. Ming waited at the front door when they walked in, informing Kendal there'd been no calls while they were out. Mac and Molly retired as soon as they got back, and by one in the morning the house was completely quiet. Lenore and Morgaine were together going over the information again, along with all they'd kept on Julius and his history.

Kendal told Piper everything about her conversation with Rolla, and that Julius's body was gone.

"Do you really think this guy's walking around?" Piper lay next to her and had rested her head on her naked chest.

Piper had come to bed in the shirt Kendal had taken off, and she'd stripped down to her underwear and was going through the stack of books Lenore had given her to find passages about Julius.

The old book she'd started with was actually a text of weapons that resembled a catalog. "Why did you keep this?" Piper pointed to the page she'd stopped at since the sword resembled the Sea Serpent Sword.

"The Elders have hoarder tendencies when it comes to the written word, no matter the subject matter. I'm sure Lenore forgot she had this and just put it in the thousands of piles she has all over the world."

"Remind me to go through all my catalogs and recycle the old ones. I doubt we'll need anything from Pottery Barn or Victoria's Secret two thousand years from now." Piper slowly ran her hand down Kendal's abdomen and under the elastic of her underwear.

"Speak for yourself, pipsqueak. I enjoy buying you things from the Victoria's Secret catalog."

Piper snorted as she pinched the skin above Kendal's navel. "Sure you do, but I'd rather only keep more educational books around. I'd rather read—" Piper stopped talking when Kendal cocked her head and held her hand up for silence.

Without a word, Kendal jumped up and ran out of the bedroom, not stopping to get dressed. "Where are you going?" Piper yelled after her.

Kendal turned to see Piper hang on to the banister as if to stay on her feet, but she couldn't comfort Piper yet and hoped she stayed put. The reason she'd bolted from the bedroom stood on the landing, but at least ten more were ready to pounce when the woman holding Mac gave them the word. Two of them held Molly between them on the first floor, and the Marmandes appeared completely terrified.

"Asra, how nice of you to join us," the woman holding Mac said, and that was enough for Kendal to know she was indeed in charge. Even though she was at the head of the stairs she could see the rapid pulse of Mac's carotid when the redheaded vampire pulled his head back by the hair.

"What do you want?" she asked, keeping her voice calm. It wouldn't make a difference if this woman really meant the Marmandes harm, but she didn't want to escalate the situation for Mac and Molly's sake.

"Honey, please," Piper said emotionally, and Kendal could tell she was crying, but she raised her hand for silence. Vampires fed not only on blood but on the terror of others.

"Do you really see yourself in any position to ask questions and, before you think about them, demands?" The redhead made Mac whimper when she ran her tongue along his cheek.

Coming closer to them, Kendal could see that Mac's focus was on the elongated incisors the woman seemed to proudly show off. Just as quickly Mac glanced at her and she smiled at him to assure him. "You're in my house, and you're bothering my guests, so I do have the right to make demands. I'll start with your name."

"My name is Vadoma and I'm the new queen."

Something about her speech pattern tickled Kendal's memory, and she tried to think of why, ignoring the way Molly was whimpering below them. "Tell me why you're here before I rip your heart out and nail it to my door to greet the sun." She had to concentrate but remembered the language of the Gypsies. That's what the accent she recognized was, so she used the old language to lower Vadoma's aggressiveness.

Vadoma seemed to almost forget Mac for a moment and let his head come forward as if she'd relaxed her grip. "I was told you were a worthy adversary, but I specifically chose this time of night for a reason."

"Why's that?" She moved closer and stopped when Vadoma, her tongue flat, licked the trickles of blood that had dripped from Mac's neck. She had to get Vadoma away from Mac before the smell made her thirsty and she went into a feeding frenzy that would also consume Molly.

"Judging from the way you're dressed and your lack of weapons, you weren't expecting company and couldn't have guessed I could get inside." Vadoma laughed, but she made her first mistake when she pushed Mac to his knees, to further humiliate him, Kendal was sure. "And save the spiel of how you don't care for these people and I can do with them whatever I want. I've watched you and I know better."

Kendal went down another step with her hands out in front of her. "I can see you're in charge, and I'd never tell you I don't care about anyone here, so if it's me you want, let them go." She smiled down at Mac, then Molly to get them to relax, although she knew that was impossible. Behind Vadoma and her followers, Lenore, Morgaine, and Charlie moved into the room undetected.

"My cousin made too many mistakes with you, but she will smile in hell tonight. I've watched you long enough to know you're nothing special," Vadoma said, and was bending down to feed on Mac, or so Kendal assumed, when she heard Hill yell at the top of the steps. It was enough of a distraction.

"You should've watched me a little closer, witch." Kendal moved quickly to press on one of the wood panels, opening a secret compartment on the staircase wall, and armed herself.

She threw the first dagger up and impaled the fledging that had been creeping up on Piper and Hill, and Piper gasped when he dissolved to dust. Five more fledglings died instantly when Morgaine, Charlie, and Lenore attacked. That left Molly free and only five others, as well as Vadoma, to be dealt with.

Next Kendal jumped headfirst down the last of the steps separating her from Vadoma, flying over Mac and knocking a shocked Vadoma down the last flight of stairs. She could tell Vadoma's minions were anxious to help her, but they stood still when they saw the blade pressed to their mistress's neck.

"You brought them with you because they're the best of your legions." She had Vadoma's red hair wrapped firmly around her free hand and pressed the knife into the delicate-looking flesh at her throat with the other. She didn't think to be gentle, though, since she knew what Vadoma was under that beautiful façade. "And if they are, you're screwed."

"What do you want?" Vadoma said, but sounded in control.

"I want the dust of your dead body dirtying my carpet, but we'll get to that." She pulled harder on Vadoma's hair and turned her to face the fledglings she had left. "Tell them to stand down right now or I'll gut you like the minnow you are."

Vadoma lifted her head as much as she could and looked at the young man closest to her. "Go back to the lair and wait for me."

"We won't leave you, mistress." His face contorted in an effort to scare Kendal into letting Vadoma go, and to show she was serious Kendal pulled the dagger away from Vadoma's throat and threw it so fast, his only recourse was to howl in outrage before it pierced his heart.

"Care to try again?" By the time she asked, Morgaine had handed her another large knife.

"Leave now, we're not welcome here." Vadoma gave the order in the old language, and this time the remaining four obeyed and left her behind to her fate.

"You and I are going to have a talk," Kendal said to Vadoma, now more aware of Mac and Molly. They stood staring at her as if they were mentally processing what they'd seen but didn't have a reference to compare it to. "Piper, are you all right?"

Piper nodded, rooted in place like she wasn't sure what she should do next. "This has been the most bizarre night of my life, and I met your brother and his girlfriend."

Kendal laughed at that remark and followed where Piper's eyes were focused—on her grandparents. She'd help her explain the situation later, but now she couldn't take the time.

"Take your grandparents back to their room and I'll be there in a minute." The sound of her voice made Piper move, but before Piper reached the landing, Kendal took Vadoma through a hidden door at the bottom of the stairs.

Piper was momentarily panicked when she saw Kendal disappear into the space that swung open when Kendal pressed on a spot on the wall. She had to deal with the aftermath of what'd happened before she could join Kendal, but as scared as her grandparents appeared, this was the best of all outcomes. No one had been hurt except for those who'd come to do harm.

"Gran and Pops, come on." She waved to them, hoping they'd save their questions until morning.

"What in the Sam Hill is going on here?" Mac said loudly as Molly made her way to him with Lenore's help, and he opened his arms to her. "What were those things?" Lenore and Charlie herded them up the stairs, but Mac stopped at the pile of dust that was created when Kendal destroyed the man who'd gotten close to her and Hill. Hill touched it like she'd figure out the trick if she thought about it long enough.

"How'd she do that, and why right now?" Hill rubbed the dust between her fingers. "It was a great magic trick, but scaring the crap out of people wasn't the way to pull it off."

"I promise that Kendal and I will talk about all this and explain exactly what happened and why, but tomorrow, okay?" Piper maneuvered them toward their rooms with Lenore and Charlie's help.

"What if I don't want to wait until morning?" Mac asked, but her grandmother stayed silent.

"I agree with him, Piper. This was way out there," Hill said.

"I understand and I'm sorry, but you're all going to have to wait until we're done with this. My place is with Kendal and she needs me right now. Please try to understand that." They stopped in front of her grandparents' door, and Charlie opened it for them and Hill so the people who'd come with Lenore and Morgaine would stand guard.

"We've lost you to all this, haven't we?" Mac asked as he put his arms around Piper before she was able to leave.

"I'm not lost, Pops. I've finally found who I am and where I want to be."

"I don't know what's going on, but you're going to be okay, right?"

"Pops, I trust Kendal with my life. We're all okay tonight because of her, so don't condemn her until we have a chance to talk." She hugged her grandparents before she urged them into their room. "I know what you saw tonight is crazy, but please be patient. As soon as we're done, Kendal and I will come back and explain everything. I promise."

"Just make sure you're okay, and the rest can wait."

"Do you want me to come with you?" Hill asked, the pistol in her hand pointed to the floor.

"Not yet, but tonight's probably going to be the only night you'll be left behind, if I know Kendal. Only if you're interested, that is," Piper said, and smiled when Hill followed her grandparents into their room.

"I'm interested, but make sure you listen to Mac. And don't take any chances you don't have to."

"For the first time in a long time, I actually feel great." And she did, considering the only thing about her vision that had come to be was the attack.

CHAPTER FIFTEEN

Vadoma appeared calm as she sat strapped in a chair in the middle of a room with no windows somewhere in the bowels of the house. After getting her grandparents and Hill situated, Piper headed to the spot where Kendal had disappeared and found Morgaine waiting, since she would've never been able to navigate the maze of secret corridors to reach Kendal and Vadoma.

Kendal, who sat across from Vadoma, had put on a robe, and another dagger lay across her lap. Piper sat on the arm of the chair and took Kendal's hand so she could study Vadoma. Right now, she appeared normal. It was hard to believe that this beauty lived on the blood of others; how many people had she killed to survive?

"When my hunger grows these bindings won't hold me," Vadoma said, and moved the chair closer to them.

"I wouldn't worry about that." Kendal pushed her back with her foot and pressed the tip of her dagger to Vadoma's forehead. "You'll be long gone before you get the chance to drain another soul." Kendal faced Piper and offered her hand. "Morgaine, if she tries anything, destroy her." She handed Morgaine what looked like a small crossbow with a wooden stake. "We'll be right back."

When they were alone in the corridor Piper put her arms around Kendal and rested her ear against her chest. "Thank you for saving them."

"You don't need to thank me for that, and I hope you see now that the rest of the visions *can* be changed."

"When I was talking to my grandparents, as horrible as this was, I was happy we all came out all right because of you. Even if the sword holds something as evil as that woman, we can beat it."

Kendal led her out and up to their bedroom, where she sat her on the bed so she could kneel between her legs. "I'm going to have to deal with Vadoma so she can't come back here, but before I drive a sword though her heart, I have to know why she was here. She mentioned a cousin that I have to think is Ora, so this might've only had to do with revenge." Kendal kissed her. "But I have to know that's all this was."

"Please don't leave me alone. I can't be away from you right now," Piper said as she pressed her forehead to Kendal's.

"My darling, your days of being left behind are over. Don't you know that by now? I'm not taking her anywhere without you, and Vadoma's not motivated to talk yet. But like all the others, she's got an internal clock that's essential to her survival. When she's outside right before sunrise, she'll tell us whatever we want to know." Kendal laid her back and got in the bed next to her.

"I do know those days are over, but I wanted to remind you just in case." Piper smiled.

"Before we head back down, did you see Vadoma in your vision?"

"The thing I saw was already feeding on Pops, so I never saw its face." The happiness that her vision had been wrong left her suddenly, and a coldness enveloped her. "Honey, do you think my visions are useless?"

"Why do you think so?"

"I see things but they never turn out the way I see them. I may be putting us all in danger because I'm so wrong."

"Some seers look into the future, and what they see is written in stone. No matter what we do, the outcomes never vary. Then some see the possibilities, but our actions have the power to create better outcomes." Kendal took her hands and kissed each knuckle. "If we'd been given a choice, I'd have chosen your sight, love. Your real gift, the ability to see the worst-case scenario when there's danger to be faced, gives us a chance to plan for it."

"Then don't you wish I'd had a vision about you going out there in your underwear and how my grandfather would react," she said as she got on top of Kendal, laughing.

"Breakfast should be interesting tomorrow."

"You'll have to come up with a good explanation as to what you were doing in here with just your shorts on. Had it been anything other than some spawn from hell trying to make a snack out of Pops and Gran, he'd probably tease you for months to come about your fighting outfit."

Kendal's laugh shook Piper's fear off, and she got up to help Kendal dress. "I don't usually show this much skin, but sometimes you have to just jump into the action no matter what." Kendal squeezed her before steering them to the closet.

"At least Hill will stop wondering what I found so alluring about you," Piper teased as she got a shirt and sweater out for Kendal.

Kendal picked out jeans and a pair of hiking boots, and Piper laughed when she thought of Kendal's aversion to bugs. When they left the bedroom it was well after three in the morning and the house had once again grown quiet. She felt better that the guards in front of her family's room were vigilant.

"How do you get her to talk? Drive bamboo under her fingernails or drip water on her head?" Piper hung on to Kendal's pants as they went down the dark stairs.

"Bamboo and waterboarding? Is this gift for torture something you're waiting to tell me about? Some hidden talent for making people squirm, perhaps?" Kendal reached out for her hand when they were close to the hidden door. "They're not in there anymore." They stopped at the fireplace and Kendal took down one of the crossed swords that hung up there as a decoration.

"I only like making you squirm," she said as they headed out the back of the house through the large kitchen. "Where are they?"

"I'm sure there's a string of vendors back in New Orleans who might disagree about your torturing methods." The outside air was heavy with dampness, and the cold immediately seeped through Piper's clothing, making her move closer to Kendal to stay warm.

"You're so funny." Piper let Kendal guide her deeper into the woods at the back of the estate. "Where are we going?"

"If you want the truth out of someone like Vadoma, there's only one foolproof way." Kendal held the sword away from Piper but kept it at the ready, not trusting that the fledglings had really left.

After thirty minutes or so Kendal pointed to a clearing with an outcropping of rocks, and Piper followed her. Morgaine, Charlie, and

Lenore had obeyed Kendal's instructions and chained Vadoma to the rock so all she could really move was her head. Vadoma didn't look as smug as she had back at the house, and even in the lamplight, Kendal could tell she was starting to sweat since, despite the temperature, her forehead was smeared with blood.

Kendal took a deep breath and exhaled in Vadoma's direction, her breath visible as the vapor swirled around Vadoma's head. "Do you smell that? The dawn is still my favorite time of day."

"Were you this cruel with Ora?" Vadoma asked.

"You don't have time to ask questions. I have so many that the sun will rise before I'm done. Why did you come into my house uninvited?"

Kendal pressed her sword to Vadoma's chin, and Vadoma pulled her head as far back from the tip of her sword as she could, but the rock behind her wouldn't give.

"I need no invitation to enter a place where I want to go," she said, and Kendal let up a little on the pressure on her chin.

"Was it your cousin who taught you the skills to be a witch before she dragged you into the darkness?"

"My family was known for their talents in Romania for centuries, so yes. I was no different until Ora gave me true life. The darkness has never been my enemy."

Kendal heard the others moving around behind her, as if patrolling the area, and she could see Vadoma peering in the direction behind them, but she had the lamp so close to her face she doubted she could make out anything. "So you came only to seek revenge?"

"That's all you want to know?" Vadoma asked as she started to squirm more.

"Like I said, I have a lot more questions than that."

"Why do you want to know?"

"What's your name?"

"I am Vadoma Decebal, daughter of—"

"Inacu Decebal, or at least one of his descendants." Her lineage explained how Vadoma had gotten into the house without an invitation. Her ancestors were well known to the Elders, so combined with her immortality from Ora, she came from one of the most talented families that practiced witchcraft. Considering how long Vadoma had been at it almost made her shiver.

"How do you know my family name?"

"Why the sudden interest in those close to me?" Kendal asked, already realizing she'd have to lock Vadoma away if she didn't get all the information she needed. The silence stretched out, so it was time to put a little fear into the new queen. "I asked you a question, but if you don't want to answer, fine." She blew out the lantern and motioned for everyone to follow her back to the house. No matter how desperate Vadoma was to get loose, she'd never break through the chains in time. Her age and power would guarantee she wouldn't die immediately at sunrise, and the pain would be excruciating.

They got about thirty yards away before Vadoma broke. "Wait," she screamed out. "What do you want to know?"

"Just answer my question. You're powerful, but you and those puppies you brought weren't ready to face that many slayers at once. Why were you here?" She listened to the explanation about Vadoma's meeting with the men who told her they were Elders of the Genesis Clan.

"That sounds like Julius," Lenore said, and her shoulders slumped. "So it's true."

However he had managed it, Kendal thought, they'd have to worry about that later. He was back and he knew about the sword. That he'd used vampires to retrieve it made her crave to cut his head off again.

"I told you what you wanted to know." Vadoma gazed up at her and struggled with her bindings in earnest. "Please release me before it's too late."

"I want one more thing from you." Her explanation was as short as she could make it since the dawn was already starting to change the color of the sky around her. "What's your answer?" she asked when she was finished.

"What's in it for me?" Vadoma asked. She was struggling with the chains so hard the veins in her throat were visible.

"Aside from living out the night?"

Vadoma laughed and finally relaxed, as if she'd resigned herself to her two very limited options. "Yes, aside from that."

"I'll grant you a century of peace, if you leave my family alone and do what I ask." She put her hand up before Vadoma answered. "Before you think to lie, let me warn you. If you enter my home again, any home, without an invitation I'll kill you. If you touch someone under my protection again, I'll kill you. There'll be no negotiation and no bit of mercy ever again. Do we understand each other?"

"Perfectly, and I give you my word I won't let you down." As swift as Vadoma's answer was as swift as Kendal's sword came down on the lock that held the chains together.

Piper looked like she was in shock as Vadoma ran into the woods away from them. "You let her go?" Piper asked.

"I let her go," she said, expecting Piper's anger.

"You don't think we should've talked about it first? She would've killed Gran and Pops without remorse if you hadn't been there to stop her. They're the only family I have left. She deserved more than you just letting her go."

"I'm your family too, and I know you don't understand what I'm doing, but I'd like you to trust me." If they'd been closer to the house, the Marmandes would've heard every word Piper screamed. "We need her alive for now."

"For now." Piper kept yelling. "Try for the next hundred years. I know you, and your word is sacred to you. She gave you hers, but I bet it means nothing to her. That thing would've said anything for you to unchain her."

"Piper, please." Kendal moved closer to Piper. "We don't have that much time to figure out how some psycho from my past is going to get to us, so forgive me for trying to do what I can to give us an advantage. Julius has the element of surprise, and that puts him in a better position. He made this deal with Vadoma and her followers in London, so he's close, but I don't have the first clue as to where to even start looking for him."

The air directly in front of Piper's mouth condensed, showing her long exhale. "I'm sorry. I'm sure you know what you're doing." She sounded so dejected Kendal almost heard the iron gates closing around her heart and locking her out. The others must have picked up on that as well, because they started back toward the house as if they realized their conversation didn't need an audience.

"If you shut me out now, we'll never make it through this." Kendal moved away from Piper to give her the space she obviously needed. "If you shut me out now, the reality of eternity will become a nightmare for us both."

"I'm not, but I'm not happy with you right now." Piper crossed her arms over her chest, her mouth in a thin line. "Am I not ever supposed to get upset with you?"

"You're free to do whatever you like." For once the phrase "I'm too old for this" made perfect sense to her, and she started the walk back. "Let's go. I'm sure your grandparents will be up soon and they'll demand an explanation."

"You promised me," Piper said, which stopped Kendal.

"Promised you what?" she asked, but still hadn't turned around.

"You said you'd never leave me behind." Piper sounded small and vulnerable again, a tone Kendal hadn't heard in months.

"Leave you behind?" She had to take a deep breath to control her anger.

She was furious, but it had nothing to do with Piper, so she tried to control her tone before she said anything else. It'd been so long since she'd felt so lost and in the dark. Vadoma had gotten too close, and she'd been working for Julius.

"You may not want to see it, but I'm doing everything I can to keep my promises to you. I want a future with you, but some asshole I should've cut into so many little pieces it would've taken eternity to find them all is trying his best to get in the way of that." She heard Piper run and then felt arms wrap around her waist from behind.

"I'm sorry, I know you're doing your best. It's just that I keep seeing those fangs so close to Pops's neck and it's making me crazy."

"No matter what we face, I will never do anything to endanger you or those you love." She turned around and drove the sword into the ground so she could pick Piper up. "Your family is as sacred to me as you are. I wouldn't have done this if it meant they'd be in danger."

With a ferocity she didn't know Piper possessed, Piper pressed their lips together and kissed her as if it were the last time. "I'm sorry for doubting you."

"No, I'm sorry for not talking to you first, but Vadoma was working against the clock." She bent to retrieve her sword and started walking with Piper's legs wrapped around her waist.

"I can walk, you know."

"So can I, even when I'm carrying a light load." She easily moved through the trees and reached the house after the sun had come up. As she put Piper down she wondered if Vadoma had found a place to sleep.

The Marmandes and Hill sat close to the fire in the library, sipping coffee, when she entered with Piper, and they all stayed silent as she handed her sword to Ming. When she sat, Piper chose the arm of her chair, as if showing her grandparents and her friend she stood with her.

"I don't know where to begin asking questions," Mac said as he held Molly's hand.

"I do, and I need you to pay very close attention." She glanced up at Piper and smiled. "All of you."

CHAPTER SIXTEEN

Find out where she's going." Julius watched through the chain-link fence as Asra boarded a large, strange vessel alone. Behind her, an Oriental man carried two urns, the kind that held cremated human remains.

The man followed her to the top of the steps and handed them to Asra, then went back to the car for one last urn. Asra's expression was so solemn and sad, Julius could see the pain clearly etched on every part of her face and her posture. He'd laughed at Vadoma's success a few days earlier, but it wasn't time to celebrate yet. Asra wasn't done paying him in pain what she owed him.

Behind him Bailey talked softly into the phone, and judging from the conversations, he was trying to find the answer to his question. More bags were unloaded from Asra's vehicle, and the men with her loaded them on the plane. As they finished, another car arrived with Lenore, Morgaine, and Charlie, and they all took turns embracing Asra.

"Do you know what Asra's problem has always been?" Julius asked Travis, who'd been able to get away from Rolla for the next couple of weeks without raising the Elder's suspicions.

"I'm sure you're going to tell me, so why waste time asking."

"She cares too deeply for those things in her life that are fragile. Why fall in love so easily if you'll never be rewarded for those efforts?" He glanced back at Bailey and smiled as he rubbed along the scarred line where Asra had separated his head from his shoulders. The elixir had brought him back, but he wasn't completely healed. "Loving and taking care of these idiots who die as easily as if swatting a fly has been her life's ambition. She should've concentrated instead on how best to control them to do her bidding."

"The night she took me by surprise and embarrassed me in front of Rolla, I thought I'd never hate someone that much, so tell me you're not done with her," Travis said, and the links in the fence bent under the pressure of his fingers.

"She is headed back to New Orleans. That's all the man in the airport tower knew after reviewing their flight plan," Bailey said. "I'm still shocked Vadoma was able to kill Asra's bedmate while they were under her protection."

"There's always safety in numbers, Bailey, and when we get to where she's going, that lesson will be clear to you. Asra is their best warrior, but now she's useless to them because of her grief." The workers around the big vehicle Asra had entered were closing it up. "Where is this place, New Orleans?"

"It's west of here over the ocean," Bailey said.

"And this thing they're loading, it will take her there?" He'd slept so long that at times he found himself at a loss as to how much the world had changed. "Is it slow enough that we can follow?"

"Julius, I explained this before." Bailey, though, explained it again. "It flies, so she and the others will be home by tonight."

"Then we must fly as well and finish this. We have a very short time before—" He caught himself and stopped before giving Travis too much information.

"Before what?" Travis asked, seemingly brighter than he gave him credit for.

"We must get to her while we still have the advantage we've fought hard for." Julius returned to watching what was going on with the thing called an airplane. "After all, from what you said yourself, you didn't pose much of a threat to her." He couldn't restrain the small dig.

"She caught me off guard. We've been through this." Travis sounded like he was about to turn his anger on him, but the roar that came from the vehicle made Julius lose interest in tormenting Travis.

He watched it streak toward them, then magically lift off the ground like a large bird. The sight made him feel like a fascinated little boy, and he was anticipating learning all that was available to him in this era. He had time for that, but he had much to do before his real fun began.

"We'll see you soon, Asra." He whispered the promise as he followed the plane's ascent until it was completely out of sight. "And then I will finish what I started with Attila so long ago."

❖

Kendal's plane landed at a private airstrip about fifty miles away to pick up the rest of their passengers, who'd arrived by helicopter. If Julius was watching, he'd concentrate on her and not the house, especially after Vadoma had told him she and her followers were able to kill Piper and her family.

Kendal's conversation with Vadoma had been interesting, since she'd never entered into a partnership with a child of the night, but Vadoma had called to update her, so far keeping her word. Vadoma might be playing both sides, but Kendal couldn't worry about that now.

Their talk with the Marmandes and Hill the night before had ended in a tenuous truce of sorts, and they had all agreed to Kendal's plan. If whatever had attacked them had agreed to help them, and the people who'd hired them thought they were dead, that was for the best. The one subject neither Kendal nor Piper had talked about was the elixir of the sun and the fact Piper had consumed a cup of it.

Bruik had arrived, and Kendal hoped neither Julius nor anyone he had watching the house had noticed the clan's best seer enter. He'd spent the night before talking to Piper and, from what Piper had said, taught her a few exercises that'd make the visions become easier to remember.

Over the Atlantic, Piper followed Bruik's instructions, then went quiet, and her face took on a pensive expression that made Kendal believe her mind had flown off in its own direction. Piper stayed in her trance for almost two hours, closing her eyes as if trying to lock away whatever she was seeing in her mind.

When Piper became aware of her surroundings again, Kendal leaned closer to her and kissed her. "Are you okay?"

Piper nodded and put her head on her shoulder. "Believe me, this isn't the time to get into it."

"No hints?"

"You're the only one I'm telling, but I have to wait until the right time. It won't work otherwise."

They stopped to refuel a couple of times, and the first part of their trip ended in California. A car waited in the hangar to drive them into the hills of an estate between Sonoma and Napa, to another piece of Kendal's history. They turned off a scenic highway and drove through a gate very similar to the one at Farthington House. The drive up to the house wound around vineyards now bare following the recent harvest.

Sparrow, an attractive older woman of American Indian descent, waited for them at the front of the house. She was dressed in jeans with a native-print jacket, and her beautiful black hair pulled into the familiar ponytail was mixed with a little gray.

"How are you?" Kendal asked when she opened her arms to her old friend.

"Old and cold, but I'm feeling better now after looking at such a beautiful sight," Sparrow said as she gazed up at her. "Come give an old woman a kiss."

For a second Piper held her back as if she had something to fear. Sparrow didn't talk to Kendal like a servant or employee, and the expression on Sparrow's face telegraphed the intimate history between them.

"Behave," Kendal admonished her in the Hopi language as she let Sparrow go so she could hug Sparrow's tall sons. "Everyone, this is Sparrow and her sons Josh and Jeremiah Brown Bear." After the introductions Sparrow waved toward the house, doing her best to make everyone feel welcome.

The staff served a wonderful meal that Mac and Molly ate methodically, still appearing to be in shock from what had happened. Sparrow and her children brought her Kendal to date on what was going on around the vineyard as well as in town. When the dishes were cleared, the Marmandes retired to the room Sparrow led them to, and they knew it would be their new home until all this mystery was over.

Sparrow and her boys retired to their own home, also on the property, and Kendal took Piper for a walk. The moon was almost full, and they took advantage of the light to stroll along the rows of grapevines. Some of the fruit that had been dropped during the harvest lay dried and shriveled, waiting to be tilled back into the soil.

"Now I understand the comment you made about being a winemaker," Piper said, repeating her statement from the night Lenore and Morgaine joined them.

"So you do," Kendal said with a smile, and walked as if she knew this land.

Piper pulled them toward a tree in the distance, wanting to hear about this part of Kendal's life. Kendal sat with her back against the tree, and Piper sat between her legs.

"Tell me about her?"

Kendal didn't ask who she was talking about, and started her story. "When she was about nineteen, Sparrow was married to a man who loved the bottle more than her and their two sons. To keep her family off the streets, Sparrow made jewelry to sell in town and tried to make the best of what the gods saw fit to give her. It wasn't enough to make her happy, but it was a bearable life, from what she told me, until the beatings started."

Piper pinched the skin of Kendal's forearms and became irrationally angry. "Wait, she was out making money and he thanked her by beating her?"

"She wanted to use the money to feed her boys and not his whiskey habit." Kendal kissed her temple and held her tighter. "You try to hide it from the world, but you're a caring soul, my love." With no effort, Kendal picked her up and turned her a little so she straddled her lap and they were facing each other.

"What are you doing?"

"I want to see this beautiful face while I'm talking to you." Kendal ran a finger along Piper's lips and smiled when she bit her fingertip.

"Some big tough warrior you are. It's all this mush that makes them fall in love with you and pine for you even after you leave. Finish your story, honey."

"I bought this place about a hundred years ago because I thought the area was as peaceful as it was breathtaking and a good place where I could retreat every so often, not because I knew a lot about grapes and wine. It's about eighty acres, and the wine pressed here fills the cellars of places like Farthington and Oakgrove. I was here for a visit close to forty-four years ago and saw a truly pathetic sight."

Kendal took a deep breath and let it out slowly. "Sparrow was huddled on a corner in town with a split lip and two black eyes. Her husband had really gone after her the night before, so she was out trying to sell her jewelry with her two little boys and as many possessions as she could bring with her. She had finally had enough. I went and got my truck and just opened the door and offered my help. Going with me and accepting my offer was up to her."

"And she did." Piper pressed her palm to Kendal's cheek, then turned her head enough so she could kiss her.

"She came here with me and her boys, and they never left. I couldn't stay, so I asked the man I had running the vineyard to look out for them and teach Joshua and Jeremiah the business. Eventually they moved closer to a small lake on the property where I had a house built for them, since Sparrow liked the main house, but it really wasn't her style."

Piper kissed Kendal again and knew exactly why Sparrow had moved. "It wasn't that she didn't like the house, my love. She didn't like that you weren't there to share it with her. She fell in love with you, but she didn't get to keep you. I think that hurt her more than that bastard's fists."

"Two lonely people found comfort in each other, but I don't know about love. I won't lie and tell you I don't care for Sparrow and her sons, because I do. They've been good to me and work hard to make this place successful."

"I didn't say that to make you feel bad. That you care so much is why I fell in love with you, and I would've begged you, like her, to stay if I hadn't drunk the elixir. I know I don't have to worry about anyone alive. Thank you for cementing that truth in my mind with your honesty." She leaned back a little and started to unbutton Kendal's shirt. "Did her husband ever bother her again?"

Looking down at her chest and how much more of it she could see as Piper kept unbuttoning her shirt, Kendal smiled. "He returned once and tried to force her back, threatening me and telling me he owned her. I convinced him what a bad idea it would be for him to try it again."

Piper nodded and pulled the shirt free of Kendal's pants.

"Do you have something in mind?" Kendal asked as Piper started on her belt.

The tree had surprised Piper when she saw it during their walk. The new vision on the plane had driven her crazy with a desire to touch Kendal, but it was important to be patient. She didn't tell Kendal or Bruik when they'd asked, not wanting the outcome to change. All Hallows' Eve, or Halloween as everyone in the modern world knew it, was close and it was time to start to awaken a sleeping dragon.

"It seems like such a long time ago, but during an important afternoon of my life, someone very wise told me to share myself only with someone who ignited my passion and owned my heart." Piper took off her own shirt and pressed their bodies together, sighing when skin met skin. "I found you and I want you to show me your passion. Show me that your heart belongs to me as much as mine belongs to you."

"I will always belong to you, my love." Kendal held her hands as she stood to remove her pants and shoes. Piper was strong enough to pull her to her feet so she could finish undressing her as well.

"Then show me," she said, when they were seated again. As they came together the cold night air was forgotten, and Piper felt like every inch of her body had come alive in a search for a way to become one with Kendal's.

"Do you belong to me?" she asked, trying to remember everything from the vision. It was the first time she'd had a guide to show her what needed to be done. The woman had been so helpful and had explained to Piper why this night had to happen in a certain way. She'd showed it to her over and over until she'd memorized every aspect of the process. "Answer me," she demanded, when Kendal took too long to speak.

"Only you." Kendal willingly let her take control, leaning against the bark of the tree and putting her hands to the sides of her thighs.

"In a tent a long time ago you were marked." She took one of Kendal's hands and entwined their fingers, and it was like she was becoming someone else who sounded commanding and in control. "The woman who marked you did so because one day you'd find someone who'd claim you as their own, and then the brand would come to life and the dragon would know your true mate." Piper hesitated before placing her hand on the spot she knew from her vision held the hidden tattoo. If it didn't appear after what she had to do, it would break her heart because of what that would mean.

"Piper, look at me," Kendal said softly when she hesitated and couldn't stop staring at their hands. As Piper glanced up, Kendal's eyes filled with tears for the uncertainty she probably saw on her face. The fear came from not knowing her place. She loved Kendal more than life, but would the mark know how she felt? "What did you see on the plane?"

"I saw this place." She let Kendal's hand go and pointed to the tree and the rows of grapevines around them.

"Do you trust me and what we have?" Piper nodded. "Then trust that my heart knows who you are and what you mean to me." Kendal took their still-linked hands and pressed them over her heart. "Trust yourself and claim everything that belongs to you." When she nodded again, Kendal moved their hands until they were lying over the spot where the woman had run her finger all those years ago, as if knowing what had to happen.

"In the name of the goddess, awaken from your watery sleep. Your time has come to stand and fight with the one true of heart." She chanted this three times in the strange language the woman had made her repeat until she had gotten it right. After the third time, their linked hands started to glow and the warmth moved up Piper's arm and across her chest.

When the ritual was done they lifted their hands, and there on Kendal's skin was the dragon ready for battle. It was coiled like it was on the sword, and its jaws were open, ready to incinerate anyone who meant them harm. Piper's relief almost made her forget the next part. With their hands still glowing, she moved them to rest over her heart so she could finish the chant.

"I am ready to stand by her side and accept the responsibility of keeping her whole." She said it three times, and after the third time something slammed into her chest over her heart.

When they lifted their hands this time, Kendal saw a tattoo of a dragon on Piper's chest. Instead of looking as if it were prepared for battle, this one held what appeared to be an orb in one claw, the other claw hovering over it as if to keep it safe.

"Where did you learn that language?" She sounded like she was in awe of what had happened. "I've only heard it once before, and I didn't understand it then either."

The heated, uncontrolled desire was starting to grow, like it had the first time they held the sword together, and Piper wasn't in the mood to answer any more questions. Whatever the power of the dragon was, because Aphrodite had made it, it centered on the connection they had to each other. The dragon had seemingly taken the love they shared and magnified it so that it became all-enveloping.

Kendal brought her forward and crushed their mouths together, as if she needed to feel as much of Piper as she could. Kendal's usual control had seemingly broken its leash and she started to lay her down, but Piper stopped her.

"Easy, baby, let's take this slow and enjoy it." That was hard to say since she wanted Kendal to possess her, to take her like she had in the sword room at Farthington, but the images of her vision made her take control. "I need to be close to you, but I want to see you." She caressed Kendal's face with her fingertips, then followed by placing kisses over her eyes and mouth as she went. "Make love to me while you hold me." She tipped her hips forward and painted Kendal's lower abdomen with her wetness.

Kendal closed her eyes as Piper kissed her, and she could tell Kendal wanted desperately to take control because of her clenched hands and rigid body. "Look at me," she said, and Kendal finally opened her eyes. She took Kendal's fist and kissed the top of her fingers. The act made her hand open like a blossoming flower.

"That's it, let me see you." Kendal's eyes stayed glued to hers as she lifted her hips and maneuvered Kendal's hand between their bodies. Kendal let out a moan when Piper rubbed herself against the length of her fingers, getting them wet. "Do you feel how much I need you inside me?"

She lowered herself slowly, enjoying the way Kendal completely filled her. "God," she said as she slowly moved her hips, and the feel of Kendal's fingers going in and out made her let go, the overwhelming power of the orgasm coming much too soon for her taste. Before it robbed her of all awareness, she reached down and found Kendal wet, hard, and throbbing. She squeezed two fingers together, confident the rocking of her hips would provide all the stimulation Kendal needed to join her as she came.

She clenched the walls of her sex around Kendal's fingers and could sense when Kendal flew off the abyss with her. Kendal let out

a roar that scattered a few birds in the tree above them, but Piper
slumped forward and sighed when Kendal wrapped her arms around
her. Everything had been like what she'd seen in her vision, but they
still had to do one thing to prove they were ready to move to the next
phase of unleashing the sword's power.

With one last kiss to Kendal's chest, she sat up and looked first to
Kendal's mark, then at the new one on her chest. They were still vivid
and visible, and hadn't faded as it did the first time the dragon had been
painted on Kendal's skin.

"The goddess has chosen her champion." She moved so Kendal
could ease her hand out of her slowly, making her shiver. "The mark is
now a part of you."

Kendal ran her finger along the tattoo on Piper's chest and seemed
to study every part of it. "And what does this mark mean?"

"In my vision, my guide said if I accepted, I'd be marked as
well, and it'd mean I belong to you. Every great warrior needs a mate,
especially if they are fighting for the right side, or in this case, the side
of love and not the power of conquest." Kendal laughed and Piper
joined her. "I don't think in this case it means the candies-and-flowers
kind of love, but for the good in the world."

"I'm sorry. I promise I'm not making fun." Kendal reclined against
the tree again, putting both arms around Piper's hips. "What else did
you see?"

"It was nice to have a spirit guide this time, but it would've been
better if she'd told me what happens from this point to the end. How
the sword fits into all this is still a mystery, but she did give me one
warning."

"Take your time."

"Like it says in the prophecy, the sword will awaken on Halloween,
but it has the ability to serve two masters."

"Two masters like love and evil?"

She exhaled loudly and shook her head. "That's what she wasn't
willing to give up, and I asked a few times as we memorized all the
stuff I had to say. She refused and only showed me a glimpse of a
great sex scene, gave me that warning, then left me hanging." She felt
Kendal's chest moving as if she was trying not to laugh. "Laugh it up,
Asra, but do you realize how hard it was not to ravish you somewhere

over the Atlantic with my grandparents on the plane? So now that I can be more rational, what do you think it all means?"

This time Kendal didn't hold her laugh in, and it sounded so carefree it warmed her.

"Let's just concentrate on what she gave us for now. Tomorrow will come soon enough."

CHAPTER SEVENTEEN

"What do you think that was?" Morgaine asked as she stood by the window, looking out. She meant the yell they'd heard earlier, but Lenore was more interested in watching the shadows the moonlight painted on Morgaine's body as the trees swayed in the wind outside.

"See anything?"

"Nothing out of the ordinary," Morgaine said, but stayed put, and Lenore sensed she didn't want to turn around.

"Then come back over here." Lenore lifted the blanket in invitation. "You don't regret what happened, do you?"

It'd been the strangest thing, considering nothing like it had ever happened with anyone before, but as they'd discussed some new passages she'd found in a few books from the Farthington library, something took hold. Whatever it was, they'd dropped to the bed and started ripping off their clothes like the world would end if they hadn't made love. She wanted to find the right words to talk about it, since whatever had brought them together was still skittering around the room, ready to make her lose her mind again.

"Not regret, no," Morgaine said slowly. "I just find it interesting."

"I've been alive for a long time, and I've made love thousands of times, but 'interesting' usually translates to regret." Lenore dropped the blanket and tried to hide her disappointment at Morgaine's rejection. "If you want, you can leave. Go ahead. I'm sure you'll feel better if you go out and look around."

"Don't do that," Morgaine said, and sat next to her. "It's true that we've known each other for centuries, but we've always been occupied with other things, other interests, so it's made me blind to a lot of things. That's my fault, but I've been weighed down by my own collection of rejection and failures." Lenore put her hand on Morgaine's thigh and hoped she'd continue. "What did you tell me not that long ago? Love would find me the minute I stopped looking."

"Stop now if you don't mean it."

"Listen to me. Tonight you stripped me bare of any pretense, and I welcomed you. I found something in you that no one before you has ever come close to having."

"Not even Asra?" she said as Morgaine moved over her. "She never wrote it in any of her chronicles, but I've always known how it was between the two of you."

"Asra was never mine, and I could never be hers, but this is something you and I can build on. Don't punish me for being a complete idiot. You fit so well with me I want to cry from the pure joy of it."

"Thanks for that, but if it'll make you feel better, go outside and check the grounds."

"I don't want to go outside," Morgaine said, pressing her to the bed. "The only thing I want is you." Morgaine moved her hand down the middle of Lenore's chest. "I want to start the fire between us again, but how about a slow burn this time?"

"Touch me," she said, and opened her heart to Morgaine.

❖

In the morning, despite whatever danger they were about to face, everyone at the table had a large smile except Hill. The Marmandes appeared well rested and happier than when they'd arrived. They all ate breakfast together, Kendal and Piper knowing it would be their last meal with them and Hill until they got back.

"How about a walk?" Kendal asked the Marmandes after they were done.

They took the same path she and Piper had taken the night before, and Kendal let Piper go ahead, holding Molly's hand.

"I know back in England we exchanged promises, but I want you to make me another one," Mac said as he slowed down even more, so they were out of earshot.

She held her hand out for him to shake. "I'll promise whatever you like."

"I know you're leaving Molly and me here to keep us safe, and that you tried to talk Piper into staying on with us," Mac said as he kept his eyes on his family. "Piper is the image of her mother. She's as stubborn as the day is long, and it's what got my son all fired up about marrying her and what killed his spirit when she died."

"The first day I came to have lunch with you two was the day she grabbed me by the heart, and I pray she never lets go." Kendal smiled and winked at Piper when she glanced back at them.

"Just like her mama," Mac said, and put his hand on her shoulder. "No matter where my son went or what he was into, my daughter-in-law was always right there, and vice versa."

"I don't want you to think I'd put Piper in danger if I could avoid it."

"I know that, and that isn't what I wanted to talk to you about. I want you to promise me you'll go back to New Orleans and kick whoever's ass you have to so you can come back here for us."

"You, Molly, and Hill will be on the first plane home as soon as we're done."

"Think you can promise me one more thing?"

She smiled and waved him on. "If I can, I'll be happy to."

"Once you get back, I want to take another walk with you so you can tell me a story." He slapped her on the back and laughed. "I have a feeling your story will be the most interesting spin I'm ever going to have the honor of hearing. You aren't what you appear to be, Kendal Richoux, but goddamn if I don't like you."

"Thank you, sir." She stepped into his embrace when he held his arms out and smiled at the affection Mac was still willing to give.

They finished their walk, and when they got back the staff had packed their bags. Hill held the locked box containing the Sea Serpent Sword and hesitated to hand it over when Kendal held her hands out for it.

"Take me with you," Hill said, gripping the box with white fingers.

"You don't know what you're asking," Kendal said, and squeezed Piper's fingers as she took her hand. "You're not equipped to handle this, and don't take that as an insult."

"If whatever you're going to face is anything like what we saw in England, you have to take me. Wouldn't it be better if you have more than one person keeping an eye on Piper? If something happens to her—"

"Wait a second, Hill, don't do that," Piper said as she held Kendal back.

"I've known you longer than Kendal has, and I don't care what you told us about the freaks that made us run here. Those things were real, and I've seen enough movies to know they're vampires, as crazy as that sounds," Hill screamed as she clutched the box against her chest. "Logically we all know they don't exist, but those things were real."

"And Kendal took care of them, so hand that box over and calm down." Piper let Kendal go and went to Hill. "Don't fight us on this one."

"You can't stop me from following you."

"If you're smart, you won't step foot in New Orleans until we're done," Kendal said as she forcibly took the sword away from Hill. "You can accept that or not, but know that we'll have enough to worry about without you getting in the middle of something beyond your comprehension."

"Promise me you'll stay here," Piper said to Hill. "She's right and I trust her with my life, no matter how short a time we've been together."

"I can't do that because I care about you too much to throw you to the wolves."

"There won't be a wolf within a thousand miles of where we're going." Kendal pointed to the car.

"Take care of yourself and call us if you need anything," Molly said as she held Piper. "Come back to me."

"Gran, life always won't be perfect, but you can count on me and Kendal being with you and Pops for years to come."

Mac hugged Piper next with the same words of advice, then treated Kendal to them too. Piper didn't want to leave them behind, but this time she couldn't avoid it. They boarded with Lenore and Morgaine holding hands, and Charlie and Bruik coming in last. Whatever All Hallows' Eve held for them, it was upon them.

❖

When they drove through the gates of Oakgrove, the house and the grounds looked quiet and peaceful, and they all headed for their rooms. They had one more night to make plans before it was too late.

Kendal went down to talk to Charlie a few hours later about the idea she'd come up with, but he wasn't at his place, though his bags sat in the front room of his house. She dialed the stables and the other spots on the grounds he might be, but she couldn't locate a note or anything explaining his absence. Kendal walked through all the rooms looking for anything out of the ordinary, but aside from the luggage, it looked as if Charlie had stepped out for a while.

"Did you find him?" Piper asked as she sat and listened to Lenore read from the book she'd first found on the sword. Once Kendal voiced a concern, Lenore and Morgaine came down.

"Something's not right." She could feel it in her gut. Charlie's place was too tidy, and the painting of his family didn't hold the vase of flowers he always put out for them. "He knows how important tonight is, so he hasn't just decided to take a drive or something."

"He'll be back, honey." Piper got up and took a piece of candy from the bowl close to the door. "Are we entertaining the little ones for Halloween?"

"We get the occasional trick-or-treater, so the staff likes to be prepared. It's the one time of year strangers can wander in from the road without the fear of being arrested for trespassing." She accepted the chocolate from Piper and smiled. "I'm not sure why they'd put it out this year, since we're not unlocking the gate."

"You mean I missed my chance to get in here all those years ago?"

"If you'd shown up in some sexy costume, I would've insisted you come in, no matter what day of the year it was."

"Flatterer."

"On my oath as a soldier of Egypt, I tell only the truth when it comes to you."

Piper blushed and Morgaine made gagging noises when she came in with drinks for her and Lenore. "No comments from the peanut gallery, thank you."

Kendal reached for another piece of chocolate. "Did you spot Charlie?"

"He's not back, but I'm sure he knows we're counting on him." Morgaine sat and looked around the room.

"You must forget Charlie for now," Bruik said as he sat in a meditative pose by the fireplace.

"What have you seen?" Piper asked.

"He's close but won't be up for the fight. Asra and Morgaine, you can't let that take your mind off what needs to be done," Bruik said.

"Have you seen anything else about what happens tomorrow?" Piper asked.

"That vision belongs to you, child. Whatever there is to be seen, it's for your sight, not mine."

"Where'd you put the sword?" Piper asked as she remembered the vision, which still hadn't changed at all.

"I locked it in the sword room. I'd rather see it sleep for another two thousand years than let it awaken something we can't fight."

"I don't have a clue, but I think you two will be up to fighting whatever's awakened," Lenore said. "I had my assistant drop off a few things for me." She held up Bruik's writings and he shook his head. "When you did have sight of this, you were certain this would be the year the dragon awoke. If we add that to what Piper has seen, we can safely say we can't stop it."

"But my visions have changed when we worked to change them," Piper said.

"With training, eventually you'll hone your talent," Bruik said as he stood and came close to Piper. "Your visions are just that, a possibility of what can happen. I've been able to sort through the different scenarios of what I see and come to an absolute outcome." He smiled, and the lines around his eyes became more pronounced. Bruik was the only Elder Kendal had ever met who actually appeared old. "It doesn't mean your insights haven't been important to us, sweet child. Long ago I may have seen you in a series of visions and written extensively of how important you'll be to us. Of that I have always been certain, and even if you're not sure of your gift, you have gotten all those you love to this point unscathed."

"Can we try again tonight? Maybe now that it's so close, something else will come to me."

"Save your energy for what needs to be done," Bruik said, and returned to his meditation after he kissed Piper's cheek.

"We have a starting place for tomorrow night, Piper, and together we'll bend it to our will."

CHAPTER EIGHTEEN

The morning and afternoon were quiet, and as soon as the sun went down, Kendal sent everyone to their positions before she went out to the front porch alone to smoke a cigar. She watched the road but wasn't really expecting Julius and his friends to drive up and announce themselves. If they were watching, though, she wanted to face the oncoming battle like any other lord protecting her domain, showing no fear.

The temperature had gotten a little cooler, and she could feel the chill through the open collar of her shirt. Wearing her boots and soft buckskin pants, she looked very much like the ghost of Jacques St. Louis come to life once more.

"Still no sign of him," Morgaine said when she dropped into the rocker next to her. "I ran the perimeter of the house but there's still no sign of Charlie."

"No, but if you look in the tree to my left you'll find signs of someone else."

Morgaine's face never turned from Kendal's, but her eyes looked to where Kendal said. Kendal had spotted him the minute she came out, and whoever he was he was dressed in black, including the pommel of his sword, though she could still see the whiteness of his skin as he sat hidden in one of the high branches.

"And if you look to your right, you'll see he brought a friend." She stayed still and closed her eyes to concentrate on the sounds around her. She heard faint whispering and the sounds of people climbing the walls and dropping onto the grounds. "He brought a few more as well."

"How many?" Morgaine asked as she stood and leaned on the banister.

"I'm thinking six more at the wall, and the two in the tree." The katana she'd used to fight Henri and Ora was lying across her lap, the Sea Serpent Sword locked in the house. "Eight of them and two of us. I'll take those odds," she said in case the intruders could hear their conversation. Morgaine snorted, since they'd fought alongside each other enough times for her to know she was getting ready to engage and try to mess up whatever timeline Julius's men had.

"I tried to up our numbers," Morgaine said, "but it was hard to know who to trust. If some power comes to light tonight with the capability to take over the world, I'd rather not tempt someone who's on the fence as far as honor is concerned."

"True. After all, that's what the Republicans are for."

Morgaine laughed. "Smart-ass. You keep saying things like that and eventually you'll get audited."

"That might be a scarier thought than facing off against some evil bastards trying to take over the world."

"Do you really think we need reinforcements?"

She nodded and smiled. "Remind me the next time we're in the same situation to buy Lenore and Piper the latest issue of *Swordplay for Dummies*, to bolster our defenses."

"I'll make a note of it, but tonight you're going to have to be happy with me."

"I am happy, and for more reasons than that you're here." She stood as well and moved next to Morgaine so she could put her arm around her waist. "I'm glad to see what's building between you and Lenore. I've only known that kind of love for a short time, but it does give me a renewed sense of something to fight for." She stubbed out her cigar and walked down the steps to the front yard.

"Let's get this over with."

❖

Piper, Lenore, and Bruik watched from the windows in the front parlor, and Piper cringed when Kendal unsheathed her sword and descended the steps to the yard. Even through the double-paned glass they could hear the scraping noise as Kendal dragged the tip of her sword along the drive.

"What's she doing?" Piper asked.

"I'm not sure, but I believe it's what's referred to as calling someone out."

"Sometimes it's best when you don't get what you're asking for, because she's in no way ready for what's coming."

The male voice seemed to send a chill up Lenore's spine, because she stiffened, then shivered. She appreciated that Lenore subtly placed herself between her and their unexpected visitor. How he had gotten past both Kendal and Morgaine baffled her, but it didn't matter now.

"You don't look surprised to see me, Lenore." The man was tall, but not as tall as Kendal, and wore robes that looked like the ones she'd seen in pictures of ancient Romans. He was handsome but seemed overwhelmingly cruel. "And you've brought the mighty Bruik with you. Thank you for saving me the trouble of digging him out of that mausoleum in Egypt that Rolla loves so much."

"What are you doing, and who helped you escape?" Lenore asked.

"Those who'll share in my rise to power released me, and only they will be safe once I conquer the world. All your planning and scheming against me will come to nothing. Asra has only Morgaine and you, since her beloved Charlie lies in darkness. She taught him well, and he showed promise, but he refused to join us, so he was eliminated. But he won't be alone long."

"Answer my question. What do you want?"

"We don't have enough time right now for me to list all the things I want, but I'll be happy to start while the ruffians finish their childish games outside." Julius sat in the middle of the couch and crossed his legs. "Sit down, I insist."

Julius picked up the journal of Bruik's writings and flipped through the pages. "In my time, I memorized all of your writings and held my tongue about the numerous insults you put in here about me." He laughed and snapped the book closed. "I'm willing to let you live, since your sight of the future will come in handy."

"You've been asleep so long you might not realize Asra has become the type of warrior you can't beat," Bruik said. "I've seen nothing but her survival, no matter what or who you brought with you. This is a battle you can't and won't win."

"Don't lie, Bruik. It's unbecoming in someone who's sworn to tell the truth in all things." He glared at Bruik and showed no interest in Piper yet. "You saw it long ago." The clang of metal hitting metal came from outside, but he didn't seem interested in that either. "Your vision spoke of a sword fired by a god that would give its owner the world, and he'd be unstoppable."

"No such vision exists," Lenore said with heat. "I've read them all, so don't try to rewrite our history."

"Bruik was as eloquent as ever in his endless quest to impress Rolla, but that scroll never made it to his desk. Since Bruik assumed every one of his hallucinations made it to Rolla, no one ever missed it." He threw the journal close to the fire as if disgusted by it. "I memorized every line, then burned it, but it added to my knowledge of the sword that no one believed existed. My quest led me to Attila, and just as I thought all was lost, there it was. I don't know how Asra got it, but once the time was right I knew exactly where to look for it."

"There's no sword," Piper said, and his eyes whipped in her direction.

She'd never seen his face, but his hands were the ones from her vision. That part had always been clear to her. Julius's hands had held the sword when the eyes glowed red right before the evil thing was unleashed on the world, and he welcomed it. These were the same slender fingers, almost delicate in their appearance, and his laugh was the same as well.

"I'll find out in time if you're a good bed warmer, but you're a terrible liar. The sword can't be destroyed by any mortal. Asra might think it's safely hidden, but she'll give it up soon enough."

"She can't give you what she doesn't have." She moved closer to Lenore's back.

"It exists and I want it now," he screamed as he slapped Lenore viciously across the face.

"Piper, run," Lenore said as she held her hands up to her cheek, and it sounded like a balloon was losing air slowly when the knife Julius threw pierced her chest. "Please, Piper, go."

She started for the door, knowing Lenore would be fine as soon as the sun came up, but she couldn't abandon her. The elixir would save her life, but not from the torture she figured Julius had in store for her to make her tell him where the sword was.

"No," Lenore gasped, but it was too late. Piper had fallen into Julius's trap and he had her around the neck.

"Release me or Asra will cut you into pieces this time."

"Let's see what is stronger in her, love for you or hatred of me."

❖

Kendal and Morgaine were close to disarming Travis and two others fighting with him, and Bailey was bleeding from the wound she'd given him in the leg. He was still crying when the front door opened and Piper stumbled out. Kendal took her eyes off Travis and lowered her sword when she saw the large hunting knife pressed to Piper's throat.

"Remember he can't kill her," Morgaine said as she stood next to her. "Remember that and keep your wits about you."

"Asra, your turn to be judged has come," Julius said as he pressed hard enough on Piper's neck to break the skin and draw blood. "In my time with Attila he came to appreciate my talent for strategy."

"I always thought he appreciated your sick mind, since the Hun was a psychopath like you."

"Don't tempt me," he said, and pressed again, making Piper gasp in pain. "I told Travis from the beginning that you and the bitch who taught you had to be destroyed."

Since Kendal was riveted on Piper, she couldn't stop Travis in time when he sliced through Morgaine's spine, dropping her instantly. She brought her sword up, but the other two men were behind her, and she didn't see which one of them drove his sword all the way through her. It was as if they'd taken the lesson of what Henri and Ora had done and improved on it.

The wound hurt, but as she started to get up again, Travis and Bailey stabbed her as well. She was too weak, and against all hope it seemed Piper's vision of doom was in this case one she couldn't change. By the time the sun rose, Julius would have won.

"Where is it?" Julius yelled down at her as she tried her best to stay on her knees. "Tell me or I'll gut her right here."

"You can't kill me," Piper said, and Kendal grimaced for more than her wounds. Julius took the knife away and whipped Piper around to look at her face, or, more precisely, her eyes, if Kendal had to guess. "By the gods, this is better than I thought. Bruik saw you too, lovely girl."

"Let her go," Kendal gasped. "She'll be of no use to you."

"I may not be able to kill her, but I'll return the favor you bestowed on me when Rolla asked it of you. Only I'll have a bit of fun before I show her any mercy." The clock inside the house chimed once, announcing they had thirty minutes before it would strike twelve. "Where is it?"

"Let her go and I'll tell you."

"Kendal, no," Piper said, but Julius let her go immediately.

"Inside the house." Kendal fought to get the words out, feeling the strength slip slowly out of her. When she finished telling him where he could find the sword, he grabbed Piper by the hair and pulled her with him.

"Why does he want this sword so badly?" Travis asked her.

"I don't know, but whatever it is, he used you to get to it. He and his friend Bailey won't need you for anything once he has it, though. You've been played."

Travis and Bailey stared at each other before they ran up the stairs into the house.

"Do you have any idea what we should do next, since I can't feel anything below the neck?" Morgaine asked.

Kendal was about to answer when someone came into her line of sight. Vadoma's red hair was down and loose, and she wore an outfit that made her look like she was trying out for a new Catwoman movie. It was a seductively attractive shell that hid the ugliness inside.

"Trick or treat," Vadoma said as she helped her back to her knees.

"Oh, fuck me," Morgaine said with a groan. "This day keeps the surprises coming, don't you think?"

"Is the fuck offer one of my choices?" Vadoma said as she ran her finger down Kendal's chest and licked it clean. "Yummy, this is a rare vintage definitely worth coming out for."

"It's nice to see you again," Kendal said with effort.

"Your greeting is warm, warrior, but don't show such enthusiasm yet. The night's young and I have yet to feed." She snapped her fingers and some of her followers picked up Kendal and Morgaine and followed her toward the house.

"This is the deal you made?" Morgaine said with a tear-stained face as one of Vadoma's followers carried her over his shoulder.

"Sometimes the road to light can only be found through the darkness."

❖

Julius had finally broken into the sword room and was obviously tearing the walls apart to find the Sea Serpent Sword. That's what it sounded like to Piper as two men held her in place. As Julius walked out with the sword in his hand, Piper noticed the dragon's eyes were starting to change. The center of the green stones glowed red, and if not stopped, the change would forever alter the essence of the weapon.

"What are you doing here?" Julius said when he saw Vadoma standing close to Piper, and Morgaine and Kendal lying on the floor at her feet.

"Collecting on your promises," Vadoma said, her incisors drawn as she moved closer to Piper.

"Anyone but her," he said. "I don't know how she fits into this, but I can't afford to lose her yet. And before you think to ask, stay away from her too." He pointed to Kendal.

From her vantage point Piper could see that the stones held more red than green, which meant the sword was close to awakening the dragon that would serve Ares. Kendal seemed better off than Morgaine, but in no shape to stop Julius and the men with him.

"Tsk," Vadoma said to Julius. "I want to have as much fun as you do." Vadoma glanced to Kendal and Kendal nodded slightly. The grandfather clock in the corner read one minute to midnight, and Vadoma moved until she was standing right next to Julius. With a motion so fast he was powerless to stop her, she grabbed him as her face contorted to its most hideous form.

Quicker than anything on earth, Vadoma drained Julius until he looked like a gaunt ghost of himself. Piper gagged when Vadoma used her fangs to open the vein at own her wrist with a savagery that made no sense at first, but like a mother with her baby, she thrust her wrist to Julius's mouth and pressed it to his lips.

"Drink," she commanded him. The clock had started to chime and had already rung four times when he seemed to have gotten his fill.

"I thought the elixir held the answers to the universe, but it's nothing like this," Julius said as he got to his feet and lifted the sword over his head and claimed it as his. "Ares, show yourself. Give me what's rightfully mine."

Piper looked on as the dragon at the end of the pommel came to life and started to coil itself around Julius's arm. They'd lost, and, alone, she was helpless to stop what was happening. The clock was at its sixth chime, and they were running out of time. Once midnight passed, the sword would forever serve only one master, and Julius must've felt that truth, since he was laughing as the dragon started to become a part of him. He looked up again and called to Ares, his and the other two men's total attention focused on the ceiling.

They didn't see Kendal struggle to pick up the katana Vadoma had brought and left close to her. With what looked like the last of her strength Kendal threw it like a javelin.

The moment it pierced Julius's heart he exploded into dust and the dragon returned to the sword hilt. As soon as it did, Bailey and Travis made a run for it as the clock struck the tenth chime. Vadoma kicked it to Piper before they reached it, and once she had it in hand she ran to Kendal, knowing she was the only one there with the right to claim it.

As the clock struck twelve, she picked up Kendal's limp hand and wrapped it around the hilt. Everyone in the room closed their eyes from the bright light as the dragon uncoiled again and floated over them, its wings unfurled as if in protection. Piper opened her eyes in time to see it open its jaws and let out a stream of fire that encircled not only Kendal and her, but Lenore and Morgaine as well.

The heat didn't burn, but healed the wounds Kendal, Morgaine, and Lenore had suffered. Piper felt Kendal grow stronger beside her. They all stood and faced the dragon.

The heat intensified on Piper's chest, and Kendal had to have felt the same thing, since her hand went to her thigh. In a flash both dragons flew from their spots on the women's bodies and met above them. The one from Kendal reared back and shot a ball of fire to the one that had come from Piper. Piper's held up the orb in its claw, as if accepting the gift of fire. The orb started to glow, then split in two so her dragon now had an orb in each claw.

When they were the brightest thing in the room, the dragon threw them toward the ceiling, where they disappeared. After that both of the dragons returned to their owners.

As quickly as the ritual began, it ended. No one said anything, as if not having words for what had happened. Kendal picked up the Sea Serpent Sword, now very plain because the dragon decorating its handle had been released.

After one strike, Travis's head bloodied the floor, and then she turned to Bailey. "Tell me what he did with Charlie or you'll beg for me to do that to you."

"Julius put him in a box and sank him in the lake out back." When she pressed him to the wall with the tip of the sword, he started crying. "I swear it. He had Travis and me throw it in."

"Morgaine, would you see to his comfort while I thank our savior," Kendal said.

Vadoma cocked her head to the side and smiled when Kendal moved close enough to take her hand. Her smile widened when Kendal bowed over it and kissed it. "Thank you for keeping your promises, and I hope you know I intend to keep mine. If you so choose, we'll see each other in a hundred years."

"I think we'll see each other before that, Asra. Tonight has shown us there's a place in this world for both of us. Don't you agree?"

"Why didn't you keep the sword for yourself when you saw the potential it held?" Piper asked as she moved to Kendal's side.

"Because, Lady Richoux," Vadoma said, "in life, even a life like mine, there must be balance. If power like we saw tonight is to be released, it's better with you than with someone like Julius. The only thing I want from life is the same thing you do—to simply live it." She snapped her fingers and her fledglings moved behind her. "I am not your enemy, Piper. Nor yours, Asra, so may you enjoy whatever you have gained tonight, and may our fragile truce hold for longer than a hundred years. Neither of you has anything to fear from me."

"Is it over?" Piper asked when they were alone with just Lenore.

Kendal picked her up and held her close before answering. "I find that because of who we are and what we do, it's never completely over. But for tonight, and as far as Julius is concerned, it's over." Kendal kissed her forehead and touched where Julius had cut her, but like Kendal's wounds, it had been healed by the dragon's fire. "Are you all right?"

"I'm fine, honey. Now would be a good time to promise me, though, that you'll stop getting stabbed in the heart on these grounds. I realize it can't kill you, but it's a little disconcerting to watch." Slowly she ran her hand over the place on Kendal's chest that was still stained with blood, reassuring herself that Kendal was fine.

"I'll try my best to make it the last."

"What happened to the sword?" Piper looked to the weapon lying on the floor, expecting it to do something else. "When Julius held it I could see the power going into him. Now it looks drained."

"That can wait until tomorrow. Since I don't feel any different, I think we defused whatever it was supposed to do. Right now we need to get Charlie out of the lake." Kendal put her down and kissed her again. "Do you feel any different?"

"Not really, but we'll do what you said and talk about it later."

"Let me go help Morgaine." Kendal headed to the back of the house, but stopped at the parlor door. "I almost forgot about you," Kendal said to Travis.

"You bitch." His head was a good four feet from his body, but it was still functioning, like some incredible magician's trick. "The sun will be up before long and I'll have my revenge."

"The sun is something you'll never have to worry about again, no-neck. If anyone bothers to look for you they'll be looking for a very long time, trying to put the very small pieces together." She grabbed him by the hair and by the front of his shirt and dragged both pieces out.

"Do you agree with that assessment?" Piper asked as she took Bruik's and Lenore's hands in hers.

Lenore shook her head. "I feel very different, but I can't really explain it. How do you feel?"

"I don't think different begins to cover it, but you're right. It's hard to explain." She glanced toward Bruik, and he only smiled as he led them back to the couch. "I saw you, and I saw the end of this tale, but I was forbidden to say anything."

"Who stopped you from telling us? Knowing the outcome would've saved us a lot of worry."

"For this part of my vision I had a guide, and I gave her my word to not share it with anyone or risk the outcome."

As Bruik spoke, Lenore's book about the sword floated from the coffee table to the chair across from them. Piper rubbed her eyes, hoping to clear the image, but opened them wide when the woman from her vision on the plane materialized in the chair. She opened the book and flipped to the end, where, magically, more pages appeared. They filled with writing when the woman ran her finger down each one.

"I see that I've chosen my champions well." The woman looked at her and laughed at what she assumed to be her shocked expression. "Your love is as ingenious as I believed her to be, so I think her trick to win deserves a treat."

"Who are you?" Piper asked.

"I am many things to those in need of me, but because of you and the strength you have given me, I too will live forever."

"That sounds like a riddle," Lenore said, but Bruik put his hand up to stop her from saying anything else.

"How may we serve you?" Bruik asked, his head bowed.

The woman looked to Lenore first. "I don't deal in riddles, Lenore. I'm what you find when you look up from your books and dream of what's in store for you. You'll see me in the center of what you hope to find when you close your eyes and imagine how your life will transform when you find someone to share it with you." The woman laughed again, as if enjoying herself. "But if you need the comfort of what you know best, I leave you this as a gift." She handed over the book, then kissed Lenore and Piper each on the cheek.

"Remember well your promise, Piper." The woman's image was starting to grow faint, but she left behind an overwhelming sense of peace.

"What promise?"

"'I am ready to stand by her side and accept the responsibility of keeping her whole.'" The language still sounded strange, but Piper understood every word. "You began tonight, but the job is far from over."

"I will never disappoint you, or her," Piper said, and bowed her head like Bruik.

"I know, little one, and it's why I have left you with a gift. It will allow me to fulfill a promise I made so long ago."

The woman was gone, and Piper reviewed the conversation, trying to figure out what the woman meant. Behind her, Lenore sat on the sofa and flipped through the book the woman had handed her, with Bruik reading over her shoulder.

"Holy shit." Lenore's comment was so out of character, Piper looked at her like she'd gone mad.

"What?"

"She left the answer to the mystery of the Sea Serpent Sword and what power it held. At least what power her side held."

"So?" She held her hands up, waiting. "What's the answer?"

"You," Lenore and Bruik said together.

CHAPTER NINETEEN

D on't be ridiculous," Piper said as she reflexively started laughing and kept on until tears streamed down her face. "As far as this immortal thing goes, I'm the new kid on the block, but I highly doubt I'm the key to any puzzle you all have been working on for years."

"Piper, it's all here in what she left us," Lenore said, and held up the book. "The woman wrote the end of the Sea Serpent's legend."

"She couldn't write it until the story was done so her brother couldn't accuse her of giving her champions an unfair advantage," Bruik said.

"Who's her brother?" she asked, sure she already knew.

"Ares, the god of war, and while I don't have proof Julius was his champion, that red dragon is as close as I ever want to be to him," Bruik said.

The room still held the sights and scents of the recent battle, which were starting to make Piper queasy, so she motioned for Lenore and Bruik to follow her into the kitchen. "Okay, tell me." She put on a kettle of water.

That was the last thing she remembered doing until after Lenore stopped talking and the whistle of the kettle finally broke through the fog. What the woman had left behind held ramifications for both of them, and Lenore seemed to be in as much shock as she was.

"That can't be true." Piper shook her head, causing an unruly lock of hair to fall into her eyes, and she pushed it back with impatience. "Things like that just don't happen. I may be blond, but I do have some idea how the world works."

"You mean things like some nut who was beheaded and put to

sleep for hundreds of years comes back to get you, you're saved from his attack by a friendly vampire, after which you watch a big dragon come to life in your living room? Those kinds of things?"

"Well, when you're that literal, it doesn't sound all that improbable but—" She looked at Lenore and started laughing again. "I really don't know how in the hell to finish that sentence."

"As the old saying goes, what's done is done," Bruik said. "I didn't see this, but it's a happy ending, don't you think?"

"I'm not unhappy, if it's true, but one thing in there's wrong, so maybe the rest of it's wrong too."

"What's wrong?" Kendal asked when she stepped into the kitchen, followed by Morgaine and Charlie. They were all wet and Charlie looked a little weak, but fine. Their swim had washed off some of the blood from the battle earlier, and to Piper, Kendal looked better. "Well?" Kendal said, as she reached for the teacup in Piper's hand.

"While you were out we had another visitor." She jumped up to put her arms around Kendal to keep her from running to the front of the house. "A good visitor, honey, calm down."

"Who was it?" Morgaine asked, and Lenore put her arms around her as well.

"Just listen to what Piper has to say." Lenore looked from Kendal to Morgaine.

"Our visitor thought we might want to know the end of the Sea Serpent Sword's legend." Piper pointed to the counter where Lenore had placed the book, open to the last section. "She left us that, but the end doesn't gel with our reality, and that's what I was telling Lenore when you got back."

"What ending?"

Piper had to laugh and pinch Kendal's butt. "My darling, you take the term 'strong, silent type' to a whole new level. You're allowed, if you want, to use more than two words to phrase your questions."

After the night they had lived through, the humor was welcome and made Kendal laugh. Not caring if they had an audience, Piper lowered Kendal's head and kissed her for a very long, sweet moment. Kendal seemed to pour all her feelings for her into that one simple, loving act, and it healed the nightmares the night had caused.

"This isn't a question," Kendal said as she pressed their lips together. "And it has more than two words." Kendal kissed her again. "I love you, and I'm so happy you were here with me. Without you I don't know if I could've won."

Piper stood with her eyes closed, wanting to enjoy the words a little longer. "Is it any wonder she always gets the girl," she said when she finally looked back to the others.

"I believe she asked you something about an ending," Morgaine said as she made a circle with her hand.

"It says if Aphrodite's chosen claimed the sword, the markings of the two would remain, but they'd reverse themselves. They're in the wrong spots for the prophecy to be true."

"Wrong spots?" Kendal asked, and Piper pinched her for the two-word question.

"Well, according to the book mine isn't supposed to be over my heart, yours is, but we both know where yours is." The white shirt Kendal was wearing was still damp, letting the skin show even through the remnants of the bloodstains. "Yours is…" She looked at Kendal's chest, to the spot over her heart.

Slowly she brought her hands up, scared the image would disappear, and gripped the ends of Kendal's shirt. In one rapid movement she ripped it open, sending buttons flying all over the room.

"Are you having a flashback of our robe incident the day you came over with the deputy?" Kendal said, and laughed as she stood there with her chest exposed. "We can go upstairs if you want." She tried to turn a little so the others didn't have such a good view.

"Look," Piper said as her brain tried to wrap around what she was seeing and what it meant.

"What?" Kendal's eyes were still on Piper, as if she was afraid she'd snapped.

"Look," she repeated, and watched Kendal's head drop.

"What the—" Kendal stared at her own chest and the dragon tattoo that was now there. The drawing had changed, and while the beast still appeared ready for battle, it held the Sea Serpent Sword in one claw and the orb from Piper's tattoo in the other. "What does this mean?"

"It means…" Piper said as she started unbuttoning her own jeans.

"There's no way in hell you're taking your pants off down here."

When she didn't stop, Kendal picked her up, headed upstairs, and only stopped when she kicked the door to their bedroom closed. "Start from the beginning and tell me what's going on."

"I can't prove it, because she never offered her name, but the guide I had for my vineyard vision was Aphrodite. And I can't prove what happened to you a long time ago, but I think she's the woman who gave you the sword."

"The goddess of love is on a first-name basis with both of us." Kendal laughed.

"Do you want to hear this or not?" Piper asked as she stripped her pants off.

"Sorry, go on." Kendal dropped to her knees to examine the new tattoo in the same spot Kendal's had been.

"If Aphrodite's chosen won the battle for the sword and the dragon it held, it would release something, but not the power to rule the world. Only we both have to choose the future of the prophecy, because it's a hard thing to just thrust on us."

"All that happened was us defusing that thing, so it's done," Kendal said, but she traced the tattoo on her thigh with her finger.

"It's not over. Do you want to decide or not?" Piper asked as she stripped off her shirt, wanting to get completely naked.

"If we're going to be naked for this talk, I might agree to whatever you want."

"It shocked me at first, but the more I think about it, the more I want this with you."

"What?"

She lay back on the bed and spread her legs before she put her hand between them. "If you make love to me, the orb will come to life, and we'll finish the prophecy by unlocking what it held."

CHAPTER TWENTY

Kendal stopped talking to take a sip of wine. They'd returned to Oakgrove months before, and Piper's grandparents had moved in with them for now, so Kendal and Mac had the opportunity on most afternoons to talk. They had been sitting outside under the trees where she and Piper had shared lunch one afternoon in the beginning of their relationship, and she answered a lot more of his questions.

As with most of their talks, she could tell he still wasn't buying the whole immortality, elixir-of-the-sun thing, so she finally proved it to him. Just once she wished someone would just take the story at face value and not demand a demonstration that she'd live forever. At least this time it only took nailing her hand to the table with the cheese knife with a nice noon sun overhead to get him to believe her.

It'd take a lot longer for him to hear about her whole history, so she'd only hit the highlights, ending with what Piper now meant to her. From his comments, the reality that Piper would live forever both thrilled and terrified him. It was the last part of her and Piper's story he was the most interested in, wanting to understand the outcome of their battle here at Oakgrove.

"So what is the legend of the Sea Serpent?"

Another bottle was uncorked, bringing the total to four that Kendal had consumed almost alone. If Mac had tried to keep up with her, the afternoon would have ended with her carrying him inside to sleep off his hangover. "Ready for the wrap-up, huh?"

"As fascinating as your life has been, Asra, the ending is the best part, and not only because it's about Piper as well." He held his glass out and laughed when she poured him only a little.

"Once upon a time there lived two lovers." She laughed when he frowned. "Well, there were two according to this story. When we first read it, though, we thought it was something along the lines of *Romeo and Juliet*."

"Only it wasn't." Mac popped a grape into his mouth and relaxed back into the cushion of his chair.

"Only if the play had been renamed *Juliet and Her Really Good Friend Sally*," she said with a smile. "One of the girls came from an influential family, and as open-minded as the Greeks were, they'd never have allowed her to spend the rest of her life with the daughter of a farmer who was in a blood feud with the other girl's father. With no other choices, the girls ran off together, hoping to find a better life somewhere—not in another part of Greece, but in the future."

"Is that even possible? Did the ancient Greeks believe in reincarnation?"

In the distance she could see Molly and Piper slowly walking toward them, making Kendal realize how much she'd missed Piper even though they'd been apart for just the afternoon. "I can't tell you what their religious beliefs were, but they ran to the sea and found a quiet place to do what lovers do in romantic settings. They thought it was the beginning of a life together, but it was short-lived because their families were close to tracking them down. So instead they made love one last time and sacrificed their lives to Aphrodite."

"The goddess is real?"

"My life is living proof that she is real, Mac."

"No wonder you've turned my granddaughter into a passionate woman," he said. "I can't complain about the results, though, since I'm thrilled for both of you, and I've gotten my greatest wish."

The heat of what she was sure was a blush worked up her neck, and she shook her finger at him. "Let me finish, troublemaker. Their sacrifice really touched the goddess, and she vowed to make them whole again in a time and place where they'd be free to love each other without prejudice and with a family who would support their choices. Until that time she took the crest of the rich family and created what up to then had only been a mythical creature, to hold the love they shared—the Sea Serpent."

"So back then the dragon was real?"

"According to the rest of the story that came after the battle, this particular dragon lived in the waters close to where the girls died and was given the gift of immortality by Aphrodite. Ares complained to their father that she had delved into his realm, and he wanted the dragon for himself since he saw the power it was capable of."

"How did the sword come to be?" Mac asked.

"I can see where Piper gets all her patience," she said, teasing him. "Zeus gave Aphrodite a choice. She could either destroy the dragon or find a way for the dragon to choose to serve either her or Ares. The Sea Serpent was captured, and with the help of her husband, the god of the forge, they trapped the dragon in what came to be known as the Sea Serpent Sword."

"How did you end up with it?"

"Aphrodite won the battle over who'd get the sword first, and I believe she already knew who Ares had chosen to fight for him. I was the complete opposite of Julius. It didn't hurt that I was so close by, and once she figured out why I was there, she gave it to me along with her mark."

She left out how Aphrodite gave it to her, since that story was a part of her past that was hers alone. Piper knew most of the story, but not every detail of what had happened in that tent a long time ago. She doubted that many people, immortal or not, were blessed enough to spend an intimate night with the goddess of love.

"It was a gift I didn't really treasure at first because I didn't know the prophecy, but I do now because it's become more than a key to me. Looking back now I realize that it took forever, but it would only come to life for me if I found the other half of my soul. When I did, the sword marked me as its true owner and Piper as my mate, as it were. So on Halloween night, at the stroke of midnight, the sword and the markings were able to break free at the precise time the world has no barriers against such things, and they fulfilled the goddess's vow to the lovers."

She stood and went to help Piper walk the rest of the way, holding her hand as she took Kendal's place under the tree. "Thank you, love," Piper said as she looked up at her.

"How are you feeling?" she asked.

"The same way I did the last time you asked me that, which I believe was less than four hours ago." It wasn't a reprimand, just a gentle teasing she heard more than a couple times a day. Molly and Mac smiled as Piper pinched her cheek for her concern. "Are you two done yet?" Piper asked about her and Mac.

"We just got to the part about some markings and Aphrodite fulfilling her vow," Mac told Piper.

"This was an excuse to sit out here and drink wine, wasn't it?" Piper's question was directed at Kendal, and she felt the heat of another blush. "Did the booze put you in the mood to be long-winded?"

"I'm not as talented a storyteller as you or Lenore, and your grandfather asks lots of questions. I'm sorry we took so long."

"Long-winded or not, finish the story," Mac said, patting the spot next to him so Molly would join him.

"On that night, the part of the dragon that had marked me came to life, looking for the other part of itself. It found it in the marking Piper had over her heart. One had fire and the other passion, and together they had enough of each to create life." She started the end of the story as she placed her hand over Piper's lower abdomen. "The orb that the one held in its claw was the container for the soul of a young woman who lived long ago and died with her lover by the sea. The love they had for each other was strong enough to split the orb into two separate vessels so they could live again with the chance to love once more."

"From your fire as a warrior," Piper said.

"And from your passion as a woman who believes in the power of love came the seed that now grows within you," Kendal said. The strong kick against her side was evidently a kind of sign the baby agreed with its mothers. "It was Aphrodite who put us all together that night so the rest of Bruik's prophecy could come to light."

"I thought his prophecy was only about Piper and who'd she be to the Elders?" Molly said.

"It was, but Rolla had kept another scroll hidden, not believing it'd ever come to pass. Bruik knew Piper was the missing part of the puzzle, but to make the prophecy work we needed Morgaine and Lenore as well. From one strong spirit came two souls, and we had to have another set of true hearts to bring the other to life."

"So you carry one," Mac said.

"And Lenore carries the other for her and Morgaine. I guess these two bundles of joy will have the choice to love whomever they choose to, but with us they'll have the freedom to become the women or men they want to because they'll be raised with love and respect." She received a kiss for her words from a very pregnant Piper.

Kendal had never considered having a family, since it wasn't something within her reach. Leaving everyone in her life had been hard enough, but leaving a child to keep her secret would've been impossible for her, even if she'd ever possessed the power to sire one.

When Piper told her otherwise almost nine months ago, before she asked her to make love to her to make it so, it was the closest she had ever come to passing out from shock. In Piper's womb grew a seed they'd both planted. True, it would hold the essence of two people who'd once loved each other centuries before, but it would also be graced with the essence of her and Piper, just as if they'd created the baby themselves.

From there, neither of them knew what the future held for the two miracles who would soon come into the world. What the two expectant mothers and the Marmandes did know was that she and Morgaine were about to rattle apart from worry over their mates. No two women had been so coddled during their pregnancies as Piper and Lenore.

"So, Mac, you get your wish after all," she said.

"What wish?"

"Soon there'll be a little Marmande-Richoux running around Marmande's, guaranteeing the business will survive for another generation."

"Do you think the baby will be immortal as well, with you two as parents?" Molly asked.

"Since we're frozen at the age we are when we drink the elixir, I hope not," she said, and helped Piper up.

They headed back to the house to join the others for dinner. After they'd come home to Louisiana, they'd started constructing a house for Lenore and Morgaine, built to their specifications, which included a sprawling library and sword room. Soon most of the places Kendal owned around the world would finish all the new construction she'd ordered. Close to each house she owned would stand a new home, so their children could grow up together.

The Elders had met and determined the fate of Bailey, since Kendal had decided Travis's fate for them. She assured them his remains would never be found, and she'd never record how to find them. Rolla accepted her choice since it was his lax judgments that had allowed Travis to join their ranks in the first place. Bailey was placed whole in the crypt where Julius's body had lain for so many years. With luck, Rolla wouldn't order his release for at least a thousand years, but she'd fight it when he did.

At the conclusion of their meeting, Asra was given the status of Elder and provided more rooms in the main compound in Egypt. The others accepted Piper for who she was now in her life and who she'd eventually become to them. Piper hadn't made the trip with her, but had been comforted that Bruik had stayed to continue her training.

Bruik had always been a bit of a recluse but had found he enjoyed his afternoon walks with Piper and vowed to stay at her side until Piper felt she no longer needed him. He'd become a welcomed part of their family.

The other thing Rolla and the others had insisted on was leaving a healer with them. Two pregnancies that had resulted from the power released from a sword would be hard to explain to a doctor in a normal setting. Some of the best medical minds had trained the young woman who saw to their needs. She tried not to bother them too much and had moved into one of the guest rooms to wait for the big day.

"Coming?" Piper asked as she stood at the base of the stairs after dinner.

"In a minute, love. I just remembered I left the book about the sword and the Sea Serpent legend outside. If something happens to it, Lenore might have me drawn and quartered, or something equally bad."

"Hurry back." Piper started up the stairs to their room.

It wasn't that she needed the rest. So far the pregnancy had been great and her energy level had remained the same. Piper just liked to spend time with Kendal, pressed skin to skin as they marveled at how her body had changed and why. The fact that the baby was theirs overwhelmed them at times.

It was completely dark by the time Kendal made it to the trees. The staff had left the book she was looking for on one of the chaises, but the evidence of her picnic with Mac had been cleared away. She didn't see anyone until she bent to retrieve the leather-covered volume that'd come to mean the world to Lenore as well as Piper.

"Tell me, warrior, how are you handling life lately?" Aphrodite materialized, stretched out on the chaise lounge, and stared up at her.

Aphrodite's voluptuous figure hadn't changed at all, and her voice still had the ability to wrap around Kendal like a velvet glove. Those were the first two things Kendal had noticed about the goddess when she initially visited her, even in the disguise of an old woman. Aside from Piper, only a handful of women had been able to affect her like this. It was a night that, before Piper had come into her life, she thought of often.

"It was incredible, I'd have to agree," Aphrodite said, as if she'd spoken her thoughts out loud. "But now you have the woman who will cater to your every want just like you will to hers, do you not?"

"I do, and I wonder if I have you to thank for that as well," she said before lowering her head, "Goddess."

Aphrodite clapped her hands together and laughed. "I told your partner I chose well, but Piper was completely your choice to make. You're smart as well as strong and incredibly sexy, and I congratulate you for having such good taste. Piper is your perfect match, but she didn't make out so bad either."

"Thank you for the compliment, and I'm glad you came back so I could also thank you for all you did for us."

"Actually, I came back to answer all those questions you've had rolling around in here." Aphrodite tapped the side of her head with a perfectly manicured nail. "It's a shame you can't sleep. You could use some downtime every so often from all this thinking. It's making me tired, and all I'm doing is listening."

"It's the soldier in me."

"Then allow me to help put your mind at ease. I meant what I told Piper. The baby you and Piper will bring into this world will be yours, with only a touch of love that started a long time ago. It was my promise to the lovers, who gave me so much, to allow them another opportunity at a life together, but I feel they'd be better off starting fresh without the burdens of their pasts. The same is true of Lenore and Morgaine's child."

Kendal let out a long breath of relief. Not that she minded what the sword had given them, but raising someone who had her own mind-set from birth was a little much to think about. Before she could say or ask anything else, Aphrodite changed form to become the old woman she'd met in the woods after her visit with the Roman general.

"Sometimes someone who comes bearing gifts is just that. They don't always have ulterior motives or strings attached. They're just someone giving you something to make you happy. Learn to listen to your heart, Asra, for it has served you well up to now." Again Aphrodite changed to another woman Kendal had known from a distant past. "I've been with you always to make sure the hope in here never fully died away with the horrors you've faced." She tapped gently over her heart.

"I never realized."

"You gave me your heart because, as I told you before, you were always true and pure when it came to the things you wanted. Someone so kindhearted deserves my rewards and all the gifts I can bestow on you."

Kendal looked down as the goddess unfastened enough buttons to see the tattoo that still graced the skin over her heart. The dragon now holding the sword and the orb had become Piper's favorite place to run her fingers when they were alone.

"You have given me, as well as my sisters, the depth of your love, the virtue of your wisdom, and the infinite strength of your courage." Aphrodite pressed her hand harder over her heart, and it was incredibly warm. "We in turn have given you the will to continue the fight." Aphrodite traced over the claw that held the sword with her finger. "And the reason to do so," she said, then moved to the claw that held the orb. "The markings changed so you would always remember that it is your heart that makes you who you are, Asra. A heart that now belongs as much to the woman who owns it and the child who will soon lay its own claim. And through it all you will have my sisters and me to look over you."

"I thank you again, Goddess." Kendal covered Aphrodite's hand, pulling it away and kissing the palm with as much tenderness as she could.

"So, little one, are you happy as well?" Aphrodite said with a smile that made Kendal turn around.

"Had you undone one more button I'd be thinking of ways to kill you, but I'm happy for the most part," Piper said, her hand on the small of her back, helping her to support the growing weight she was privileged to lug around all day. Aphrodite had come to Piper more than once when she practiced expanding her sight for visions, and they'd formed a friendship.

"I just wanted to come for one more visit before the blessed event." Aphrodite moved away from Kendal so she could place her hands over their active child. She laughed at the healthy kicks that probably followed, since the baby loved to be caressed. "I believe this one will act much like that one." She pointed to Kendal, warning Piper. "And that one I've watched for a long time. Are you sure you can handle two of them?"

"I can handle anything as long as she loves me." Piper sounded like she was at peace. Kendal placed her hands on her shoulders. Piper smiled back at her but turned back to the goddess.

"Good." Aphrodite moved her hands to Piper's head. "Enjoy the calm of what's coming, for the war will begin again soon enough. Those who dare to live life to the fullest are those who have the most to lose."

"But they are also the ones with the most to gain." The language they used was the language of the gods, and Kendal stood still behind her since Piper knew she didn't understand.

"True, but know that my protection over you will be eternal. All you need do is call my name if you have need of me, and I'll come to you."

"I appreciate that, and I really do thank you for this gift." Piper put her hands over her midsection and smiled. She planned to give this child all the love and devotion she had missed out on from her own parents.

"Take care of her, warrior." Aphrodite's voice drifted to them in the wind when she disappeared.

"I'll take care of you, all right," Kendal said as she pressed Piper back against her chest and put her hands over Piper's on their child. "I'll take care of you both." After Kendal kissed the side of her head she guided them back to the house.

"Anything I should be worried about since I can't make out any of that language?" Kendal asked.

"Eventually, but for now I'm going to enjoy you and the life we have together. The rest will just have to wait until I've had my fill." She leaned heavily into Kendal to take the pressure off her back.

"The world doesn't always wait until you're ready for the bad things flung our way." Kendal kissed the side of her neck.

"That's true, but we'll have powerful protectors going forward."

"The gods of old don't hold too much power anymore, my love," Kendal said, the baby active under her hands. "Granted, it's amazing to me they exist at all, but I doubt they'll be much help when battles like this one come our way."

"Do you remember the night you mixed the elixir for me?" Piper turned around and faced Kendal.

"That's not something I'll forget anytime soon." Kendal shook her head slightly, as if she didn't understand where Piper was taking the conversation.

"I told you then with my rusty French that the words that came to me were *toujours ici*. 'Always here' is what's most important for you to remember about me going forward. That was my promise to you then, and it's my promise to you always." Kendal immediately lowered her head when she placed her hands behind her neck and kissed her. "You are my balance and the person who completes the other half of my soul, and nothing will ever sever that bond."

"Maybe I should promise something in return." Kendal picked Piper up and cradled her against her chest for the walk back to the house.

"At the threat of sounding like a composer of Hallmark greeting cards for Valentine's Day, you've already given me more happiness than I ever thought I deserved. That you love me has been the greatest gift any god or supreme being has been gracious enough to give me."

"Let's see if you remember any more of your high school French," Kendal said as she kissed her again. "You said *toujours ici*," she whispered.

"Always here for you, love," she said softly back.

"*Sera toujours*," Kendal said, and it took Piper a moment to translate the words in her head.

"Always will be." She smiled.

"No matter the road, the fight, or the years," Kendal said as she neared the back of the house. "I'll always be at your side."

"Thank you and I love you," Piper said—and her water broke.

The next chapter of their story started now.

About the Author

Originally from Cuba, Ali Vali has retained much of her family's traditions and language and uses them frequently in her stories. Having her father read her stories and poetry before bed every night as a child infused her with a love of reading, which carries till today. In 2000, Ali decided to embark on a new path and started writing.

Ali now lives in the suburbs of New Orleans with her partner of twenty-nine years, and finds that living in such a history-rich area provides plenty of material to draw from in creating her novels and short stories. Mixing imagination with different life experiences makes it easier to create a slew of different characters that are engaging to the reader on many levels. Ali states that "The feedback from readers encourages me to continue to hone my skills as a writer."

Books Available From Bold Strokes Books

Homestead by Radclyffe. R. Clayton Sutter figures getting NorthAm Fuel's newest refinery operational on a rolling tract of land in upstate New York should take a month or two, but then, she hadn't counted on local resistance in the form of vandalism, petitions, and one furious farmer named Tess Rogers. (978-1-60282-956-5)

Battle of Forces: Sera Toujours by Ali Vali. Kendal and Piper return to New Orleans to start the rest of eternity together, but the return of an old enemy makes their peaceful reunion short-lived, especially when they join forces with the new queen of the vampires. (978-1-60282-957-2)

How Sweet It Is by Melissa Brayden. Some things are better than chocolate. Molly O'Brien enjoys her quiet life running the bakeshop in a small town. When the beautiful Jordan Tuscana returns home, Molly can't deny the attraction—or the stirrings of something more. (978-1-60282-958-9)

The Missing Juliet: A Fisher Key Adventure by Sam Cameron. A teenage detective and her friends search for a kidnapped Hollywood star in the Florida Keys. (978-1-60282-959-6)

Amor and More: Love Everafter, edited by Radclyffe and Stacia Seaman. Rediscover favorite couples as Bold Strokes Books authors reveal glimpses of life and love beyond the honeymoon in short stories featuring main characters from favorite BSB novels. (978-1-60282-963-3)

First Love by CJ Harte. Finding true love is hard enough, but for Jordan Thompson, daughter of a conservative president, it's challenging, especially when that love is a female rodeo cowgirl. (978-1-60282-949-7)

Pale Wings Protecting by Lesley Davis. Posing as a couple to investigate the abduction of infants, Special Agent Blythe Kent and Detective Daryl Chandler find themselves drawn into a battle over the innocents, with demons on one side and the unlikeliest of protectors on the other. (978-1-60282-964-0)

Mounting Danger by Karis Walsh. Sergeant Rachel Bryce, an outcast on the police force, is put in charge of the department's newly formed mounted division. Can she and polo champion Callan Lanford resist their growing attraction as they struggle to safeguard the disaster-prone unit? (978-1-60282-951-0)

Show of Force by AJ Quinn. A chance meeting between navy pilot Evan Kane and correspondent Tate McKenna takes them on a roller-coaster ride where the stakes are high, but the reward is higher: a chance at love. (978-1-60282-942-8)

Clean Slate by Andrea Bramhall. Can Erin and Morgan work through their individual demons to rediscover their love for each other, or are the unexplainable wounds too deep to heal? (978-1-60282-943-5)

Hold Me Forever by D. Jackson Leigh. An investigation into illegal cloning in the quarter horse racing industry threatens to destroy the growing attraction between Georgia debutante Mae St. John and Louisiana horse trainer Whit Casey. (978-1-60282-944-2)

At Her Feet by Rebekah Weatherspoon. Digital marketing producer Suzanne Kim knows she has found the perfect love in her new mistress Pilar, but before they can make the ultimate commitment, Suzanne's professional life threatens to disrupt their perfectly balanced bliss. (978-1-60282-948-0)

Trusting Tomorrow by P.J. Trebelhorn. Funeral director Logan Swift thinks she's perfectly happy with her solitary life devoted to helping others cope with loss until Brooke Collier moves in next door to care for her elderly grandparents. (978-1-60282-891-9)

Forsaking All Others by Kathleen Knowles. What if what you think you want is the opposite of what makes you happy? (978-1-60282-892-6)

Exit Wounds by VK Powell. When Officer Loane Landry falls in love with ATF informant Abigail Mancuso, she realizes that nothing is as it seems—not the case, not her lover, not even the dead. (978-1-60282-893-3)

Dirty Power by Ashley Bartlett. Cooper's been through hell and back, and she's still broke and on the run. But at least she found the twins. They'll keep her alive. Right? (978-1-60282-896-4)

The Rarest Rose by I. Beacham. After a decade of living in her beloved house, Ele disturbs its past and finds her life being haunted by the presence of a ghost who will show her that true love never dies. (978-1-60282-884-1)

Code of Honor by Radclyffe. The face of terror is hard to recognize— especially when it's homegrown. The next book in the Honor series. (978-1-60282-885-8)

Does She Love You by Rachel Spangler. When Annabelle and Davis find out they are in a relationship with the same woman, it leaves them facing life-altering questions about trust, redemption, and the possibility of finding love in the wake of betrayal. (978-1-60282-886-5)

The Road to Her by KE Payne. Sparks fly when actress Holly Croft, star of UK soap *Portobello Road*, meets her new on-screen love interest, the enigmatic and sexy Elise Manford. (978-1-60282-887-2)

Shadows of Something Real by Sophia Kell Hagin. Trying to escape flashbacks and nightmares, ex-POW Jamie Gwynmorgan stumbles into the heart of former Red Cross worker Adele Sabellius and uncovers a deadly conspiracy against everything and everyone she loves. (978-1-60282-889-6)

Date with Destiny by Mason Dixon. When sophisticated bank executive Rashida Ivey meets unemployed blue-collar worker Destiny Jackson, will her life ever be the same? (978-1-60282-878-0)

The Devil's Orchard by Ali Vali. Cain and Emma plan a wedding before the birth of their third child while Juan Luis is still lurking, and as Cain plans for his death, an unexpected visitor arrives and challenges her belief in her father, Dalton Casey. (978-1-60282-879-7)

Secrets and Shadows by L.T. Marie. A bodyguard and the woman she protects run from a madman and into each other's arms. (978-1-60282-880-3)

Change Horizons: Three Novellas by Gun Brooke. Three stories of courageous women who dare to love as they fight to claim a future in a hostile universe. (978-1-60282-881-0)

Scarlett Thirst by Crin Claxton. When hot, feisty Rani meets cool vampire Rob, one lifetime isn't enough, and the road from human to vampire is shorter than you think… (978-1-60282-856-8)

Battle Axe by Carsen Taite. How close is too close? Bounty hunter Luca Bennett will soon find out. (978-1-60282-871-1)

Improvisation by Karis Walsh. High school geometry teacher Jan Carroll thinks she's figured out the shape of her life and her future, until graphic artist and fiddle player Tina Nelson comes along and teaches her to improvise. (978-1-60282-872-8)

For Want of a Fiend by Barbara Ann Wright. Without her Fiendish power, can Princess Katya and her consort Starbride stop a magic-wielding madman from sparking an uprising in the kingdom of Farraday? (978-1-60282-873-5)

Swans & Clons by Nora Olsen. In a future world where there are no males, sixteen-year-old Rubric and her girlfriend Salmon Jo must fight to survive when everything they believed in turns out to be a lie. (978-1-60282-874-2)

Broken in Soft Places by Fiona Zedde. The instant Sara Chambers meets the seductive and sinful Merille Thompson, she falls hard, but knowing the difference between love and a dangerous, all-consuming desire is just one of the lessons Sara must learn before it's too late. (978-1-60282-876-6)

Healing Hearts by Donna K. Ford. Running from tragedy, the women of Willow Springs find that with friendship, there is hope, and with love, there is everything. (978-1-60282-877-3)

Desolation Point by Cari Hunter. When a storm strands Sarah Kent in the North Cascades, Alex Pascal is determined to find her. Neither imagines the dangers they will face when a ruthless criminal begins to hunt them down. (978-1-60282-865-0)

I Remember by Julie Cannon. What happens when you can never forget the first kiss, the first touch, the first taste of lips on skin? What happens when you know you will remember every single detail of a mysterious woman? (978-1-60282-866-7)

The Gemini Deception by Kim Baldwin and Xenia Alexiou. The truth, the whole truth, and nothing but lies. Book six in the Elite Operatives series. (978-1-60282-867-4)

Scarlet Revenge by Sheri Lewis Wohl. When faith alone isn't enough, will the love of one woman be strong enough to save a vampire from damnation? (978-1-60282-868-1)

Ghost Trio by Lillian Q. Irwin. When Lee Howe hears the voice of her dead lover singing to her, is it a hallucination, a ghost, or something more sinister? (978-1-60282-869-8)

The Princess Affair by Nell Stark. Rhodes Scholar Kerry Donovan arrives at Oxford ready to focus on her studies, but her life and her priorities are thrown into chaos when she catches the eye of Her Royal Highness Princess Sasha. (978-1-60282-858-2)

The Chase by Jesse J. Thoma. When Isabelle Rochat's life is threatened, she receives the unwelcome protection and attention of bounty hunter Holt Lasher who vows to keep Isabelle safe at all costs. (978-1-60282-859-9)

The Lone Hunt by L.L. Raand. In a world where humans and Praeterns conspire for the ultimate power, violence is a way of life…and death. A Midnight Hunters novel. (978-1-60282-860-5)

The Supernatural Detective by Crin Claxton. Tony Carson sees dead people. With a drag queen for a spirit guide and a devastatingly attractive herbalist for a client, she's about to discover the spirit world can be a very dangerous world indeed. (978-1-60282-861-2)

Beloved Gomorrah by Justine Saracen. Undersea artists creating their own City on the Plain uncover the truth about Sodom and Gomorrah, whose "one righteous man" is a murderer, rapist, and conspirator in genocide. (978-1-60282-862-9)

The Left Hand of Justice by Jess Faraday. A kidnapped heiress, a heretical cult, a corrupt police chief, and an accused witch. Paris is burning, and the only one who can put out the fire is Detective Inspector Elise Corbeau…whose boss wants her dead. (978-1-60282-863-6)

Cut to the Chase by Lisa Girolami. Careful and methodical author Paige Cornish falls for brash and wild Hollywood actress Avalon Randolph, but can these opposites find a happy middle ground in a town that never lives in the middle? (978-1-60282-783-7)

Every Second Counts by D. Jackson Leigh. Every second counts in Bridgette LeRoy's desperate mission to protect her heart and stop Marc Ryder's suicidal return to riding rodeo bulls. (978-1-60282-785-1)

More Than Friends by Erin Dutton. Evelyn Fisher thinks she has the perfect role model for a long-term relationship, until her best friends, Kendall and Melanie, split up and all three women must reevaluate their lives and their relationships. (978-1-60282-784-4)

Dirty Money by Ashley Bartlett. Vivian Cooper and Reese DiGiovanni just found out that falling in love is hard. It's even harder when you're running for your life. (978-1-60282-786-8)

Sea Glass Inn by Karis Walsh. When Melinda Andrews commissions a series of mosaics by Pamela Whitford for her new inn, she doesn't expect to be more captivated by the artist than by the paintings. (978-1-60282-771-4)

The Awakening: A Sisterhood of Spirits novel by Yvonne Heidt. Sunny Skye has interacted with spirits her entire life, but when she runs into Officer Jordan Lawson during a ghost investigation, she discovers more than just facts in a missing girl's cold case file. (978-1-60282-772-1)

Blacker Than Blue by Rebekah Weatherspoon. Threatened with losing her first love to a powerful demon, vampire Cleo Jones is willing to break the ultimate law of the undead to rebuild the family she has lost. (978-1-60282-774-5)

Murphy's Law by Yolanda Wallace. No matter how high you climb, you can't escape your past. (978-1-60282-773-8)